I0831245

Veil of Illusions

Genevieve McPartlin-Bryant

Book 1
of the
The Shattered Veil Series

Veil of Illusions

Cover design by Genevieve McPartlin-Bryant
Interior formatting by Genevieve McPartlin-Bryant

ISBN: 979-8-9985840-2-2
First Edition

Printed in the United States of America

For those who have ever felt silenced.
For the ones still finding their voice.
This story is yours, too.
And for the girl I once was—
You survived.
And now, you speak.

Table of Contents

KING'S
REALM
CITY OF
STARLIGHT
SORROM S RIVIR
RUINED
CITY
FOREST
OF VEILS
SHADOW
MARSH
MUNTAIN PASS
SEA
OF MIST
SANCTUARY
SHADOW
MARSH
ELARION

ASHIRA'S
REALM
THE
SANCTUARY
THE
GROVE
PATH OF RUNES
THE
WELLSPRING
THE
WELL
THE
VAULT
EMOTION-BORN
REALMS
THE
WELL
LIRIA

Prologue

The sky over Elarion never fully darkened. Suspended in a timeless twilight, the air shimmered faintly with the scent of wild jasmine, gentle as a lullaby. Peace reigned effortlessly, or so it seemed.

The kingdom was perfection crafted from illusion, a world free from pain, grief, or even inconvenient truths. From birth, citizens wore enchanted lenses that painted their world with serene lies – lies whispered soothingly by King Aurik himself. No one questioned it, because no one remembered there was anything to question.

But beneath this fragile peace, something stirred.

Elira Veyne, the quiet, obedient princess with the silenced voice, sensed it most clearly at night, when shadows stretched, and secrets whispered from forgotten places. Dreams plagued her, dreams that were not her own – memories and faces she didn't recognize yet felt achingly familiar. Among them was a figure whose presence made her heart ache: a woman with hair like starlight, warmth radiating from her very being. Her mother, perhaps – but that truth, too, had long been buried beneath enchantment.

The dreams grew stronger, more insistent, until one night, Elira woke trembling. The silver choker at her throat, placed there long ago by her father, burned against her skin. Her dreams had shown her a truth hidden behind the shimmering veil, a truth that resonated in her bones and hummed in her blood.

Beside her dream-mother stood another figure, luminous yet ethereal: Ashira, the guardian of souls, The Twin Flame of the Veil. Ashira had appeared to guide her, to remind her of the truths she once knew but had forgotten.

In that instant, Elira knew the world she saw was a carefully crafted lie – beautiful, yet dangerously fragile. Her father's gentle smile concealed a cruel secret. Her heart raced with both terror and hope.

The veil had cracked, and with it, Elira's silence.

It was time to remember who she truly was and break the illusion once and for all.

Chapter 1:

Journal Entry – Elira Veyne

There's something I can't quite place – a feeling that's settled deep within my chest. A whisper that tugs at my consciousness, urging me to wake from a slumber I never knew I was in. It's as if my soul is yearning, reaching desperately for something just beyond my fingertips. Something real.

My father says that Elarion is a kingdom of eternal peace, a haven untouched by suffering. I've spent my whole life believing it – smiling, obeying, grateful for the tranquil that surrounds me. Yet, when twilight falls and my room grows silent, doubt creeps in like shadows beneath my door.

My dreams have become my truth-tellers, persistent messengers showing me faces I feel I should recognize, memories I don't recall making. Last night's vision was especially vivid, tangled with grief and longing, haunted by eyes filled with warmth – eyes so much like my own. My mother's eyes. She spoke my name, a whisper powerful enough to shatter the silence that binds me.

I awoke gasping, heart racing, the familiar silver choker icy cold around my neck. Father placed it there himself long ago, assuring me of its beauty, a symbol of his love. Yet now, it feels like a chain, binding me to silence, tethering me to a carefully crafted lie.

My dreams and waking thoughts are beginning to merge into one undeniable truth: something in Elarion is deeply wrong. This perfect existence is no longer enough. My heart beats harder now, stirred by whispers of rebellion and the burning desire for authenticity.

I fear what truths I might uncover. But more than fear, I feel a fierce, growing courage.

Whatever lies beyond this veil, I must find it. I must break free.

Elira blinked slowly, adjusting her vision to the gentle glow of the morning light filtering through her silk curtains. She inhaled deeply, feeling her pulse steady after the vivid remnants of her dream had finally loosened their grip. Her fingertips rose instinctively to touch the cold, silver choker around her neck – a habit born of both comfort and resentment.

She sat up slowly, letting the silken covers slip around her waist. The expansive room surrounding her was decorated elegantly, with muted shades of cream and gold, furnishings carefully curated to represent tranquility and elegance. Yet today, everything felt foreign, tainted somehow by the echo of the truths whispered in her dreams.

Elira rose from her bed, her bare feet meeting the cold marble floor. She approached the large window that overlooked Elarion's capital city. From this vantage, it appeared flawless, bathed in golden hues that shimmered gently under the eternal dawn. But now, she saw it differently. The city's perfection felt strained, artificial, as though a thin veneer covered a much darker reality.

"Your Highness?" a gentle voice called from behind her, pulling her from her thoughts.

Elira turned to see Mara, her handmaiden, standing cautiously by the doorway. Mara's smile was kind but uncertain, as if she sensed the tension Elira herself couldn't fully name.

"Morning, Mara," Elira responded softly, offering a faint smile. She knew she had to maintain appearances, even as the disquiet grew within her.

Mara stepped forward, holding a delicate gown in shades of pale lavender, its fabric shimmering faintly. "The King requests your presence at breakfast today," Mara said hesitantly, watching Elira closely.

Elira suppressed the slight shiver that danced down her spine. Her father's invitations were never truly requests.

"Very well," she murmured, stepping toward Mara. Her heartbeat quickened; each step closer to confronting the man whose gentle smiles concealed far more than she ever dared to imagine.

As Mara helped her into the gown, Elira's mind wandered again to the image of her mother's gentle eyes, full of warmth she longed to feel again. She wondered if the woman from her dreams had ever truly existed or if she was merely another creation of her mind, another illusion she was desperate to believe.

Mara began to arrange Elira's hair, her fingers skilled and careful. "Is everything alright, Your Highness?" Mara's voice was gentle, laced with concern.

Elira hesitated, meeting Mara's gaze through the mirror's reflection. There was trust in Mara's eyes, something sincere and reassuring. For a moment, Elira considered telling her everything – the dreams, the doubts, the whispering truths. But the memory of her father's warnings silenced her.

"Everything's fine," Elira whispered, offering another faint smile. "Just a restless night."

Mara nodded slowly, accepting her answer but clearly sensing there was more left unspoken. "If you ever need to talk, Your Highness, you know I am here."

Elira's chest tightened with gratitude. "Thank you, Mara. Truly."

She took a steadying breath as she rose, her appearance once again perfect, her mask flawlessly back in place. But beneath it, determination took toot, fierce and unyielding.

The truth awaited her – and she would find it, whatever it took.

As Elira stepped into the corridor, guards clad in polished armor straightened respectfully. She nodded politely, moving gracefully past them. The hallway, adorned with exquisite tapestries depicting heroic victories and grand celebrations, felt colder today. Each image seemed more distant and meaningless, part of a story that no longer resonated with her.

Her steps echoed softly on the polished stone floor; the rhythm steady but her mind racing ahead. The grand dining hall awaited her, and with it, her father. King Aurik. The man whose gentle smiles masked secrets darker than night. Today, Elira vowed silently, would be different. Today, she would watch carefully, searching for cracks in his carefully maintained façade. Today, she would begin to unravel the lies.

She paused at the grand double doors leading into the dining hall, steeling herself. The guards pulled open the heavy doors, revealing the vast room where sunlight spilled through tall windows onto a lavishly set table. King Aurik sat at its head, his posture relaxed but his eyes sharp and observant. He smiled warmly, a gesture that, for the first time, felt calculated rather than comforting.

"Good morning, Elira," his voice smooth and controlled, echoed across the hall. "Join me. We have much to discuss."

Taking a deep breath, Elira lifted her chin, moving forward with practiced grace and quiet resolve. "Good morning, Father."

He studied her carefully, his gaze lingering just a moment too long. "You look beautiful, my dear," he said, the warmth of his voice not quite reaching his eyes. "I trust you slept well?"

"Well enough," Elira replied calmly, meeting his stare evenly as she took her seat beside him. She watched as servants began to serve their meal, the room filling with the aroma of fresh bread and fruits. Yet her appetite was nonexistent, suppressed by the weight of the unspoken tension.

"I've arranged a gathering in your honor," her father began casually, slicing into a perfectly ripened pear. "Many will be attending. It's important to me that you make a lasting impression."

Elira's heart quickened, dread curling around her spine. "Of course, Father."

His eyes locked onto hers, the intensity startling. "I expect nothing short of perfection, Elira. Remember, appearances are everything."

Elira forced herself to hold, her voice steady despite the turmoil inside. "Understood, Father."

King Aurik leaned closer, his voice lowering. "And, Elira," he added, his tone sharper, "do keep those dreams of yours to yourself. They can be quite misleading, can't they?"

A chill rippled through Elira's body, but she maintained her composure. "Yes, Father," she replied smoothly, fully aware that a silent battle had begun.

Chapter 2:

Elira's heart continued to race as she departed the dining hall, the doors closing behind her with an echoing finality. Her father's words replayed incessantly in her min, each syllable coated in an unsettling mixture of warning and veiled threat.

She walked slowly down the corridor, thoughts spinning wildly, until she reached the grand balcony overlooking the gardens below. Her eyes scanned the perfectly arranged flowerbeds, vibrant in the perpetual dawn. Yet even their beauty couldn't quell the growing unease within her.

"Elira?" a familiar voice gently interrupted her spiraling thoughts.

Turning sharply, Elira felt immediate relief at the sight of her lifelong friend and confidante. Ashira's presence had always been a calming force, her warm smile a comforting balm against the cold façade of royal life.

"Ashira," Elira exhaled softly, moving to embrace her friend tightly.

Ashira held her close for a moment before pulling back, studying Elira carefully. Her striking violet eyes searched Elira's face with genuine concern. "You look troubled. Was it your father again?"

Elira hesitated briefly, the instinctive need for caution rising within her, even with Ashira. But the heavy burden of secrecy had grown too immense to carry alone. "Yes," she admitted quietly. "He… he knows something. About my dreams. He warned me."

Ashira's expression shifted instantly, darkening with worry. "He knows? How? You've been careful, haven't you?"

Elira nodded quickly. "I've told only you. Yet, somehow, he knows. It's as if he can see straight into my thoughts."

Ashira took Elira's hand, guiding her gently toward a nearby bench hidden beneath the cascading wisteria. "Then me must be even more cautious," she whispered urgently. "The king is powerful. Far more than he allows anyone to see."

"I know," Elira breathed shakily, leaning into Ashira's comforting presence. "But I can't keep living like this – pretending, lying, feeling trapped. I need to know the truth."

Ashira squeezed her hand reassuringly. "Then we'll find the truth together. You're not alone in this, Elira. You never were."

Elira smiled weakly, gratitude welling in her heart. Ashira's unwavering support was a beacon of hope amidst the shadows that threatened to engulf her.

"Where do we begin?" Elira whispered, determination reigniting in her eyes.

Ashira glanced carefully around them, ensuring no unwanted ears were nearby before leaning in closer. "I think it's time you meet someone who knows far more about this kingdom – and your father – than either of us could imagine."

"Who?" Elira asked cautiously, heart quickening in anticipation.

Ashira's voice lowered further; her tone filled with intensity Elira had rarely heard. "His name is Kaelen. And if anyone can help us uncover the truth, it's him."

Elira's curiosity surged, but she tempered her excitement with caution. "Kaelen? How have I never heard of him before?"

Ashira cast a wary glance around once more. "He's been hidden away, Elira. Kaelen was once one of your father's most trusted advisers. But something happened. He discovered something, something your father wanted buried. Ever since, he's lived quietly in the shadows, waiting for the right moment."

Elira felt a shiver trail down her spine. "How do you know we can trust him?"

Ashira's eyes grew distant, filled with an old pain. "Because he's, my uncle. And he's been waiting years for this day, for someone to finally ask the questions that need answering."

Stunned into silence, Elira stared into her friend's resolute gaze. Ashira, always composed and gentle, now showed an unwavering strength she'd never fully revealed before. Elira felt a surge of determination ripple through her, erasing the last traces of hesitation.

"Then let's not keep him waiting any longer," she whispered resolutely. "It's time we discover the truth."

Ashira nodded sharply, standing with a newfound resolve. "Tonight, then. Meet me at midnight, at the old willow near the edge of the western gardens. We'll go together."

Elira's pulse quickened with anticipation and anxiety. The reality of what she was about to do finally settled over her, but alongside her fear was an unshakable clarity. She nodded firmly. "I'll be there."

With a brief, reassuring smile, Ashira turned and departed down the hall, leaving Elira alone once more with her thoughts. Taking a deep, steadying breath, Elira turned her gaze back toward the gardens, heart pounding in her chest.

Everything was about to change, and for the first time in her life, Elira felt truly awake.

Midnight came swiftly, cloaking the palace grounds in a velvety darkness punctuated only by faint starlight. Elira moved silently; hooded cloak drawn tightly around her slender frame. She reached the ancient willow, its heavy branches swaying gently in the cool night breeze and found Ashira already waiting.

"Are you ready?" Ashira asked softly, her voice barely above a whisper.

Elira inhaled deeply, her gaze steady and resolute. "Yes. Take me to Kaelen."

They moved quickly and silently, slipping unnoticed through the shadows and secret passages that Elira never knew existed. Each step they took drew them further from the carefully controlled world she'd always known and deeper into the unknown.

As they approached the outskirts of the city, hidden within the dense forest, Ashira finally paused in front of a modest cottage. Lanterns flickered warmly withing, casting dancing patterns upon the aged wooden walls.

"We're here," Ashira whispered, knocking gently on the door.

The door swung open slowly, revealing a tall, stern-faced man with sharp, watchful eyes. Kaelen's gaze met Elira's directly, piercing and knowing.

"Welcome, Elira," he said gravely. "I've waited a long time for this meeting. Come inside. We have much to discuss."

Taking a deep breath, Elira stepped forward into the cottage. The door closed softly behind her, sealing away the last remnants of her old life, and heralding the beginning of a journey into the hidden truths that would change everything.

Chapter 3:

Inside the modest cottage, Elira felt a stark contrast to the opulent palace she had always known. The room was warmly lit by a hearth crackling softly in the corner, casting flickering shadows across shelves filled with ancient books and strange artifacts. Herbs hung drying from the rafters, filling the space with a comforting, earthy scent.

Kaelen moved to a sturdy wooden table at the room's center, gesturing for Elira and Ashira to sit. He took a seat across from them, his expression grave but gentle. "I know this is overwhelming," he began, his voice steady. "But I assure you, the answers you seek are closer now than ever before."

Elira glanced nervously at Ashira, whose calm presence gave her strength. Turning back to Kaelen, she found herself speaking with unexpected resolve. "My father is hiding something. I've felt it all my life, but now… now I'm certain. And I need to know why."

Kaelen nodded slowly, steepling his fingers thoughtfully. "Your instincts serve you well, Elira. Your father, King Aurik, has indeed woven a tapestry of illusions and secrets. It's no ordinary deceit – his powers extend far beyond what most believe possible."

"Powers?" Elira asked sharply. "What kind of powers?"

Kaelen leaned forward slightly; his eyes intense. "He possesses a rare magic, an ancient form known as Veil weaving. It grants him the ability to alter perception and reality itself, at least within his domain. Everyone within Elarion lives unknowingly beneath the shroud of his illusion.

A chill ran down Elira's spine, her eyes widening in shock. "And my dreams? Could they be -"

"Your dreams are glimpses of reality," Kaelen confirmed solemnly. "The Veil weakens in sleep, allowing the truth to bleed through. Your father fears this; it threatens his control."

Elira felt her heart pounding violently within her chest. "Then why me? Why do I see these things when no one else does?"

Kaelen exchanged a knowing glance with Ashira before continuing carefully. "Because, Elira, you inherited his gift. You are a Veil weaver. Perhaps the strongest one in generations."

Elira's breath caught, her world spinning at the revelation. She shook her head, struggling to comprehend. "How can that be? He never taught me-"

"Because he fears you," Kaelen said gently. "Your potential threatens his illusion, and he knows it. It's why he's watched you closely your entire life. He hoped your abilities would never awaken fully."

Ashira placed a comforting hand on Elira's shoulder, grounding her amid the torrent of emotions. "So, what can we do? How can we break this illusion and free Elarion?"

Kaelen's eyes glittered with determination. "There is a way, but it won't be easy. The Veil draws its strength from a source hidden deep within the palace – crystal known as the Heart of Illusions. If we can sever its connection to your father, his powers will weaken enough for the truth to surface."

Elira felt a sense of purpose igniting within her, mingling with fear and doubt. "Tell me how to find it."

Kaelen's expression hardened with resolve. "It will be heavily guarded. You father's most trusted servants protect it fiercely. But there is a secret passage beneath the palace, long forgotten by most. It will lead you straight to the chamber housing the crystal."

Ashira squeezed Elira's hand reassuringly. "You won't face this alone."

Elira nodded firmly, courage swelling in her chest. "When do we leave?"

Kaelen offered a faint smile, proud and solemn. "Tomorrow night, under the cover of darkness. Until then, rest and prepare. Once we begin, there is no turning back."

Elira stood slowly, her mind racing with newfound clarity and determination.

"Then tomorrow night, the illusion ends."

As she spoke, she felt something within her awaken – a strength she had never fully embraced before. The destiny she once feared now lay before her, not as a burden, but as a promise of liberation and truth.

For the first time, Elira understood the power of who she truly was – and she was ready.

Chapter 4:

The next day passed swiftly, filled with intense anticipation and careful preparation. Elira spent the daylight hours studying maps and absorbing every detail Kaelen provided about the secret passage and the guards. Ashira remained by her side, quiet yet resolute, a reassuring presence that steadied Elira's nerves.

As twilight descended upon Elarion, casting elongated shadows across the city, Kaelen handed Elira a small leather satchel containing provisions, a cloak of deep midnight blue, and a dagger engraved with delicate runes.

"This dagger," he explained gently, "we crafted specifically to disrupt the Veil's magic. Use it wisely."

Elira accepted it reverently, tracing the intricate carvings with her fingertips.

"Thank you, Kaelen."

He nodded, eyes warm with encouragement. "Remember, you possess the strength within you, Elira. Your true power is not in your bloodline alone, but in your heart and your courage."

Elira's resolve deepened; her gaze steady as she secured the dagger at her waist. She felt Ashira's gentle touch on her shoulder.

"It's time," Ashira whispered softly, guiding her towards the door.

The trio slipped silently into the night, moving quickly through the shadows cast by towering trees and moonlit buildings. As they reached the palace perimeter, Kaelen halted, turning solemnly toward them.

"This is as far as I go," he said quietly, his voice carrying the weight of all the hopes he had entrusted to them. "The entrance lies just beyond the next hedge, beneath a broken statue. I will remain here, watching for any sign of trouble."

Elira met his gaze firmly. "We won't let you down."

"I know you won't," Kaelen replied with quiet confidence. "Trust yourselves and each other."

With a final nod, Elira and Ashira moved forward, hearts pounding with each careful step. They soon found the broken statue Kaelen had described – a weathered figure of a long-forgotten queen, her marble visage cracked and worn by time.

Elira pushed aside a dense growth of ivy at the statue's base, revealing a hidden latch. She pressed it carefully, and with a faint, almost inaudible click, the ground shifted to reveal a narrow staircase spiraling downward into the darkness.

Taking a steadying breath, Elira stepped into the passageway, Ashira following close behind. The stone staircase was cold beneath their feet, lit only by the soft, pulsing glow of luminescent moss lining the ancient walls. The air grew colder and heavier with every step, laden with the weight of countless secrets.

After what felt like an eternity, they reached the passage's end. Ahead lay a heavy iron door engraved with symbols that mirrored those on Elira's dagger. She drew the weapon slowly, its blade shimmering faintly in the dim light.

With a steadying breath, she placed the dagger against the symbols. A low hum resonated, and the door swung inward silently, revealing a chamber bathed in eerie, pale light.

At its center stood a pedestal, upon which rested a large, crystal-clear gem pulsing with an unsettling, hypnotic glow. Around the pedestal, four guards stood rigidly, their eyes glazed and unseeing, clearly enchanted by the crystal's power.

"We must move quickly," Elira whispered urgently to Ashira, gripping the dagger tighter.

Suddenly, the crystal pulsed violently, emitting a blinding flash of light. Elira shielded her eyes instinctively as a deep, resonant voice echoed throughout the chamber.

"Welcome, daughter. I've been expecting you."

Elira felt her blood run cold as the familiar voice filled the air. King Aurik's presence was undeniable, his power palpable even from afar.

Determination surged through her veins, overriding her fear. "Your illusions end here," she declared firmly, stepping forward defiantly into the light. "It's time to face the truth."

Ashira moved to her side, unwaveringly loyal. The battle for Elarion's freedom had begun – and Elira knew she was ready.

Chapter 5:

Elira stood her ground, heart racing with a blend of fear and defiance, as the chamber filled with the oppressive weight of her father's presence. The guards surrounding the crystal began to stir, their enchanted eyes sharpening with awareness, turning menacingly toward her.

"You truly think you can challenge me?" King Aurik's voice echoed coldly, amusement lacing each word. "Your spirit is admirable, Elira, but your naiveté betrays you."

"I refuse to live in your lies any longer," Elira responded with unshakable resolve.

"This world deserves to know the truth."

Suddenly, the guards lunged forward, their movements swift and precise. Elira instinctively raised the dagger, its rune-etched blade flaring brilliantly as it sliced through the air, releasing pulses of light that disrupted the enchantment surrounding the guards. Their steps faltered, confusion momentarily flashing across their faces.

Ashira moved gracefully at Elira's side, deftly weaving through the chaos, protecting her friend from every approaching threat. Together, they fought desperately toward the crystal, each step forward feeling like an arduous journey.

A guard caught Ashira off-guard, striking a fierce blow that knocked her to the ground. Elira felt panic rise within her chest, her heart pounding violently as she rushed to Ashira's side.

“I’m okay,” Ashira gasped, struggling to her feet, determination gleaming fiercely in her eyes. “Don’t stop now, Elira. You must reach the crystal.”

Elira nodded sharply, adrenaline fueling her movements as she surged forward, closing the final distance to the pedestal. With a powerful swing, she drove the dagger into the crystal’s core.

An explosion of light and energy erupted from the crystal, blasting Elira backward onto the cold stone floor. The guards crumpled instantly, freed from their enchantment and rendered unconscious. The room shook violently, fragments of crystal raining down like glittering stars.

In the aftermath, a sudden silence enveloped the chamber. Elira slowly sat up, heart thundering, her body aching from the impact. Her eyes searched desperately for Ashir, who lay motionless a short distance away.

“Ashira!” she called out, scrambling to her friend’s side, heart seizing with fear. Ashira’s breathing was shallow, her eyes fluttering open weakly.

“You did it,” Ashira whispered faintly, a soft smile forming despite her evident pain. “You’ve started the change, Elira.”

Before Elira could respond, Ashira’s form began to shimmer gently, dissolving into a soft, ethereal glow that lifted into the air.

“No!” Elira cried, reaching desperately for her friend.

“I’m always with you,” Ashira’s voice echoed softly, ethereal and comforting.

“This is my path now. Trust in yours.”

Ashira's light rose higher, mingling with the dissipating magic of the shattered crystal, transforming into an ethereal presence that filled the chamber with warmth and strength.

Tears streamed down Elira's face, grief and awe intertwined. She felt Ashira's comforting presence surrounding her, a reminder that their bond transcended physical form.

As the dust settled and silence returned, Elira became aware of a new sensation – a gently pull, calling to her from beyond the now fracture Veil. The Lirians were reaching out, inviting her into their hidden realm.

Determined and filled with newfound strength, Elira rose to her feet, heart set on this new path. She knew she would honor Ashira's sacrifice and fulfill her destiny, no matter the cost. The journey had only just begun.

Chapter 6:

The sensation of falling hadn't ended – only shifted.

Elira stood in a field that glowed with a faint lavender haze, blades of grass like ribbons of light, soft under her feet. The air thrummed with warmth, like music on the verge of being heard. The sky above shimmered in watercolor hues, constantly shifting – a dream in motion. Her breath caught as she turned slowly, taking it all in.

This wasn't Elarion.

And this certainly wasn't the world she'd known.

A cool breeze brushed her cheek, carrying whispers – actual whispers – and the soft rustle of wings. She turned toward the sound. Floating lantern-like orbs, no larger than her palm, danced just above the ground, each one pulsing gently with color. They scattered as she moved toward them.

Her heart raced.

Ashira was gone. Dead.

And Elira was…where?

A sudden sharp ache rose in her chest. The weight of the loss returned in full force, stealing her breath. Her sister, her anchor to everything, was gone. She staggered to her knees in the glowing grass and pressed her hands to her face, trying not to scream.

But even as the pain cracked open her chest, something else stirred.

A pulse beneath her palms.

She froze.

"You feel it now."

The voice came from behind her, soft and sure. Elira stood slowly, wiping her face, and turned to face the speaker.

A woman stood there, tall and radiant, cloaked in flowing silver fabric that moved like mist. Her hair was pure white, not from age, but something more ethereal. Her eyes were piercing – a shade of violet that seemed to see right through Elira.

"What is this place?" Elira whispered.

The woman tilted her head, regarding her. "You've crossed the Veil."

"Veil?"

"Between what was and what is. Between illusion and truth. You broke through, and now you're here."

"Where is here?"

The woman stepped closer, her voice quieter. "You are in Lira. The realm of origin – where all emotion is born."

Elira blinked. "I don't understand."

"Few do at first. But you were called here. Your grief tore a hole through the illusion that holds your world captive. And something ancient answered."

Elira shook her head. "I don't want this. I want Ashira. I want to go back."

The woman's expression softened. "Your grief is sacred here. It will not consume you but guide you."

She gestured, and the field around them shifted – a gentle ripple revealing a pathway lined with floating stones, leading toward a glowing city in the distance. Towers of crystal rose like frozen lighting, pulsing with faint light.

"Come. There are others you must meet. You are not the only one who has broken through."

Elira hesitated. "Who are you?"

The woman gave me a faint smile. "You may call me Seris. I am one of the Remembered."

"Remembered?"

"Those who have kept their origin. Who remember what the world was before the illusion."

Elira followed Seris down the path, her thoughts spinning. With every step, the world seemed to come more alive. Flowers bloomed in response to her breath. Trees shifted their limbs to create shade for her. It felt…impossibly tender. Like the world itself saw her grief and whispered, you are not alone.

They reached a bridge of translucent stone, spanning over what appeared to be a river made entirely of light. On the other side, figures were waiting.

Lirians.

They stood tall and graceful, each of them emanating a distinct aura – colors swirling and shifting in patterns Elira couldn't name. One looked as if made of flame, their hair flickering in waves of orange and gold. Another shimmered with blue and silver, eyes like mirrors.

Seris turned to Elira. "They are born of single emotions. Pride. Sorrow. Joy. Anger. Love. The strongest of feelings. Some are balanced. Others, consumed by what created them."

Elira stepped forward, instinctively searching the crowd. She didn't know what for – but then, she saw him.

At the far end, half in the shadow, stood a figure cloaked in deep garnet and black. He was still, watching her. Not with menace, but with careful consideration.

Something in her chest twisted.

He looked familiar. Not in face. But in feeling.

Her journey had only just begun.

Chapter 7:

The Realm of Emotion

Elira followed Seris in silence, her boots crunching lightly against the crystalline path that shimmered beneath her feet. The air around them felt impossibly soft – like being wrapped in silk and mist all at once. Every breath she took felt fuller. Sharper. And yet lighter, as if her lungs were finally expanding without invisible weight pressing them down.

They passed towering flowers that pulsed with color, changing hue with the sway of the wind – lavender shifting to deep blue, then to a silvery pink. It was more than beauty. It was *alive.* Every petal seemed to respond to her presence, arching ever so slightly toward her as she walked by.

"This place feels…" Elira began, but the words escaped her.

"Like part of you already knows it," Seris finished.

She looked at her, startled. "Yes. How?"

Seris smiled. "Liria isn't just a place, Elira. It's a reflection. Of whom you are. What you feel. What you *carry.* The more open you become, the more it reveals itself to you."

As if on cue, the sky above them shifted from pale peach to the softest blue she'd ever seen. The clouds bent around the light in swirls that reminded her of her mother's old oil paintings.

They crossed a delicate bridge woven of silver vines. Below it flowed a stream – not of water, but of *light.* Soft, fluid radiance danced across its surface. When Elira looked too long, she swore she saw her own memories flickering within it.

"What is that?" she asked, slowing to peer over the edge.

Seris paused beside her. "The Vein of Memory. It weaves through all of Liria. Sometimes it shows truths not yet faced. Sometimes… echoes of who you once were."

Elira's throat tightened. The reflection below rippled and changed – showing a much younger version of herself. Alone. Crying in a hallway. Her father's voice ringing out, cold and dismissive. "Don't be so dramatic, Elira. You're too emotional for your own good."

Her nails dug into her palms.

"Can it…show me things I've forgotten?" she whispered.

"Yes," Seris said gently. "But only when you're ready." She pulled her gaze away, heart hammering, and continued walking.

Up ahead, the landscape widened into what looked like a gathering place – wide, open, ringed by glowing trees whose leaves hummed faintly with soft sound. She could feel something – *someone* – watching her. Not with malice. But with intent.

"You're not the only one who feels deeply here," Seris murmured.

From the trees emerged figures – tall, graceful, and glowing faintly from within. Lirians. Each one subtly different. One shimmered with a golden hue that radiated joy. Another carried a somber indigo light that pulsed like a heartbeat.

And then she saw *him.*

Not glowing. Not standing tall in authority like the others. But watching her with eyes that seemed to hold the storm and the calm after it.

The air shifted around her. Like the world inhaled.

"Elira," Seris said, voice lower now. "That is Carien. He is unlike the others. Born of empathy. The rarest of all."

Carien stepped forward, slow and sure. His voice, when he spoke was quiet – but every syllable felt like a balm. "Welcome, Elira. We've been waiting."

Her chest tightened. The way he said her name, like it was meant to be spoken only in kindness, unraveled something deep in her. The fear. The doubt. The question of whether she truly belonged anywhere.

Not here.

Not now.

But standing there, in a place built from emotion itself, with eyes meeting hers like he already *knew* her story – she wasn't so sure anymore that she was dreaming.

She was starting to believe.

Chapter 8:

The air felt different the next morning. Colder. Still, but not peaceful – like the world was holding its breath.

Elira rose early, stirred by restless dreams she couldn't quite hold onto. They dissolved like fog in sunlight – just enough detail to haunt her. Whispers of voices she didn't recognize. A glimpse of her mother's eyes. A pair of golden wings.

She stood at the edge of the garden, barefoot on dew-kissed grass. The sky was gray, clouded over, but no rain came. Behind her, the manor loomed – silent, pristine, and unshaken. As if nothing had happened. As is Ashira never existed.

But Elira did not forget.

And that – perhaps more than anything – was what set her apart now.

"You feel it, don't you?" Cairen's voice arrived with the breeze. He stood a few paces behind her, hands clasped loosely behind his back.

Elira turned. "Feel what?"

"The unraveling." He stepped forward, lowering his voice. "It always begins slow. A tug here, a frayed thread there. And then – snap."

Elira's brow furrowed. "I don't understand. What's coming undone?"

He tilted his head. "The lie."

Something inside her tightened. "You keep speaking in riddles. Why won't you just tell me what you know?"

"I *am* telling you. But truth cannot always be given – it must be discovered."

She exhaled sharply. "You sound like her."

Cairen's gaze softened. "Ashira?"

"She always said things like that. Things I didn't understand until they hurt." Elira paused. "Is that part of your charm? Speak in circles until we're too confused to fight back?"

"No." He stepped closer. "It's to remind you that your instincts were never broken. You just learned to silence them."

Elira looked away, throat tight. "What if I don't want to hear them anymore?"

"But you do." He said gently, without judgement. "You just don't trust them yet."

A silence fell between them.

Finally, Cairen reached into his coat and pulled something from a leather pouch – a stone, smooth and glassy, with a faint iridescent sheen that shimmered in the light. He held it out to her.

Elira took it hesitantly. The moment her skin touched its surface; a pulse ran through her fingertips. A warmth – not heat – but recognition. A strange sense of being *seen.*

"What is this?"

"A memory stone. Lirian-crafted. It responds to true emotion. If you listen, it can show you pieces of yourself you've forgotten."

Elira stared down at the stone. Its shimmer deepened, swirls of color slowly forming beneath the surface like oil in water.

"And if I don't like what it shows me?" she whispered.

Cairen's voice was calm. "Then you finally begin to heal."

⁂

Later that night, Elira sat cross-legged on the floor of her room, the memory stone resting in her palm. The house was quiet. Too quiet. Like even the walls were waiting.

She closed her eyes.

The stone pulsed once.

Then again.

And suddenly –

She wasn't in her room.

She was on a forest path.

Taller trees than she'd ever seen. A silver mist curling around her ankles.

And then she heard it – Ashira's laughter.

Bright. Alive.

Real.

Elira turned toward the sound, heart pounding.

And as she took a step forward, the mist began to clear.

The mist parted with each of Elira's steps, swirling and dispersing like it recognized her.

Ashira stood ahead, just beyond a willow tree whose silver branches dropped low to the earth. Her back was turned, hair glowing faintly under the misted light, the same way Elira remembered – but softer. Unburdened.

"Ashira?" Elira's voice cracked.

Her friend turned, slowly. Her face was radiant – not in an ethereal way, but in a *human* way. Familiar. Warm. Not touched by grief or time.

"I knew you'd find me," Ashira said, smiling.

Elira froze. "This…this isn't real."

Ashira stepped closer, the grass not bending beneath her feet. "It's more real than you think."

Tears stung Elira's eyes. "You're gone."

"I'm not." Ashira reached up, fingers grazing the willow branches. "Not completely."

Elira looked down at the memory stone, now glowing steadily in her hand. "Is this you? Is *this* what it does?"

Ashira nodded. "It allows what lives in you to speak. I never truly left you, Elira. You carry me – in your grief, in your anger, in your strength."

"I'm not strong," Elira whispered. "I was never like you."

Ashira smiled sadly. "You were never meant to be like me. You were meant to be *you.* And you are stronger than you realize. You just haven't had the chance to *remember.*"

The wind stirred through the trees like a breath.

Elira stepped forward. "Why now?"

"Because now, you're ready." Ashira's eyes gleamed. "You've started to see through it, haven't you? The veil. The illusion. The lies you've been told your whole life."

Elira blinked. "You mean my father?"

Ashira's gaze hardened slightly. "I mean the world he *built.* The illusion he cast. Not just over you, but over everyone."

Elira's chest tightened. "You tried to show me…and I didn't listen."

"You weren't supposed to then." Ashira reached for her hand – but didn't quite touch. "But you *are* supposed to now."

The forest began to dissolve. Mist rising like smoke.

"No, wait – don't go!" Elira cried.

Ashira's voice echoed as she faded:

"Trust yourself, Elira. The truth is waiting for you. You just have to be willing to see it."

Elira gasped awake, the memory stone still in her hand, now dull and lifeless.

But the warmth hadn't left her.

And for the first time since the funeral, her room didn't feel empty.

It felt…watched.

Guarded.

Held.

Ashira was still with her.

Just… in a different way now.

And Elira? She was no longer the same girl who had stood in silence and swallowed grief.

The veil was beginning to fray.

And for the first time, she *wanted* to pull it down.

Chapter 9:

"Sometimes it's not the light that reveals the truth – but the way the shadows no longer fit."

The memory stone hadn't glowed since that night.

Elira had tried everything – meditation, moonlight, even whispering Ashira's name like a prayer. But the stone remained cold and gray, its magic silent. Still, something had changed.

She could feel her. In the hush between thoughts. In the stillness of dawn. Like Ashira's presence had settled just behind the veil of her perception – out of reach but not gone.

It made the palace feel different, too.

She noticed things she'd never paid attention to. Guards who stood in the same positions each day, their movements too rehearsed. Courtiers whose smiles never quite reached their eyes. The way the King's portrait in the great hall seemed to follow her with its gaze.

Or maybe I'm finally paying attention, she thought.

She passed her father's study that morning and paused, hearing voices through the heavy oak door.

"…a few more days until the renewal ceremony. We cannot afford distraction," one of the voices muttered.

Her father's reply was hushed but urgent. "Elira is no threat. She's too absorbed in her grief."

A flicker bloomed in her chest. She stepped back, careful not to make a sound, and walked away.

No threat, she thought bitterly.

Maybe I was never supposed to be.

⁂

Later that afternoon, she sat by the stone garden, where a cool breeze whispered between the white columns. She had the journal in her lap again – Ashira's. The leather cover was worn in the corners, the ink inside slightly faded, but her voice rang clear in every entry.

"Illusions aren't always lies. Sometimes they're truths too painful to carry."

"He's changing, Elira. I don't know if you see it yet, but I do. The King we once knew – your father – is becoming something else. Or maybe he always was, and I just wanted to believe he loved you."

Elira closed her eyes, pressing her fingers to the pages.

How long had Ashira been trying to understand? How long had she *known?*

Footsteps broke her thoughts. A familiar voice followed.

"You've been quiet lately." It was Ryn, the palace gardener's son. Someone she'd grown up with. Observant. Quiet. Safe.

"I've had a lot to think about," she said softly.

He tilted his head. "You look different. Not in a bad way. Just… like you're seeing things more clearly."

She offered a small smile. "Maybe I am."

He hesitated before sitting beside her. "There are rumors."

"About?"

"The King. Whispers from the outer provinces. People are starting to… forget."

Elira's brows knit. "Forget what?"

"Their own memories. Places they've been. People they've loved. As if… someone rewrote them."

A chilled laced down her spine.

Ryn lowered his voice. "And they say it started right after the last *Veil Renewal.*"

Elira gripped the journal tighter. 'Do you believe it?"

He looked straight at her. "I believe something's wrong. And I think Ashira did too."

The stone garden fell silent except for the wind.

Maybe she hadn't imagined it. The illusion. The veil.

Maybe Ashira hadn't just died.

Maybe she had been *silenced.*

Elira returned to her room that night with her heart pounding. She lit a single candle, placed the memory stone beside it, and opened the last page of the journal.

Ashira's final entry read only two words:

"Find me."

And this time, the memory stone glowed faintly at her touch.

Chapter 10:

"The truth doesn't always scream. Sometimes, it whispers through the cracks of what you thought was real."

The memory stone glowed for only a second.

But it was enough.

Elira's breath caught in her throat. The pale blue light had flickered – just once- before fading into stillness. Not imagined. Not a trick of the candlelight. It *responded.*

She stared at it, her fingers trembling.

"Ashira…" she whispered.

She wasn't sure what she expected. A voice. A vision. Some magical apparition appearing in the room. But there was only silence, and the fading scent of wax and stone dust.

Still, something stirred in the room – like the air had shifted, thinned.

Elira moved to the window, where the moon hung low and heavy, draped in clouds. The gardens below shimmered faintly, and for a split second, the trees moved in ways they shouldn't have. Not by wind. By *something else.*

A pattern. A pulse. Like the heartbeat of the realm itself, hidden beneath layers of silence.

I'm not imagining this anymore.

The next morning, Elira woke with a start. Her dream had been vivid – a whispering voice calling her name from a forest she'd never seen before, where light bent unnaturally, and colors shimmered like mist. When she opened her eyes, her fingers were still curled around the memory stone.

It was warm.

You're leading me somewhere, she thought. *Aren't you, Ashira?*

She wrapped the stone in a cloth and tucked it into her satchel.

If this was the beginning of something – of everything – she wasn't going to wait any longer.

She slipped out of the palace quietly, her cloak drawn up around her face. She wasn't sure where she was going, only that she *had to move.* Away from the thrones. Away from the carefully crafted world her father controlled.

Ryn met her just past the stables, exactly where she'd asked him to. He didn't say much. Just handed her a small pack of food and supplies and nodded.

"You sure?" he asked softly.

"No," Elira answered honestly. "But I *have* to do this."

He hesitated. "Then…come back. Please."

Elira gave him a grateful look before returning toward the woods. Not the main roads. The forgotten ones. The ones no one used anymore.

The deeper she walked, the quieter the world became.

The air grew heavier. Trees leaned closer, ancient and gnarled; their bark etched with symbols older than the kingdom. The path narrowed. And that's when she saw it –

A shimmer in the air. Like heat rising from stone.

She reached forward – and her hand passed through it.

The illusion peeled like silk.

Beyond it was *another realm.*

And standing at its edge was **Ashira.**

Not flesh. Not ghost. Something in-between. Her form was wrapped in light and memory, flickering slightly like a candle in the wind – but her eyes were the same.

"Welcome, Elira," she said. Her voice wasn't sound – it was *felt.* A pulse beneath Elira's ribs.

"I – I thought you were gone."

Ashira smiled softly. "Not gone. Just…waiting for you to be ready."

Elira stepped closer, heart thundering. "Ready for what?"

Ashira turned, motioning toward the forest beyond the veil – where colors bled like watercolors and the air pulsed with magic.

"To see the world as it truly is. To remember. And to awaken."

And there, beneath ancient trees and trembling sky, Elira stepped fully thought the veil.

The illusion was behind her.

Ahead was the truth – and the realm of the **Lirians.**

Chapter 11:

The illusion cracks loudest in silence.

The world felt *too* still. As Elira moved through the village that morning., every step on the cobblestone felt like an echo. People smiled as they passed, waving with mechanical ease. A baker handed a warm loaf to a child, but the child didn't blink. The scent of lavender floated in the air – but there were no flowers in bloom.

It was all *too* perfect.

Her fingertips brushed the edge of the fountain in the square. The water sparkled like sunlight trapped in glass, cascading in flawless arcs. But as she looked closer, her breath caught. The reflection staring back at her was…wrong. It was her face – but her eyes weren't *hers.*

They shimmered gold. Fleeting. Gone in a blink.

"Elira," a soft voice whispered.

She froze. The voice was barely audible – like wind through leaves – but it stirred something deep inside her.

"Ashira?" she murmured.

The air trembled, subtle and strange.

"You're not imagining this."

Elira turned, heart pounding. A shimmer stood just beyond the veil of light – like heat rising from stone. A woman-shaped presence formed from threads of light and shadow, ethereal and untouchable. Ashira.

"You're here," Elira whispered.

"Always," Ashira said, her voice not from lips, but from everywhere.

"You just couldn't hear me before."

Emotion surged in Elira's chest, but Ashira raised a hand – a gesture of grounding, not distance.

"There's little time. The veil is cracking, and the king feels it. He'll tighten his grip. You must move faster."

Elira swallowed hard, the weight of destiny settling against her ribs. "I don't know how. I don't know where to go from here."

Ashira tilted her head. "Then listen to the quiet. Not the noise of the illusion – but the silence underneath it. That's where the truth lives."

The shimmer faded, but warmth lingered – inside her, around her, *with* her.

Elira turned back to the fountain. This time, her reflection looked back with *her* eyes. Deep. Awake.

And underneath the sound of flowing water, she heard it.

A hum. A pull. The heartbeat of something hidden.

The truth was calling.

And Elira was ready to follow.

The hum beneath the surface wasn't music, not exactly. It was older than melody – older than language. It vibrated through the soles of her feet and curled around her ribcage, a slow, steady pulse that matched her heartbeat, and yet… wasn't hers.

Elira stepped back from the fountain, her breath catching in her throat. Her hands trembled, not from fear, but from recognition.

This was real.

Ashira – her best friend, her almost-sister, her soul's tether – wasn't gone. Not entirely. Not where it counted.

Tears welled in her eyes, but she didn't wipe them away. She *wanted* to feel it all. The ache of longing, the spark of hope, the quiet terror of what came next.

Ashira's words circled her mind.

"The veil is cracking… he'll tighten his grip."

Elira glanced around. The village still shimmered in its fabricated perfection – children laughing too sweetly, skies too blue, a calmness that felt too close to suffocation.

Now that she had *seen* the cracks, she couldn't unsee them.

A woman in the market waved, but her smile faltered when their eyes met – just for a second. Elira saw something behind them.

Fear? Doubt? Awareness?

And then, like a puppet snapped back into place, the woman's smile returned – too wide. Too sharp.

The illusion was fighting back.

Elira clenched her fists and exhaled. "Okay," she whispered. "If you can reach me…I can find you."

Ashira's presence was still here, quiet now but warm, a tether woven between Elira's ribs. She could feel it.

A single thought bloomed in her chest:

You are not alone.

For the first time, that didn't feel like a lie.

Elira turned her back on the fountain, head high, breath steady.

She didn't know what she'd find next. Only that she had to go.

And she would not go quietly.

Chapter 12:

The truth waits for those brave enough to ask.

The path to the eastern woods was rarely traveled. Most villagers avoided it, spinning tales of haunted creatures and misfortune, warning their children never to wander nearby.

But Elira had always been curious.

As a child, she'd stood at the forest's edge, staring into its shadowed veil, wondering if magic lived there. Her father said the stories were nonsense, but something about his eyes when he spoke—too hard, too fast—told her he feared it. That was reason enough to believe it mattered.

And now, she was going back.

The hum she'd felt at the fountain hadn't faded. If anything, it grew stronger as she approached the border of the trees, vibrating just beneath the surface of her skin like a compass guiding her home.

The leaves whispered in a language she couldn't understand—but felt, deeply. They rustled not with wind, but *memory*.

Elira stepped past the first tree, and the illusion of the village fell away like a silk curtain torn down.

The light changed. Softer. More *honest.* The air was cooler, grounded. She took another step.

And that's when she saw it.

Symbols—etched into the trunks of trees, faint but glowing. They pulsed like living runes, echoing the hum inside her.

She reached out instinctively, placing her palm against the nearest one.

A sharp breath escaped her lips.

In an instant, *images* flashed through her mind:

Ashira's face—lit by moonlight.

A boy with silver eyes, standing at the edge of a cliff.

A field of flames, and Elira—standing in the center, untouched.

A throne, carved of obsidian and bone.

And eyes. So many eyes. Watching. Waiting.

She stumbled back, gasping.

What had she just touched?

The mark on the tree glowed brighter for a moment, then dimmed, returning to its subtle thrum.

Whatever this place was, it knew her.

And somehow… it was waking up.

"To find the truth, you must first be willing to lose the lie."

The trees grew denser the farther she walked, the path narrowing into a barely visible thread between trunks. The sky dimmed, though she wasn't sure if it was evening or if the canopy above was simply growing thicker, cloaking her in soft shadow.

The village was long behind her now. And the further it faded, the more her mind cleared. The silence here wasn't empty—it was *full.* Full of things unspoken, of stories buried beneath moss and bark, waiting for someone to listen.

Elira paused at the base of a massive tree, its roots tangled like serpents, its bark carved with swirling patterns that shimmered faintly in the half-light. She placed her hand on the surface again.

No visions this time.

Just a hum. A pulse. A recognition.

"I see you," she whispered.

And the tree… answered. Not in words, but in warmth. A deep thrum that echoed into her bones, welcoming her.

Suddenly, a breeze brushed past her cheek—warm, fragrant, and full of something she couldn't quite place.

"*Elira…*"

She froze.

The voice was not hers. Not imagined. It came from behind her.

She turned slowly.

At first, there was nothing.

Then—just beyond the curve of the path—stood a boy. No… a *man.* Tall. Lean. Eyes the color of silver starlight. Hair dark as midnight. He wasn't cloaked or hiding. He simply *was.* As if the forest had always held him, and only now decided to show her.

She opened her mouth, but no sound came.

He tilted his head slightly, not smiling, not frowning. Just… seeing her.

"You've stepped beyond the veil," he said quietly. His voice was calm but carried weight. "There's no going back now."

Elira's heartbeat thundered in her chest, but she stood her ground. "Who are you?"

"A guide. A guardian. A thorn in the King's side," he said dryly. "Depends on who you ask."

She blinked.

He took a slow step forward, hands visible at his sides. "My name is Vaelen. And I think you've been looking for me."

The name struck something in her. As if she'd heard it in a dream she couldn't fully recall.

"I don't know you," she said. But even as she said it, her soul whispered *yet.*

"You will," Vaelen replied gently. "But not here. This is only the edge of what you're meant to find."

He looked past her, toward the runes glowing behind her. "You've seen her, haven't you? The girl you lost."

Elira flinched.

"I see her with you," he added. "Still. Always."

She swallowed hard. "How do you know that?"

Vaelen's expression softened. "Because the Lirians have started to stir."

Her breath caught.

"Wait… the Lirians are real?"

He didn't answer. Just turned and started down a side path, one she hadn't even noticed before—covered in vines and barely wide enough to walk through.

After a moment, he looked back.

"Well? Are you coming?"

Elira hesitated only a second. Then she stepped off the path and followed him into the unknown.

Chapter 13:

The forest doesn't lie. But it doesn't give answers freely, either.

Elira followed Vaelen through the narrowing path, branches brushing her shoulders, the air thick with the scent of damp earth and something older—like lightning caught in moss. The light dimmed further, and her eyes adjusted quickly, as if her body knew this darkness before her mind did.

Neither of them spoke. Not at first.

The silence between them felt intentional. Sacred. As if the trees were listening, and Vaelen knew better than to speak too soon.

After several minutes, the path opened into a small clearing—circular, encased by high arching trees that shimmered faintly with that same soft glow she'd seen in the runes. In the center stood a flat stone, weathered and marked with unfamiliar sigils, and just beyond it… a pool of water. Still. Black as ink.

Vaelen stopped at the edge of the pool and turned to her.

"This is a threshold," he said. "One of the oldest."

Elira stepped beside him, peering into the water. It reflected nothing. No trees. No sky. Not even her own face.

"What is it?" she asked softly.

"Memory," Vaelen replied. "But not just yours. This place holds the echoes of everything that's ever passed through it. You came here because something inside you was ready to remember."

Elira glanced at him. "I don't even know what I've forgotten."

"That's the thing," he said, crouching near the edge. "The veil doesn't just hide the truth. It rewrites it."

She felt that hum again low and steady beneath her ribs. "The village. My father. Everything…"

Vaelen looked up at her. "He feared this place for a reason."

Her breath caught. "He knew."

"He helped build the illusion," Vaelen said, not unkindly. "Though I doubt he knew just how deep it ran. Most don't. They just feel the fear."

Elira stepped closer to the water, unable to look away from the void surface.

"What happens if I touch it?" she asked.

Vaelen's voice was quiet. "You see. And once you do… you can't unsee."

Her fingers hovered over the surface.

A flicker.

A voice.

"Elira…"

Ashira.

She gasped.

A ripple spread across the water, and a shape began to form—soft at first, like mist. A girl. Laughing. Braiding flowers into Elira's hair. Another ripple. A scream. Fire. Darkness. Then Ashira's face again, eyes wide with something between warning and hope.

Elira stumbled backward.

"She's here," she whispered.

Vaelen stood beside her. "She never left you. You just couldn't see her."

The trees rustled.

The runes brightened.

Elira turned to him, voice shaking. "Why now? Why is all of this waking up?"

Vaelen's silver eyes met hers. "Because you're ready. And because the King has grown careless. His illusions are cracking. The Lirians are waking."

She felt the tremor beneath her skin again.

"What do I do?" she asked.

He stepped closer. "You follow the thread that's always been yours. You let the truth ruin the lies."

She nodded slowly.

And then the pool shimmered again—this time not with Ashira, but with herself. Not who she was… but who she could become.

A woman with flame in her eyes.

A crown of stars.

A blade of light in her hand.

And a world behind her, unmasked and rising.

Elira staggered a step closer to the pool, heart pounding.

The image shimmered again. Herself—only… more. Stronger. Steadier. Wearing a dark cloak that rippled like shadow and light at once. Her eyes were bright with something unshakable. Not anger. Not fear. But truth.

She reached out, fingers grazing the water's surface.

The vision didn't ripple this time.

Instead, it *held.*

She saw herself standing in a grand hall, stone pillars carved with the same runes etched into the trees. A council gathered before her—some human, some not. Their faces were solemn, but their gazes were fixed on her. Waiting.

She raised her voice—not loud, but clear.

"This is the end of the illusion. We are not broken. We were made to forget. But no more."

The vision shifted. A battlefield of mist and shadow. Vaelen at her side. Strange, luminous beings hovering just behind them—Lirians, she realized, each one radiating a single, overwhelming emotion. Grief. Fury. Joy. Hope.

They weren't monsters. They were mirrors.

The image changed again.

A throne room, cold and sharp as obsidian.

And her father.

King Aurik stood at the center, cloaked in majesty, but the illusion flickered around him like a failing spell. His crown shimmered like oil over water—beautiful but broken.

Elira stood before him, unwavering.

"You will answer for what you've done."

The pool pulsed, and the image faded.

Elira stumbled back, breath catching in her throat.

Vaelen caught her before she could fall.

"What… what was that?" she gasped.

"A glimpse," he said, voice quiet. "Of what could be. What *must* be."

Her knees hit the ground, and she pressed her palms into the moss, grounding herself as her thoughts spun. "How do I become her? That version of me? The one who's not afraid?"

Vaelen knelt beside her.

"You already are her," he said. "But you've been taught not to see it."

Elira turned her head to him, eyes still wide. "Why me?"

"Because you're the one who remembered," he said simply. "You're the thread that couldn't be erased."

For a moment, she let that settle.

Then the whisper came again.

But this time, it wasn't Ashira.

It was *herself*.

A whisper from deep within, clear and unwavering.

"You were never meant to stay small."

Chapter 14:

The forest does not lose its way. Only those who walk without listening.

The path narrowed as they walked. What once was a trail had become a series of roots and woven vines, braided by time and something more ancient than memory. Elira moved carefully behind Vaelen, her fingers brushing against tree trunks that pulsed faintly beneath her touch.

Every step further away from the village felt like a step closer to truth.

"What are the Lirians exactly?" she finally asked, breaking the silence.

Vaelen slowed. "They were born from emotion, not flesh. Each one shaped by a single truth, a single feeling so powerful it took form. Love. Sorrow. Rage. Hope."

Elira furrowed her brow. "They're alive?"

"They are more than alive. They *remember*. They've waited."

"For what?"

He glanced over his shoulder, a faint smile tugging at his lips. "You."

She blinked, but before she could ask more, the trees opened into a clearing.

At its center stood a stone archway—ancient, covered in moss and symbols that shimmered like moonlight on water. The air here was different. Heavier, but not oppressive. Like standing in the pause between heartbeats.

"This is the crossing," Vaelen said. "Beyond this arch lies the heart of the Lirian realm."

Elira stepped closer. The hum beneath her skin intensified.

"This is where Ashira's spirit went," she whispered.

Vaelen nodded. "And where yours has always belonged."

Her breath caught.

"I don't know if I'm ready."

"No one ever is," he said. "But that's the thing about awakening. It doesn't ask for permission. Only courage."

Elira swallowed hard. She looked at the arch, then back at him. "Will you come with me?"

"I've been waiting to."

Together, they stepped through.

The moment she crossed the threshold, everything changed.

Light bent around her, not harsh, but fluid—like walking through the edge of a dream. The air shimmered with color that didn't exist in the mortal realm. Trees taller than mountains rose into the mist, their leaves glowing in every hue imaginable. The ground was soft and warm beneath her boots, like the forest itself was alive and welcoming her home.

And then… she felt them.

Not saw. *Felt.*

A presence brushing the edge of her mind.

Dozens. Hundreds. Watching. Waiting.

Some cautious. Some curious. A few, afraid.

But one—familiar. Fierce. Gentle.

Ashira.

"Elira…" came the whisper again. Closer now.

She turned.

And there—hovering just beyond the tree line—was a figure woven from starlight and memory. Ashira. Her features soft, her eyes glowing, not with tears—but peace.

"You found me," Ashira said, her voice a melody in the air.

Elira's knees gave out, and she fell to the earth in silent, shaking awe.

"I never stopped looking," she whispered.

Ashira smiled. "I know. That's why I could come back."

Ashira hovered above the forest floor, her form a shifting glow—neither ghost nor memory, but something more. A tether between worlds. Her outline flickered like firelight, but her presence was grounding. Real. Elira reached out instinctively, but her hand passed through the air like touching water and starlight.

"I'm not here the way I used to be," Ashira said gently, as if she knew Elira's heartache before it was spoken. "But I am still *with* you. Just… different now."

Tears welled in Elira's eyes, but they didn't fall. "Why did it have to be this way?"

Ashira's voice held sorrow and wisdom. "Because this world needed you to wake up. And sometimes… pain is the only thing that breaks the spell."

Vaelen stood quietly behind them, head bowed in reverence.

"I thought I'd lost you forever," Elira whispered.

"You did lose me," Ashira said softly. "But not everything that's lost is gone."

She drifted forward and placed her palm over Elira's chest—right above her heart.

"This is where I live now. This is where I guide you from."

A sudden wind rustled the trees behind them—different than before. Sharper. Charged with emotion. Vaelen turned sharply toward the sound.

"They're coming," he murmured. "They've felt your presence."

Elira stood slowly, wiping her face. "Who?"

"The Lirians."

From the shadows of the forest, shapes began to emerge.

Not quite human, not quite spirit. Each of them walked with a presence that made the air shimmer. Their forms were sculpted from light and shadow, skin glowing in hues that pulsed with their core emotion. One radiated a warm, golden hue—his eyes soft and kind, a quiet joy emanating from him. Another moved like a flicker of flame—her presence fierce, eyes like burning coals.

"They're… beautiful," Elira breathed.

"They are," Vaelen said. "And dangerous. Not because they wish to harm, but because their emotions are *pure.* Unfiltered. When they feel, the world feels with them."

The golden one stepped forward.

"We felt your arrival," he said. His voice resonated in Elira's mind, not just her ears. "You carry a wound. But you also carry a key."

Elira blinked. "A key to what?"

"To what's been hidden. To the truth buried beneath the illusion that binds this realm—and your own."

More Lirians stepped into view. A girl made of shadow and sorrow. A boy trailing leaves that grew as he walked. A tall figure cloaked in fear so thick it shimmered like smoke.

Ashira's voice whispered again, softer now. "Each of them has a gift to give you… but only if you are willing to feel what they feel."

Elira turned to her. "How do I know I'm ready?"

"You don't," Ashira said with a small smile. "But you're here. That means something."

The golden Lirian stepped closer and held out his hand.

"I am Solen," he said. "Born of joy. Will you walk with me?"

Elira hesitated only a moment—then placed her hand in his glowing palm.

And the world shifted again.

The moment Solen's hand touched hers, warmth spread up Elira's arm like sunlight pouring through winter glass. It wasn't just physical warmth—it was emotional, deep, safe. It filled the hollow places inside her with something she couldn't name. Not happiness exactly. Not yet. But a softness. A remembering.

The forest shifted around them. What had once been shadows turned golden. The trees swayed as if they, too, sighed with relief.

Solen's presence pulsed beside her—steady and grounding. He didn't speak as they walked, not at first. He didn't have to. His silence said: *You don't need to perform here. You don't have to carry the armor you were forced to wear.*

After a while, he glanced at her. "You carry joy like a stranger."

The words caught her off guard. "I… what?"

"You wear it like a borrowed cloak," he said gently. "As if it doesn't belong to you."

Elira looked away, swallowing. "Maybe it doesn't."

Solen stopped. They stood before a tree whose leaves glowed gold and lilac. Small blossoms bloomed in impossible colors along its trunk.

"When was the last time you laughed without fear of what came next?" he asked.

She opened her mouth—then stopped.

Solen tilted his head. "When was the last time you felt joy without guilt?"

Her breath caught. "I don't know."

"That is the wound," he said softly. "The one we do not see. The world taught you that joy must be earned, that peace is conditional. It lied to you."

He knelt beside the tree and brushed away moss from the roots, revealing a small, glimmering pool tucked between the roots.

"Look," he said.

Elira knelt and gazed into the pool. Her reflection stared back at her—but younger. A child with wide eyes, laughing, spinning barefoot in a sun-drenched field. The kind of joy that only innocence can know.

"I remember her," she whispered.

"She remembers you," Solen said. "And she's waiting."

Tears stung her eyes. "How do I become her again?"

"You don't," he replied. "You become something new—someone who carries that joy *with* her. Not instead of her wounds, but alongside them."

He placed a hand over her heart, light radiating from his touch.

"This is the first truth: joy is not a betrayal of pain. It is a rebellion against it."

The forest shimmered. Light danced through the canopy above. And for the first time in a long time, Elira *felt* it—real joy. Small, soft, but hers.

As Solen rose, the light around him seemed to settle—like a sunbeam choosing where to land.

Elira remained kneeling for a moment longer, her hand brushing the soft moss at the tree's base.

Joy is not a betrayal of pain…

That phrase echoed in her like a secret she'd always known but never spoken. It wasn't about forgetting. It was about *remembering differently.*

She looked up at Solen, and for the first time in what felt like forever, she smiled—and meant it.

A real smile.

He didn't say anything. He just nodded, as if to say, *yes… there you are.*

And together, they walked deeper into the wood.

Chapter 15:

The Ones Who Remember

The path grew stranger

Not darker, not brighter—just… different. The air tasted of rain and memory. The trees leaned in more closely, their bark etched with whispers she could almost understand.

Solen didn't speak, but Elira didn't mind. Something had shifted inside her, and she wasn't ready to break it with words.

After a while, the trees opened into a clearing—a circle ringed by stones glowing with faint violet light. In the center stood three figures.

Not quite human.

They were Lirian.

Each one shimmered in a hue Elira didn't have names for. Their presence was overwhelming but not frightening. It was like standing in the presence of an ancient truth—one you could feel but, couldn't explain.

Solen stepped forward first, bowing slightly.

"Elira," he said softly, "these are the Remembered Ones. Each born from a truth your world has forgotten."

The tallest figure stepped forward. Their skin glowed like moonlit water, eyes deep and endless.

"I am Caerith," they said. "I was born of Sorrow."

Elira inhaled sharply. The emotion that pressed against her chest wasn't her own—but it was familiar.

"You've buried much," Caerith said, gently. "We do not come to make you suffer. We come so you can remember how to feel without being consumed."

The next stepped forward—smaller but cloaked in smoke that pulsed like a heartbeat.

"I am Nyra," she said. "Born of Fear."

Her voice was a whisper, but it held power. "You have lived with me so long; you've mistaken me for instinct. But I am only a shadow—meant to warn, not define."

The final Lirian stepped closer—his presence colder, sharper.

"I am Thalen," he said. "Born of Anger."

Elira stiffened.

He didn't smile. "Good. You *should* be wary of me. But I am not your enemy. Anger is not destruction. It is the fire that demands change. The voice that says: *enough*."

She stared at them all, heart pounding.

"I… I don't understand. Why me?"

Solen stepped beside her again. "Because you feel everything the world told you not to. You are not broken, Elira. You are *awakening*. And they are here to show you what that means."

The clearing pulsed once, gently. A kind of welcome.

Elira stepped forward, eyes wide, breath uneven—but she didn't turn back.

The truths were waiting.

And she was finally ready to face them.

Elira's heart pounded in her chest, but not from fear. From something else - recognition. A memory she couldn't reach but that stirred like embers beneath ash. Her gaze lingered on each of them—Caerith, Nyra, Thalen. They didn't just embody emotion. They were emotion. And somehow, their presence made her feel more like herself than she ever had in the village.

"I don't understand," she said, her voice shaking. "If I'm the key… to what?"

Solen's gaze was steady. "To waking the rest. To breaking the veil."

Vaelen stepped forward, folding his arms. "The King built his rule on illusion. On silence. On forgetting. But you—your presence here, your awakening—it's a ripple that cannot be undone."

Nyra moved closer, her eyes glowing softly in the dim light. "There will be resistance. Not just from him. From the world inside you that was shaped to survive, not to feel."

"Especially the parts that were told feeling too much made you weak," Thalen added, voice quiet but unyielding.

The words pierced her, but not like a wound. More like a key sliding into a lock.

Caerith extended a hand—not demanding, just offering. "Let the sorrow surface, Elira. Not to drown in it, but to remember what it means to care so deeply."

The emotion caught in her throat. "What if I'm not strong enough?"

"You already are," Solen said simply. "You've carried this pain in silence your entire life. Strength isn't in silence. It's in the willingness to speak now."

The grove shifted. Wind stirred the leaves overhead, and the runes along the trees began to glow brighter, pulsing faster. Elira turned slowly in a circle, realizing something was… awakening. Around her. Within her.

"I feel like something's breaking inside me," she whispered.

"No," Caerith said. "Something is breaking *open*."

A sudden warmth spread from her core outward. Her skin prickled, vision blurring—not from tears, but light. She fell to her knees as the hum of the grove deepened, surrounding her like a song with no sound.

And in the space between one breath and the next, she felt *her*.

Ashira.

Not as a memory. Not as grief.

But as presence.

Soft. Radiant. Unmistakable.

Elira's tears spilled freely now. "You're here," she whispered.

The wind whispered through the trees like a sigh of confirmation.

"You are never alone," said a voice—not Ashira's, not any of the Lirians—but from the forest itself. Or perhaps... from herself.

And as Elira looked up at the gathered Lirians, her voice steadying, she said:

"Then let's begin."

Chapter 16:

The One She's Forgotten

The grove had stilled after the Lirians' retreat, but the air still vibrated with something unsaid. A hush fell over the space—reverent, alert. Elira stood beneath the boughs, her fingers twitching with a restlessness she couldn't name.

It was as though the forest itself was watching.

Vaelen had gone quiet again, his gaze sharp as always, tracking something in the distance. Solen hummed softly to himself as he traced the glowing patterns etched into a nearby tree, each line pulsing beneath his touch like breath.

Elira wrapped her arms around herself, the quiet pressing in on her chest. Not in a suffocating way—but in a way that demanded she listen.

Something inside her was stirring. Something deeper than memory.

A sound—barely more than a whisper—brushed her ear.

"Elira…"

She turned, heart lurching. "Ashira?"

But the voice was not Ashira's. It was softer. Sadder. Woven with something she hadn't heard in a long, long time.

Love.

A different kind of love.

She scanned the grove. No movement. No figure in the trees. Just the sensation that someone had reached out—not from the world of the living, but from something older. Something sacred.

The hum inside her chest shifted.

It didn't thrum like the runes or burn like Solen's light. This was different. Gentle, but ancient. Like lullabies sung from memory. Like arms she didn't remember but still longed for.

"Did you hear that?" she asked, her voice thinner than she meant it to be.

Solen looked over, brow lifted. "What did you hear?"

"A voice. A woman. Not Ashira. But… I don't know. It felt like…" She hesitated. "It felt like home."

Vaelen's eyes darkened with quiet understanding. "You're starting to remember."

"Remember what?"

Neither of them answered.

Because they didn't have to.

Something had been taken from her. Not just stolen—but erased. And now, that silence was cracking.

Solen stepped forward, his voice gentler than she'd ever heard it. "Not all truths come like thunder, Elira. Some come like whispers. But they are no less powerful."

Elira swallowed hard, the ache in her chest growing sharper, more distinct. A shape she hadn't noticed before.

A hole.

Not from Ashira's death, not from the illusions of the King, but something deeper.

A mother's absence.

And now… she was starting to feel it.

Not just the loss.

The presence.

The memory of something she never got to keep—but that still waited for her.

"She's close," Solen said, barely above a whisper. "And when the time is right, you'll see her. Truly see her."

Elira closed her eyes. Let the feeling settle.

She didn't know her mother's name. Her voice. Her touch.

But for the first time, she felt the imprint of her.

And the forest, the runes, the very magic around her—seemed to hold its breath in reverence.

Elira opened her eyes.

The path ahead still twisted, still cloaked in shadow and uncertainty.

But now, she knew something more waited at the end of it.

Not just freedom.

Not just truth.

But a piece of herself she'd never known was missing.

Chapter 17:

The air tasted of rain again.

Not like before, when it carried nostalgia and longing – but now, it tasted like **arrival.**

Elira walked in silence. The others had stayed behind, giving her space, as if they sensed what was coming next was hers alone to walk.

The path beneath her feet was soft and uneven, lined with pale moss that seemed to glow faintly in rhythm with her breath. Each step sent small pulses of light through the forest floor – a silent echo of the heartbeat she didn't remember sharing with anyone but now… maybe she had.

She stopped beside a tree older than anything she'd seen before. Its bark was carved in gentle spirals, but unlike the other runes, this one held no light. It was *quiet* – but not asleep.

Her fingers moved to the markings instinctively, brushing them like braille.

And the moment she touched it, everything changed.

The world *tilted.* The forest melted away – not violently, but gently, like curtains drawn back to reveal a stage she hadn't known she was standing on.

She was no longer in the woods.

She stood in a room made of starlight and memory.

A cradle. A lullaby. A woman's voice, singing a melody Elira had never heard – but had always known.

"You are no forgotten.

You were never lost.

You are the light I could not carry,

But still chose to give."

Elira's knees buckled. Not from pain. But from recognition.

The woman stood just ahead – hair like starlight, eyes like her own. A softness in her expression that didn't try to hold her… only to let her be seen.

"Elira," the woman whispered, "I've waited so long for you to remember."

The starlit room breathed with her, like the very walls were alive with memory. Gentle currents of energy floated around her – not wind, not magic in the way she'd known it – but something deeper. Something *remembered.*

The woman took a step forward.

Not a ghost. Not a vision.

A presence.

"Who are you?" Elira whispered, her voice cracking.

The woman smiled – not wide, not dramatic – but with softness that felt like the first light after a long night. "You already know. You've known me in every quiet ache, in every dream you were told not to trust."

Her eyes glistened, mirroring Elira's own. "I am your beginning."

Elira's breath caught in her throat. "Mother?"

A nod. A tear. And then: "My name was Ilyana. I was one of the first Lirians to be born of *hope."*

The word shattered something in Elira's chest.

Hope.

She thought of Ashira. Of Solen. Of Cairen. Of Vaelen. Of herself – struggling to breathe in a world where truth was forbidden. And here stood her mother – not just a piece of history, but a *force* that had survived illusion.

"But… how?" Elira whispered.

"Why don't I remember? Why did no one tell me you-"

"Because he buried it." Ilyana's voice was calm, but a tremor threaded through it now. "Aurik feared what you were. What *we* were. So, he severed your roots before they could grow."

Elira's hands curled into fists. "He lied to me my entire life."

Ilyana stepped closer. "He didn't just lie. He *rewrote* you. Took my name from your lips. Took your birth from your memory. But he could not destroy the bond between us. Not completely."

Elira's voice shook. "I always felt something missing. I thought it was grief… but it was *you.*"

Her mother raised a hand, and, for a moment, light wove between them – not touch, but *recognition.* A current flowed from Ilyana's heart to Elira's and back again. It hummed with warmth, with pain, with all the years that had passed in silence.

"You were meant to awaken," Ilyana said. "Not just to fight the veil. But to *heal* what it was made to hide. You are not just a weaver of truth, Elira. You are born of legacy. And legacy cannot be erased."

Elira blinked back tears, something shifting in her bones. "What do I do now?"

Ilyana's expression turned solemn. "You are nearing the edge of the illusion's hold. But you cannot tear it down alone. There is one more who must awaken beside you. One who has the power to unravel the lies from within."

Elira's breath hitched. "You mean…"

Her mother nodded. "Your father's greatest mistake was believing he could control what was born of hope and flame. But your light was never meant to serve his shadow."

The light around the room began to dim, not with fear, but with finality.

"Our time is short," Ilyana whispered. "But you carry me now. Not as a ghost Not as an echo. But as fire." She stepped back, the starlight of her form beginning to dissolve into shimmering particles of warmth and light.

"Will I see you again?" Elira asked, desperate to hold onto the moment.

Ilyana smiled. "I was never gone."

And just before her form vanished completely, she spoke once more — her voice woven into Elira's very breath:

"Break the veil. Free the truth. And remember this—
you are not made of what was taken from you.
You are made of what endured."

The grove returned around her. The forest. The moss. The silence. But Elira stood different now. Not with answers. But with *truth.*

Her mother had not been lost. Just hidden. And now, she was remembered.

Elira turned back toward the trees. Toward the Lirians. Toward the rebellion. Toward the unraveling. The veil had stolen much from her. But it could not steal what had awakened.

And it would never silence her again.

Chapter 18:

The wind had changed.

Solen noticed it first, his head tilting sharply as the grove fell still once more. Elira hadn't spoken since she returned — not with words, at least — but something radiated from her now. Not light. Not power. Something older.

Memory.

Vaelen watched her too, more carefully than before. Not with suspicion, but with the quiet reverence of someone who had just witnessed a prophecy take its first breath.

"You saw her," Solen said. Not a question.

Elira nodded.

And though her lips did not tremble, her hands were still shaking.

"She said I was born of hope," Elira murmured. "And of fire."

Solen's gaze deepened. "Then you're more dangerous to him than we thought."

Elira turned away, the edge of her cloak brushing the rune-lined bark as she passed. "Good."

They followed her in silence as she made her way deeper into the grove. No longer hesitating. No longer unsure. The soft glow of the ground pulsed beneath her feet like a heartbeat newly remembered.

Vaelen finally broke the silence. "Then it's time."

Elira glanced at him. "Time for what?"

"For the mirror trial."

Solen flinched. "Already?"

"She's ready."

Elira frowned. "What is it?"

Vaelen's voice was low. "The mirror trial doesn't show you the past. Or the future. It shows you what others saw while you were blind. How they perceived you. How the illusion shaped not only your life — but your *reflection*."

Elira's stomach twisted. She had faced her own memories. Faced the absence of her mother. But this? This was different.

This was about *truth* as seen through the eyes of those who never knew hers.

"It's not a punishment," Solen said gently, "but it will hurt."

Elira breathed deeply. "Then let it hurt."

Elira didn't ask where they were going.

Her feet already knew.

They crossed through the edge of the grove into a part of the forest that felt untouched by time. The trees grew taller here — impossibly tall — their trunks twisting into one another like ancient sentinels guarding something sacred. The light dimmed, filtered through thick leaves and shifting mist that carried no scent, only stillness.

Solen walked beside her in silence, but his hands were tight at his sides. He hadn't touched any of the runes here. Hadn't hummed. Hadn't spoken.

Even he feared what came next.

Vaelen led the way, his steps precise, like someone who had taken this path before — and never forgotten it.

Finally, the forest opened into a clearing. No birdsong. No wind.

Only a single stone circle, carved into the earth like a wound.

At the center stood a structure — not quite a pool, not quite a mirror — a basin carved from black stone, filled with a liquid that shimmered like smoke and starlight. The surface moved constantly but never spilled.

It was the kind of place where truths were not found but *demanded.*

Elira stepped toward it slowly, her breath catching.

She couldn't look away.

"The Mirror of Reflection," Vaelen said. "Forged long before the illusions. Before Aurik twisted truth into weapon. This is not Lirian magic. This is *older.*"

Elira's fingers twitched at her sides. "What does it show?"

Vaelen looked at her, solemn. "It shows *what was seen.* Not by you — but by those around you. The way the world perceived you under the veil. The way your silence was interpreted. Your obedience. Your fear."

Elira's throat tightened. "So, I'll see… their thoughts?"

"No," Solen said softly, his voice almost a warning. "Worse. You'll see their *truths.* The way they justified what was done to you. The way they didn't see you at all. It can break people."

Elira's jaw clenched. "But I won't break."

Neither of them argued.

The mirror pulsed.

And Elira felt it — like a heartbeat deep beneath the ground, responding to her presence.

She stepped closer, until the edge of the basin was just inches from her hands. The smoke inside shifted, curling upward like it sensed her arrival.

But it didn't show her anything. Not yet.

"Why now?" she asked, still staring at the surface. "Why is this the next step?"

Solen finally spoke, quiet and certain. "Because if you are to free others from the veil, you must first see how it lived in *you.* How it shaped you through their eyes. Until you do, you will always carry their silence in your voice."

Elira looked up at him, her chest heavy. "I'm not afraid of the truth."

Vaelen tilted his head. "Then prove it."

She turned back to the mirror.

It was waiting.

Calling.

But still… silent.

"I'll do it," she whispered.

Not for them. Not even for her mother.

For *herself.*

Because she needed to know — needed to see — who she had been to the world that forgot her. Not just the pain. But the shadows. The shame. The misunderstanding.

Because until she faced *that*, she would never fully awaken.

Solen stepped forward, placing a hand gently on her shoulder.

"Once you begin, there is no stopping. You must witness it all."

"I understand."

Vaelen moved to the far edge of the circle and touched a rune carved into the ground — one that hadn't glowed before. At his touch, it lit up with silver fire, rippling outward until the entire circle pulsed with light.

The smoke in the mirror surged.

The ground beneath Elira's feet began to hum.

The air thickened.

Not with magic.

With *memory*.

Vaelen looked at her once more. "When you are ready… step forward."

Elira stared into the smoke.

And for just a moment — just a flicker — she thought she saw a familiar face swirl through the mist.

Ashira.

Not as she remembered her — not soft or laughing — but looking straight through her, eyes filled with confusion. Or was it pity?

The image vanished.

Elira's breath hitched.

And she stepped toward the mirror.

Not in fear.

But in *defiance*.

The veil had stolen her reflection for too long.

It was time to see what remained beneath it.

Chapter 19:

The moment her foot crossed the threshold of the stone circle, the world shifted.

Not violently.

But entirely.

The forest vanished, replaced by swirling smoke and light — not darkness, but *distortion.* Like staring into water stirred too hard to settle.

Then the air stilled.

And the mirror opened.

A room appeared in front of her — not imagined, but real, drawn from memory. Her memory. Or perhaps… someone else's.

The throne room of Elarion.

Polished marble floors. Crimson banners. And her — standing at the base of the steps like a statue carved from silence.

Her posture was perfect. Her chin lowered. Her eyes downcast.

And still, the voices whispered around her.

"The girl never speaks unless spoken to. A blessing, really."

"Pretty thing. But there's nothing behind the eyes."

"Obedient. Unremarkable. Easy to forget."

Each word sliced sharper than the last.

Elira's stomach turned. She remembered this day — a royal event, a celebration for something meaningless. She'd stood there for hours.

But she hadn't known how they *saw* her.

She turned, and the scene blurred.

Reformed.

Ashira.

Sitting across from her at a quiet table in the garden.

Elira — younger, hollow-eyed, fidgeting with a glass. Ashira's face was bright, but her smile was tight, uncertain.

"I wish you'd tell me what you're thinking," her voice echoed, not to Elira — but to *herself.*

"Sometimes it feels like you're not really… here."

"I want to reach you. But I don't know how."

Elira reached toward the memory, desperate to speak — but her hand passed through it like mist. She had been there. She had *been loved.* And still… she'd been unreachable. Not because she didn't care.

But because she hadn't *known* how to be seen.

The image faded again.

This time slower.

More painful.

A golden hallway.

Her father.

Standing beside an advisor, watching her from a distance.

"She's quiet. Compliant. The illusion is holding well."

"And if it breaks?"

"It won't. Not without a trigger. She has no memory of the mother. No reason to question."

"And if she does?"

"Then we silence her again."

Elira staggered back, heart slamming in her chest.

He hadn't feared her.

He'd *controlled* her. Contained her. As if she were nothing but a tool he'd locked away.

The smoke darkened.

A shadow moved through it — not a scene, but a flicker.

Solen.

Younger. Alone.

Standing just beyond the palace gardens, watching her through a window.

"There's something wrong," his voice whispered. "She doesn't move like someone asleep. She moves like someone *erased*."

"But who am I to question the King?"

The vision pulsed.

And faded.

One by one, the reflections slipped away, each one leaving behind a bitter taste of forgotten truths.

Elira fell to her knees.

The mirror pulsed in front of her — not with judgment, but with weight.

It had shown her what she asked for.

And what she needed to remember.

They hadn't seen her.

Not really.

They'd seen a reflection of a reflection — a girl shaped by silence, mistaken for simplicity. A ghost who smiled when commanded and vanished when not needed.

But that girl…

That wasn't who she *was*.

Elira stood.

Slowly.

And the smoke around her began to part.
The trial wasn't over.
But she had taken the first step.
She had seen what was stolen.
And now… she could begin reclaiming it.

Chapter 20:

The grove felt different when she stepped back into it.

Not changed. Just… *clearer.*

The edges of the world seemed sharper, like the trees had been waiting for her to return with new eyes.

And she had.

Elira's limbs ached from the trial, but not from pain. From the weight of having carried so many lies for so long.

She hadn't cried.

Not when Ashira's voice echoed with confusion. Not when her father spoke of erasure like it was strategy. Not even when she saw herself, hollow and small, through eyes that never truly looked. Instead, something inside her had settled.

A flame.

Not born of rage.

But of *recognition.*

Solen stood a few paces away, waiting in stillness, as if afraid to speak first.

"You knew," Elira said softly, breaking the silence.

He met her eyes. "I suspected."

"But you didn't say anything."

His voice cracked, barely audible. "I was afraid if I named it… it would hurt you more. Or worse — undo the veil too soon."

She nodded slowly. "It did hurt."

"I'm sorry."

"I'm not," she said.

Solen's eyes widened.

"Because now," she continued, stepping past him, "I know what was taken. And I know what I'm taking back."

She didn't say it with fury.

She said it with certainty.

Vaelen stepped forward from the shadows beyond the trees, eyes unreadable. "How much did it show you?"

"Enough," Elira replied. "Enough to know I was never truly seen."

A long pause.

Then: "And now?"

She looked up, the wind brushing strands of hair across her face. "Now, I will never be unseen again."

The light shifted through the grove, dappling her skin in silver and gold.

Solen exhaled. "Then the next step is yours to choose."

She turned toward him. "What do you mean?"

"There are many forms of awakening. You've seen your past. Faced the reflection. But what do you want to reclaim next?"

He stepped closer and held out his hand. In it — a small orb of Lirian crystal, flickering with soft light. "This is a conduit. It will lead you to the part of your truth you are ready for. But only if you ask the right question."

Elira stared at it.

Her fingers curled around the crystal.

It was warm.

Alive.

She closed her eyes, the forest silent around her. And she asked — not aloud, but with everything in her: *"What part of me still hides in silence?"*

The crystal flared.

A gust of wind tore through the grove — not violent, but purposeful. And a whisper, soft and certain, echoed through the trees:

"Your voice."

Elira opened her eyes.

And for the first time, she didn't just hear the world around her. She heard herself.

Clear.

Unshaken.

Undeniable.

The path ahead shifted — winding deeper into the forest, toward something older than memory. Elira didn't hesitate. Because this time, she wasn't just following the truth.

She *was* the truth. And she was done being quiet.

Chapter 21:

The path called to her.

Not with light. Not with words.

But with *resonance.*

Each step Elira took pulsed beneath her soles like a drumbeat long forgotten — steady, deliberate, alive. The forest had grown denser here, the trees bowing overhead, their branches interlacing like they, too, were listening.

She held the crystal tight in her palm.

It hummed softly, in time with her heartbeat. Or maybe… it was leading it.

Solen and Vaelen had stayed behind.

This part, they said, she had to do alone.

She didn't argue.

For once, she *wanted* the silence.

Because this silence didn't suffocate her.

It *belonged* to her.

She followed the trail of silver runes glowing faintly on the ground — not etched, not carved, but grown from the earth itself. Flowers with petal-shaped glyphs opened as she passed, whispering in languages she couldn't name, only feel.

And then… the path ended.

A hollow, cradled by trees whose trunks spiraled upward like cathedral columns. Moss covered the stones like velvet, and in the center stood a structure — ancient and low, more altar than platform. Floating above it, a ring of crystal shards hovered in the air, spinning slowly around a single point of stillness.

The moment she entered, the forest hushed.

Even the wind stilled.

The crystal in her palm flashed — once — and dissolved into dust.

And her voice left her.

Not stolen.

Released.

Elira opened her mouth, but no sound came.

Not fear. Not pain. Just… *absence.*

She fell to her knees, breath shallow.

Not again, she thought. Please, not again.

But this was different.

This silence was not a prison.

It was an invitation.

A soft warmth moved through the air — brushing her skin like memory, like breath.

And then… a voice.

Not outside her.

Within.

"You were not born voiceless."

The words weren't heard but *felt.*

"Your silence was never weakness. It was survival."

Elira closed her eyes.

And the visions came.

Faster now. Sharper.

A child, standing behind marble pillars, watching her father speak lies with honey on his tongue.

A young girl trying to scream during her nightmares, and finding only silence.

A teenager nodding at court decrees she didn't believe in, because to disagree was to disappear.

And then—

A song.

Faint. Familiar.

A lullaby once lost.

Her mother's voice.

"Speak, and the veil will tremble.
Sing, and the silence will crack."

The shards above her pulsed.

And something in Elira *opened.*

Not her throat.

Her soul.

She drew in a slow, shaking breath. And exhaled — not sound, but *light.*

It poured from her chest in soft golden threads, winding upward into the crystal ring.

The forest responded — trees bending inward, runes igniting around her, flowers blooming all at once.

And then, as if the magic itself had been holding its breath—

Elira sang.

No melody she had ever learned.

No words she had ever spoken.

Only truth.

Only *her.*

The voice that left her as a child had returned not as a whisper — but as a force.

It rippled through the trees, echoed down unseen corridors of magic, brushing against the edge of the veil like fingers against glass.

And somewhere — far away, in the palace halls where illusions still held — something *cracked.*

A servant paused mid-step, blinking hard. A guard frowned; shaken by a feeling he couldn't name.

The veil quivered.

Not shattered.

But no longer unshakable.

Elira's voice faded into silence.

And this time… it was *hers.*

Chapter 22:

Far away, in a palace wrapped in gold and silence, something stirred.

It began with a sound.

Soft. Barely a whisper.

But wrong.

A note that didn't belong — curling down polished halls, threading through columns and corridors like a breeze that knew too much.

A servant paused mid-step, her tray rattling as her hands began to tremble. She turned, expecting someone behind her. No one.

She pressed a hand to her chest.

Her heart was racing.

She didn't know why.

In the eastern wing, a young scholar blinked down at a page he'd read a dozen times. The ink swam. The words blurred.

He rubbed his eyes, tried again.

But the sentence had changed.

"She is not forgotten."

He snapped the book shut; breath shallow.

The message was gone.

But the echo remained.

And deeper still, in a vaulted chamber beneath the throne room — where the magic of the illusion pulsed like a second heartbeat for the kingdom — a thread of light sparked across the runes.

Tiny.

But *wrong*.

The High Seer noticed first. She rose from her kneeling position and crossed the chamber, robes whispering over stone.

She reached for the glyphs lining the floor, brushing her fingers over one.

The rune flared.

Then flickered.

Then faded.

"…Impossible," she whispered.

The Veil's energy had never wavered.

Not since the day it was woven.

She moved faster now, climbing the tower where the King sat alone on his throne — back straight, expression bored, as if ruling an empire made of lies required no effort at all.

But the moment she entered, he turned.

Eyes sharp.

Cold.

"What is it?" Aurik asked.

She bowed, but her hands trembled. "Something… shifted."

He stood. "Where?"

"Everywhere."

His jaw clenched.

A pause.

Then: "She's remembering."

He didn't say her name.

He didn't have to.

The very walls of the palace seemed to draw tighter around them, like the illusion itself knew it had been *seen.*

Aurik's voice was ice. "Send the shadows. Track the energy spike. Find her."

The Seer hesitated. "If the veil is breaking—"

"Then we reinforce it," he snapped. "Before it unravels."

Outside the window, storm clouds gathered.

And far away, in the quiet wilds of the Lirian forest, Elira stood at the center of a growing circle of light.

She didn't know that the palace had felt her voice.

She didn't know that Aurik had ordered her found.

But she *did* know one thing:

The world had shifted.

And there was no going back.

Chapter 23:

Elira stood at the edge of the terrace, wind curling through the open arches of the Lirian stronghold. Below, the forest of Lira stretched endlessly, trees whispering secrets she had yet to learn. The sky shimmered a dusky lavender, the hour between day and night — when truth seemed to breathe loudest.

Her fingers curled against the stone railing. Ever since Solen's blessing, something within her had changed. She was more aware. Of everything. Her surroundings. Her thoughts. Her emotions. And most of all… of Vaelen.

He hadn't spoken much since they'd returned from the Grove of Echoes. But he lingered. In the quiet corners. In her periphery. Like a shadow she didn't want to banish.

"Thinking of jumping?" his voice came from behind, low and rich.

She didn't turn. "Would it be that surprising?"

"Only if you didn't fly instead," he replied.

She smiled faintly. "I'm not sure I know how."

Vaelen stepped beside her, resting his forearms against the railing, his shoulder brushing hers. "Not yet. But you will."

Elira glanced at him. There it was again — that unwavering belief. As if he already saw who she could become. As if he was waiting for her to catch up.

The wind shifted, carrying the scent of wild mint and woodsmoke. It wrapped around them like something alive.

"Do you ever miss your world?" she asked suddenly. "Before the illusions. Before… all of this."

Vaelen's eyes darkened. "There wasn't much to miss. My world was built on sacrifice. On pretending emotions were weakness. But here…" He paused. "Here, everything is raw. Honest. Painful, yes. But also, real."

She nodded slowly. "It's exhausting. Feeling this much."

"It's also power," he said, voice quieter now. "The kind your father fears. The kind he tried to bury in you."

Elira swallowed. "And now?"

"Now," Vaelen said, turning to her fully, "you're starting to burn."

Their eyes locked. The air thickened. Something in her chest twisted and stretched — not like pain, but like awakening.

She could feel the weight of his gaze. The steady storm of it. And beneath that… a tension she could no longer pretend wasn't there.

He stepped closer.

"Elira," he said softly, "You don't need to be afraid of how you feel."

She wanted to argue. To deflect. To retreat into sarcasm or silence.

But she didn't.

Instead, she whispered, "I'm not afraid of how I feel."

Her gaze dropped to his lips. Then back to his eyes.

"I'm afraid of what it will mean."

Vaelen's voice was like velvet. "It'll mean you're alive."

And before she could stop herself — or maybe because she didn't want to anymore — she leaned in.

Their lips met in a kiss that didn't ask permission.

It claimed. It cracked. It burned.

And it broke something wide open inside her.

Not in destruction. But in truth.

The way his hands framed her face. The way her fingers curled in his shirt. The way their breath caught together like two sparks colliding midair.

When they finally pulled apart, Elira's heart thundered.

"That…" she murmured.

"Was only the beginning," Vaelen finished.

And she knew he was right.

Because the fire inside her wasn't just hers anymore.

It was theirs.

And it would light the way forward.

Even through the coming dark.

Elira couldn't sleep.

Not because of dreams — but because of what she felt when she closed her eyes. It was heat. Memory. The ghost of his lips still lingering on hers.

She sat up from the woven bedding Solen had given her, the glow stones in the wall humming with a low blue pulse. Her fingertips drifted to her mouth.

She hadn't imagined it.

The kiss.

The way his hands had steadied her, like she was something rare — not fragile, but powerful. Not dangerous, but sacred.

And she wanted more.

She stepped into the corridor, following the curve of the stone hallways lit by Lirian runes. The night was thick with silence, the kind that made everything feel sharper — emotions, wants, questions.

Vaelen was outside, as if he'd been waiting for her.

He turned before she even said his name.

"Elira."

That one word held more than a greeting. It held awareness.

She stepped closer, her voice soft. "Can we talk?"

His brow lifted. "About what?"

She hesitated. "About... what happened."

A pause. He searched her face, then nodded once and motioned to the nearby archway that led to a quiet alcove tucked beneath a canopy of Lirian vines.

There, under soft moonlight filtered through enchanted leaves, she turned to face him.

"I don't know what I'm doing," she admitted. "But I keep thinking about it. About you."

Vaelen's gaze held hers, unflinching. "You don't have to justify how you feel."

"That's the thing," she said. "I'm not used to *feeling* anything this clearly. It terrifies me."

He stepped closer, slow, deliberate. "Then let's stop thinking for a moment."

His hand brushed her cheek.

Elira inhaled sharply — not because of fear, but anticipation.

And then she kissed him.

This time, *she* initiated it.

And God, the way he responded—

It wasn't gentle like before.

It was fire meeting wind.

His hands found her waist, pulling her to him as her arms wrapped around his neck. The kiss deepened, and she gasped into his mouth, not from surprise, but from the sensation of *being wanted.*

Vaelen pulled back just enough to breathe.

"You're shaking," he whispered, his forehead pressed to hers.

"I don't want you to stop," she breathed.

"I won't," he said, voice rough with restraint, "unless you ask me to."

She kissed him again — harder this time, her fingers threading into his hair.

The ache inside her wasn't just emotional anymore. It was physical. A slow-blooming need, fierce and unfamiliar. A hunger that frightened her *only because it mattered.*

One of his hands slipped beneath the edge of her tunic, resting lightly against her back — and she arched into him.

The pressure between them built like a wave, and Elira could feel the edge of something rising, cresting—

And then he stopped.

Not pulled away.

Just… paused.

Breathing heavy.

Eyes dark.

"Elira," he murmured, voice roughened with restraint. "When we cross that line, there's no going back. I want all of you. But not unless you're ready to give it."

She was quiet.

Then: "Soon."

Vaelen nodded once, brushing his lips against her brow.

"I'll wait."

She stayed in his arms a while longer, heart still pounding, desire still coiled tight in her core. But for now, this — *this* — was enough.

Because it wasn't just a kiss anymore.

It was a *promise.*

Elira lay awake long after the forest had gone still.

The warmth of Vaelen's touch still clung to her skin, like a memory etched into her bones. Not just the kiss — but everything behind it. The way he held her like she wouldn't break. Like he didn't want to own her, only see her.

She stared at the soft glow stones above her, their light pulsing like a quiet heartbeat.

So much of her life had been about silence. Control. Shame disguised as discipline. Fear masked as obedience.

But this… what she'd felt in his arms… wasn't fear.

It was *freedom.*

And that terrified her more than anything else.

Because freedom meant choice.

And choice meant facing what she wanted.

Not what she was told to want.

Not what was permitted.

But what she *felt.*

Vaelen didn't ask for anything. He didn't press. He just... *waited.* Like he trusted she'd find her way. Like he believed she could.

Elira turned onto her side, curling her fingers into the edge of the blanket.

She hadn't known touch could feel like that.

Hadn't known closeness could be a gift instead of a threat.

And now, she wasn't sure she could go back to the world where her body was only ever meant to be hidden, silenced, controlled.

A single tear slipped from the corner of her eye.

Not from pain.

From release.

From realizing that maybe — just maybe — she didn't have to carry all of this alone anymore.

That maybe she *wasn't* alone at all.

Chapter 24

They didn't make it far that night.

Not because of danger.

But because of stillness.

There was something about the hush of the grove, the glow of distant runes still pulsing in her blood, that made Elira want to stop running.

They made camp near the edge of the glade. A soft, mossy rise near a hollowed tree. Mirae curled near the fire, and Solen—his usual chaotic hum dimmed—watched the stars in silence.

Elira had barely laid down when Vaelen joined her. No words. Just his presence.

He lay behind her, one arm around her waist, the other resting beneath her head. His breath on her neck was slow and steady.

Her pulse, however, was anything but.

"You're quiet," he murmured, voice rough from exhaustion and something more.

"So are you," she whispered.

A pause.

"You feel different," he said.

She didn't know what to say to that. Because it wasn't just about magic. It was about *her*.

He pressed a kiss to the back of her neck, slow and soft.

"I won't ask you for anything," he said. "Not ever. But if you want me—truly want me—you only have to say it."

Elira turned slowly to face him, their bodies barely apart.

"I do," she whispered. "I just… I don't know what I'm doing."

Vaelen smiled, brushing a hand across her cheek.

"You don't have to. I'll show you."

And with that, he leaned in and kissed her—gently, reverently. Not rushed. Not demanding. Just *present.*

And when Elira kissed him back, something in her cracked open a little further.

It was just a kiss. One moment. But it was the beginning of something inevitable.

Chapter 25:

Elira woke to the weight of sunlight spilling through the upper vines, filtered gold and warm on her skin.

She hadn't meant to fall asleep in Vaelen's arms.

But she hadn't wanted to leave them either.

He was still beside her, one arm draped protectively around her waist, his breathing slow and even. She studied his face for a moment—the softness of it, the way the lines of tension had faded while he slept. He looked… human. Not like a soldier. Not like a weapon.

But like someone who'd learned how to hold pain without letting it harden him.

She rolled gently onto her back, careful not to wake him. Her body still thrummed with yesterday's fire—every kiss, every breath, every heartbeat that had come too close to something she couldn't name.

Or maybe she could.

Because what she felt wasn't just desire.

It was *freedom.*

In Elarion, desire was a secret. Or worse—a function. Men and women were matched for one reason: conception. It was monitored, supervised, clinical. Touch without connection. Closeness without meaning.

She remembered the lessons drilled into her in girlhood. How passion made people *unruly*. How emotional intimacy was a danger to structure. How allowing someone to want you—*truly* want you—could unravel the order the King had built.

She understood now why.

Because that kind of wanting… the kind that lived in her bones when Vaelen touched her… it *burned.*

It cracked every lie she'd ever been told.

And it left her raw, trembling, alive.

"Morning," Vaelen's voice rasped beside her.

She turned to him, startled, but not embarrassed.

"Didn't mean to wake you," she murmured.

"I don't mind," he said. "I like waking up next to you."

Her heart thudded. She lowered her gaze, lips twitching in a half-smile. "That's… not something I've ever heard before."

"It's not something I've ever said before," he replied, brushing a lock of hair from her cheek. "Seems like a first for both of us."

She sat up slowly, knees pulled to her chest. "Do you think it's dangerous?"

He tilted his head. "What is?"

"This. Us. Letting it feel like… more."

He didn't answer right away.

Then: "In Elarion, yes. That kind of feeling is dangerous. Which is exactly why the King tried to strip it from us."

She looked at him. "Because of how powerful it is?"

"Because of how *real* it is," Vaelen said. "You can't hold illusion and love in the same hand. One always burns the other away."

Elira was quiet. The truth of it settled inside her like a stone in a lake—sinking, steadying.

She reached for his hand. "Then maybe that's exactly why we need it."

He looked at her like she was something luminous.

And for the rest of the day, they barely left each other's side.

Not out of urgency.

But out of something softer.

Trust.

The day passed in gentle rhythms.

Elira moved through the Lirian stronghold with a strange lightness in her chest—like she was learning how to carry her body differently. Not because her magic had changed, or because the runes whispered louder, but because she *wasn't hiding anymore.*

Vaelen stayed nearby.

Not clinging, not hovering.

Just… present.

Their hands brushed when they passed a shared meal. He caught her when she nearly stumbled over a root near the outer archway, his hand at her waist lingering half a second too long.

No one said anything.

Solen noticed—of course he did—but he only gave her a look full of quiet amusement, then returned to weaving his latest glyph into the garden's edge.

Later, Elira found herself beside Vaelen again, seated on the wide stone steps that overlooked the treetops.

"I used to think silence meant something was wrong," she said quietly. "Now it just feels… peaceful."

"It depends on the company," he replied.

She glanced at him, caught the edge of a smile tugging at his lips. "Are you always this poetic, or just when I'm around?"

"Only when it matters."

The blush that touched her cheeks surprised her.

Not because of his words.

But because of how *safe* they made her feel.

He reached for her hand, resting his palm atop hers—fingers barely curled together.

It wasn't a kiss.

It wasn't a promise.

But it *was* something.

Something steady. Unspoken. Building.

And when he looked at her that time, it was like he already knew the question she'd ask him later.

The one he'd been ready to say yes to long before she had the courage to ask.

The moon hung heavy above the treetops, casting silver ribbons across the stone floor of the stronghold. The night air was cool, threaded with the soft hum of runes etched into the walls. Somewhere, deep within the forest, a Lirian bloom exhaled its soft, pulsing glow.

Elira stood at the threshold of Vaelen's room, her fingers brushing the frame.

She'd stood there longer than she cared to admit.

Not out of fear.

But because she knew—once she crossed that line, everything would change.

And she *wanted* it to.

She knocked once.

Vaelen opened the door almost instantly, like he'd known she'd come.

"Elira," he said, voice low, soft-edged.

She stepped inside without a word, eyes never leaving his.

The room was quiet. Dimly lit by a single orb of Lirian light floating above the hearth. The space smelled like him—clean, cedar-sweet, something steadying.

"I couldn't sleep," she whispered.

He nodded once, understanding layered into the silence.

"I don't want to be alone tonight," she said.

There was no pause.

No question.

Vaelen crossed the space between them and reached for her face—fingertips tracing along her jaw, brushing her cheek, his touch asking and waiting.

"You're not alone," he said.

Her hands slid up his chest, palms flattening over his heart. "I want this. Not because I feel like I should. Not because I'm trying to prove something. I want this because I *want* you."

Vaelen's exhale was shaky.

Not from surprise.

But from the sheer restraint it took to stay still.

"You can have me," he said. "All of me. But I need to know this is yours. That this is what *you* want."

She answered with a kiss.

No hesitation. No falter.

Just fire.

He kissed her back with the hunger of someone who had held back for too long. His hands slid into her hair, then down her back, guiding her slowly toward the bed.

Clothes fell in pieces.

Not torn.

Not rushed.

Shed like skin that no longer belonged.

When she stood bare before him, she didn't feel small.

She felt seen.

His gaze roamed her like prayer, not possession. When he touched her, it wasn't to claim—it was to connect. His hands traced reverent lines over her skin, drawing her to the bed like she was something sacred.

And when he laid her down, her body ached—not with fear, not with shame, but with *knowing.*

That this was hers.

That this was *theirs.*

The first time he entered her, it stole her breath—not from pain, but from the sheer fullness of it. The rightness.

Her fingers gripped his shoulders, her hips rising to meet his rhythm, and for the first time in her life, she didn't feel like she had to shrink.

She felt *powerful.*

Their movements were slow, intense—wordless truths spoken in gasps and touches and the tension that built between each breath.

He whispered her name like a spell.

And when she shattered beneath him, he followed—lips at her throat, arms tight around her, as if she was the one keeping him from falling apart.

They stayed tangled in the silence after.

No rush to part. No need for words.

Just heartbeats. Just breath.

Just this.

They lay together in the quiet.

Elira's head rested against his chest, her fingers drawing lazy, uncertain patterns over his skin. Vaelen's arms were wrapped around her like a shield—gentle, but sure. His breath rose and fell, slower now, steady.

But her heart… wasn't.

Not entirely.

A silence settled over them, not heavy… but questioning.

And when Elira finally spoke, it came out softer than she expected.

"I don't know what I'm doing."

Vaelen didn't move. "You don't have to."

She swallowed. "What if one day you want… more? Someone who's not learning everything for the first time."

He stilled.

"Elira," he said, voice low, a little raw, "look at me."

She did. Slowly. Her eyes glassy.

"I don't want more," he said. "I want *you*."

Her throat tightened.

She blinked, trying to push down the sting of tears, but one slipped free anyway.

And when it did—Vaelen's own eyes glistened.

He caught her tear with his thumb, but didn't wipe his own away.

"I've never done this either," he confessed. "Not like this. Not with meaning. Not with… *feeling*."

Her brow furrowed. "But you… you always seem so sure."

"I'm not," he said. "I've lived my whole life knowing how to fight. How to follow orders. How to shut things out. But this… you…" He shook his head. "I didn't realize how much I needed someone to see me. To *choose* me. Until you did."

A tear slipped from the corner of his eye.

And it broke something in her.

Not from sadness.

But from knowing—*really* knowing—that she wasn't the only one still learning how to be whole.

"I don't know what this will become," she whispered.

"Then we figure it out together," he said. "We don't have to be perfect. We just must be *true*."

She nodded, curling closer.

And in the silence that followed, it wasn't just their bodies that lay tangled.

It was everything unspoken.

Everything unfinished.

Everything waiting to be healed.

Together.

Chapter 26:

Elira awoke to golden morning light and the warmth of a body she now knew by heart.

Vaelen's arm was slung around her waist, his chest pressed against her back, breath warm against her shoulder. She didn't move—not yet. The moment was too soft, too still.

She let her eyes drift closed again, just to feel it all a little longer.

No fear. No shame.

Just breath.

Just closeness.

Her fingers toyed with the edge of the blanket, and for the first time in what felt like forever, she didn't feel like a stranger in her own skin.

When she finally turned to face him, Vaelen was already awake.

He didn't speak.

He just looked at her like he was memorizing her all over again.

Elira smiled—small, but real.

"Hi," she said, voice scratchy.

He reached up, brushing her hair from her face. "Hi."

They stayed that way for a while. No rush. No pretending they hadn't crossed a line they could never uncross.

But it didn't feel like a boundary shattered.

It felt like a doorway opened.

Eventually, they rose together—dressing slowly, pausing in between with lingering kisses and stolen touches that made Elira's cheeks flush even as she smiled against his mouth.

She didn't feel broken anymore.

She felt… *anchored.*

They walked through the stronghold side by side, not touching, but close enough that their arms brushed with every few steps. Elira noticed the subtle glances cast their way by passing Lirians—most unreadable, but one…

Solen.

He stood in the courtyard tending to a rune-laced vine, his eyes lifting just as she and Vaelen passed.

And for a fraction of a moment, he grinned.

It wasn't smug. It wasn't teasing.

It was *knowing.*

Like he saw something written between them that needed no words.

Elira felt heat rise to her cheeks, but she didn't look away.

Solen merely returned to his work, the tip of his finger glowing faintly as he coaxed a blossom into bloom.

Vaelen leaned slightly toward her as they passed. "He's going to say something. I can feel it."

"He already did," she murmured, lips twitching. "That grin said *everything.*"

Later, she found herself training again—her blade sharper, her footing surer. There was something new in the way she moved. Not just strength, but certainty.

And when her gaze found Vaelen across the courtyard, watching her with that steady, quiet pride…

She didn't look away.

Because she finally understood.

He didn't give her strength.

He reminded her that it had always been hers.

Later that afternoon, they found themselves alone again, tucked beneath a sun-dappled archway near the outer gardens. The breeze was soft here, curling around the stone columns like it didn't want to interrupt.

Elira leaned against the wall, eyes closed, soaking in the warmth of the day. Vaelen stood beside her, close enough that her arm brushed his every time she shifted.

She let out a quiet sigh—and winced.

He noticed instantly.

"Elira?"

She opened her eyes, a little too quickly. "I'm fine."

Vaelen tilted his head, unconvinced. "You made a sound."

"Just… sore," she admitted, cheeks already burning. "A little."

He blinked. "Did I hurt you?"

"No," she rushed. "No, not at all. It's not like that. I just…" She glanced away, lips twitching in embarrassment. "No one's ever… ravished me before."

Vaelen's brow arched.

She looked up at him, eyes shining with amusement. "Especially not someone built like you."

And there it was.

That smile — slow, smug, and yet softened by concern.

He stepped in close, his hand brushing her lower back. "I should've gone slower."

"You were perfect," she said, voice softer now. "I wanted every second of it."

"But you're still sore," he murmured, brushing his knuckles along her arm. "That matters to me."

Elira smiled again, leaning into him slightly. "It just means I'll remember it."

He laughed under his breath, low and quiet.

Then, in a more serious tone: "Next time…"

She looked up.

His fingers curled gently under her chin.

"Next time, we'll take our time," he said. "We'll make it slow. Soft. I want to know every inch of what makes you tremble."

Elira's breath caught.

And just like that, her heart ached in the best way.

"Next time," she whispered, "I want to know what it feels like when you love me with your whole soul."

He leaned in, pressing a kiss to her temple.

"You already do."

Chapter 27:

The wind had changed.

Elira felt it in her bones before she saw it in the sky — a low hum in the forest, a stillness between the trees that hadn't been there the day before. Even the runes in the hallways flickered slightly differently, their glow pulsing deeper, steadier. Like they were waiting for something.

Or someone.

She tightened the straps of her leathers, her hands moving with muscle memory. Vaelen was nearby, speaking in low tones with one of the Lirian sentries. His posture was more alert than usual — not tense, but ready. As if something in the air had shifted, and he could feel it too.

Elira finished adjusting her bracers and glanced up just as Solen approached.

His smile was brighter than the morning light.

"You're glowing," he said, clearly amused.

Elira rolled her eyes. "That's just sweat."

"Sure," Solen said, unconvinced. "You must've had a very *enlightening* evening."

She opened her mouth to reply — to deflect — but instead let out a soft laugh and nudged his arm. "We're not talking about that."

He grinned wider. "Noted. But for what it's worth, I haven't seen Vaelen smile like that since… ever."

She tried not to look over her shoulder toward where Vaelen stood.

She failed.

He was watching her.

Of course he was.

And when their eyes met, he didn't look away.

Neither did she.

It was just a glance. Just a heartbeat.

But it felt like a vow.

They gathered later that morning in the council chamber carved from living stone. The High Lirian, Maerys, stood at the center of the room, her silver-white braid coiled like a crown. Around her, the other elder Lirians waited with unreadable expressions.

"The veil is weakening," Maerys said, her voice carrying like wind over water. "Your awakening has accelerated it, Elira."

Elira swallowed. "That's good… right?"

Solen nodded. "Yes. But it means the King will feel the shift too."

"His illusions are tied to control," Maerys said. "If they begin to crack, he'll lash out to contain them. Or worse—reinforce them by force."

Vaelen stepped forward. "What do you need from us?"

Maerys turned her gaze to Elira. "There is a place — the Hollow of Echoes. A sacred site beneath the oldest roots of the forest. If you go there, the forest will show you truths hidden even from memory."

"Truths about me?" Elira asked quietly.

Maerys nodded. "And about what you were meant to be."

Chapter 28:

The path to the Hollow of Echoes wasn't marked.

It revealed itself only to those it deemed worthy — a winding descent carved into the earth, hidden beneath the twisted roots of the oldest trees in the forest. The air grew colder the deeper they went, the scent of moss and damp stone thickening around them like a second skin.

Elira walked in silence, flanked by Vaelen on her left and Solen on her right. Neither of them spoke.

It felt wrong to break the quiet.

The further they descended, the more the silence *felt.* Heavy. Pressurized. Like the air itself was waiting.

"I don't like this place," Solen whispered, the first to speak. "Too many things echo down here that should've been buried."

Elira glanced at him. "Then why are we here?"

"Because what's buried doesn't stay buried forever," Vaelen answered.

The Hollow opened like a great wound in the earth — vast and low-ceilinged, its walls pulsing faintly with embedded veins of glowing green crystal. Ancient runes marked the stone floor in circular patterns, too worn to read, but not forgotten.

At the center stood a platform of root and stone — a natural altar.

And something else.

Someone.

Elira stepped forward slowly, her fingers tingling as they neared the platform.

The figure was crouched, half-hidden by the curling roots — a woman, draped in tattered fabric, her hair long and tangled with moss and soil. Her shoulders trembled.

At first, Elira thought she was crying.

Then the woman lifted her head — and her eyes glowed with an eerie, unblinking light.

Not magic.

Emotion.

Pure, unfiltered, *uncontained.*

The woman let out a guttural sound — part sob, part scream — and the runes beneath her feet flared violently, casting the hollow in a sickly green light.

Elira Solen stepped forward quickly. “She’s unbalanced.”

“What does that mean?” Elira asked, already backing away.

“It means she felt something too powerful, too long ago — and she couldn’t release it. So now it *owns* her.”

The woman stood slowly, movements jerky and unnatural.

Vaelen pulled Elira behind him.

“Runes!” Solen called. “Get behind the ward line—”

But it was too late.

The woman screamed, and the sound cracked the air like lightning.

staggered, her ears ringing. Her knees hit the stone. It wasn’t just the sound — it was the *feeling.* Rage. Grief. Abandonment. All pouring from the woman like floodwater.

She was drowning in it.

Vaelen dropped beside her, shielding her with his body. “You must shield your mind. Now.”

"I—I don't know how—"

"Yes, you do," he said, taking her hands. "Feel what's yours. Let the rest fall away."

Elira closed her eyes, breath shaking.

Inside her, the roar pressed against her ribs like a storm.

But beneath it, she found something quieter.

Her name.

Her truth.

Her.

And she held onto it.

The moment she did, the pressure eased — just enough for Solen to activate the ward line, sending a shockwave of light through the Hollow.

The woman collapsed instantly, her scream cut off, her body crumpling into stillness.

They didn't speak for a long time after.

Not until they had climbed back toward the surface, the Hollow behind them sealed with new wards.

Elira sat on a stone ledge, hands still trembling, a faint bruise forming along her jaw.

"She was like me," she whispered. "Wasn't she?"

"She was what you could become," Solen said gently. "If you forget how to *feel* with intention."

"She didn't mean to hurt anyone," Elira said.

"No," Vaelen agreed. "But emotions don't care about meaning. Not when they're left to rot."

Elira stared out at the forest; her throat tight.

"I want to help them," she said. "The ones like her. I don't want to leave them behind."

Vaelen's voice was low. "That's why you'll never become one of them."

And yet… the memory of that scream lingered.

Not in her ears.

But in her chest.

Chapter 29:

Elira didn't speak for the rest of the day.

Not because she didn't want to.

Because she didn't know *how.*

The woman's scream still echoed in her head — not in sound, but in sensation. It had wrapped around her ribs like vines and squeezed, forcing her to feel everything that had ever been locked away.

And for a moment, she'd almost gotten lost in it.

That was what frightened her the most.

Not the woman's power.

But how familiar it had felt.

She found herself in the high chamber of the stronghold by nightfall, sitting beneath the arc of an ancient tree whose roots wove directly through the wall and into the floor. The room was silent, save for the occasional flicker of rune-light along the stone.

Maerys stood at the far end, a tall silhouette backlit by a pillar of pale green light.

"You saw it," the elder Lirian said, not turning. "What emotion can do when it is not honored."

Elira nodded; her throat tight. "It wasn't just rage. It was grief. Loneliness. She was drowning."

"She was forgotten," Maerys replied, finally facing her. "Like many who came before. Emotion is a force, Elira. When wielded with purpose, it can create life. Heal wounds. Break illusion. But when buried…" She shook her head. "It festers. Twists. And consumes."

"I almost lost myself," Elira whispered. "I didn't know how to stop it."

"You *felt* your way out," Maerys said. "You anchored yourself."

Elira looked up. "How?"

"Think back. What did you hold onto?"

A pause.

And then: "My name."

Maerys smiled. "More than that."

Elira blinked, and in her mind, the memory returned—not just of the Hollow, but of the weight around her, the heat of Vaelen's hands, the sound of his voice, steady and sure.

Feel what's yours. Let the rest fall away.

"I held onto him," she said softly. "Vaelen."

Maerys nodded. "Connection is not weakness. It is *structure*. Emotion is wild, yes—but bonds are what give it shape."

Elira let that settle in her chest. "So… the stronger the bond, the less likely I am to lose myself?"

"No," Maerys said gently. "The stronger the bond, the more easily you can *find* yourself again."

They were quiet for a moment.

Then Elira asked the question that had been burning in her chest since the Hollow.

"Are there others? Like her?"

Maerys didn't hesitate. "Many."

Elira's stomach sank. "Can they be saved?"

"Some. Others…" Maerys exhaled slowly. "Their emotions have been feeding the illusion for too long. They are tethered to it now."

Elira's hands curled into fists. "I want to try. I want to *free* them."

"You will try," Maerys said, voice low. "And that is what makes you dangerous."

Elira looked up.

"Not your power. Not your name," Maerys continued. "But your heart. That stubborn, aching heart that refuses to leave anyone behind."

Later, when she returned to her room, Vaelen was waiting.

He didn't say anything.

He didn't have to.

He just opened his arms.

And she stepped into them.

Vaelen didn't ask what happened.

He simply held her, arms wrapped tightly around her like he knew she needed something to press against—something solid, something *real.*

Elira buried her face into his shoulder, breathing in the steady rhythm of him. The scent of leather and wild mint. The quiet thrum of his heart.

They stood like that for a long time.

And when she finally spoke, it was barely a whisper.

"I was scared."

Vaelen's hand brushed through her hair, slow and grounding. "You had every right to be."

"I didn't realize how easy it would be to lose myself."

“You didn’t lose yourself,” he said softly. “You found a way back.”

“I don’t want to forget who I am.”

“You won’t.” He pulled back just enough to look into her eyes. “You’ve come too far to disappear now.”

Elira’s lips trembled.

He reached up, thumb brushing the corner of her mouth.

“You don’t have to carry it all alone,” he said. “Not with me here.”

Something in her chest cracked open.

She leaned forward, resting her forehead against his.

“Thank you,” she whispered.

He smiled faintly. “You don’t have to thank me for loving you.”

Her breath caught—but she didn’t pull away.

Because maybe… she didn’t need to.

Not anymore.

Chapter 30:

The palace never slept.

But tonight, it held its breath.

Captain Narel paced the northern corridor of the High Hall, his boots echoing too loudly on the polished stone. Torches lined the walls in perfect symmetry, never flickering, never fading. The illusion kept them steady. Just like everything else.

Until now.

He paused outside the mirrored atrium — a small, ornate chamber lined with silver-glass panels meant to reflect the King's eternal dominion.

He'd walked past it a hundred times.

But tonight…

He froze.

Because something was wrong.

The reflection in the far-right mirror… moved.

Not in sync. Not delayed.

Differently.

Narel stepped forward, slowly drawing his blade, his eyes narrowing.

In the glass, his reflection stood with a sword in hand — but its head turned the wrong way.

Not toward the hallway.

Toward *him.*

He staggered back, blade raised, heart pounding in his chest.

When he looked again — it was gone.

Just him.

Just his own wide-eyed reflection.

He clenched his jaw, turning sharply on his heel, trying to shake off the unease.

But as he passed the atrium, a faint sound reached his ears.

A whisper.

So soft he couldn't make out the words.

And no one behind him.

Elsewhere in the palace, a young servant girl dropped her tray as she passed the painting of the King's coronation. She stared at it, trembling.

There were faces in the background that hadn't been there before.

Faces she recognized.

Faces she'd dreamed of — but never met.

One of them had silver eyes.

High above, in the throne chamber, the King stood alone.

His fingers tapped against the arm of his throne, rhythm measured, eyes fixed on the far window where moonlight filtered in like pale judgment.

A small ripple danced across the surface of the glass.

Barely visible.

But he saw it.

Felt it.

The illusion was weakening.

And it was her.

The girl with the forgotten name.

The girl who had *survived the Grove.*

The girl he had once believed he'd broken.

He turned slowly to face the empty hall behind him.

"Find her," he said, voice cold as winter.

A guard stepped from the shadows and bowed.

"Yes, my King."

The guard's footsteps faded into the shadows, but the King remained still.

Alone in the throne chamber, surrounded by silence too complete to be natural.

It pressed in.

He turned back toward the great glass window, eyes fixed on the sliver of moon above the horizon.

A crack had appeared there—small, invisible to anyone else. A ripple that disturbed the perfect illusion blanketing his kingdom. The pulse of controlled magic that kept the people compliant. Quiet. Blind.

But *she* wasn't blind anymore.

He could feel her.

Far beyond the palace walls, the girl once called his daughter was stirring the very roots of the illusion.

His illusion.

And if she continued…

The King's jaw clenched, fingers curling tightly over the throne's carved arm.

He had erased her.

Buried her name.

Banished the mother.

Stripped her of memory, of power, of purpose.

And still—

Still, she rose.

"She is a shadow of a mistake," he muttered under his breath. "She is nothing."

But the lie rang hollow.

Because if she were nothing, the Hollow wouldn't have opened to her.

The runes wouldn't have bent in her presence.

And the veil wouldn't be bleeding at its seams.

He strode to the center of the room, pressing a palm to the obsidian sigil embedded in the floor. Magic flickered—fractured for a heartbeat before realigning. That had never happened before.

He pulled his hand away sharply.

If she wasn't stopped—

If the people *saw*—

If the illusion shattered—

His rule would crumble. And with it, everything he had sacrificed to build.

He paced now; eyes wild with thought.

"Strength must be severed before it becomes legacy," he murmured.

It was not the girl he feared.

It was the *idea* of her.

Unbroken.

Unbound.

Free.

He would not allow it.

He *could not.*

Chapter 31:

The stronghold breathed like a living thing.

Its roots stretched far beneath the ground, fed by magic older than memory. Elira sat in the garden just beyond the main hall, knees pulled to her chest, fingers combing through soft tufts of flowering moss. The light above was gentle — dappled by thick branches, filtered through enchanted leaves that shifted hue with the time of day.

For once, everything was… quiet.

Too quiet.

It wasn't the eerie stillness of the Hollow, or the sharp silence that had followed her first burst of power. It was something else.

Something *waiting.*

"Elira."

She looked up as Solen approached, his hands stained with rune-ink, a half-smile playing at his lips.

"You're brooding."

"I'm reflecting," she corrected.

"Same thing," he replied, flopping down beside her.

They sat in easy silence for a moment, the moss cool beneath them.

"You scared me yesterday," he said at last. "I've seen a lot of things in that Hollow. But watching you face her… and *survive it*... You're not like the others."

"That's not always a good thing," she murmured.

Solen nudged her shoulder gently. "It will be. In time."

Later, Elira found herself walking through one of the older corridors near the library — the ones carved deeper into the roots. They weren't used often. Too sacred. Too full of echo.

That's where she found Vaelen.

He stood at one of the arched windows, arms folded, gaze distant.

"You've been quiet," she said softly.

"I've been thinking," he replied, not looking at her.

"Dangerous habit."

That earned a faint smile.

She moved to stand beside him, her hand brushing his. And then—

He paused.

Brows furrowed.

"What's this?" he asked, fingertips brushing the chain at her neck — the one she always forgot was there. The one hidden beneath collar and rune-silk.

Elira blinked, startled. "Oh… the collar."

Vaelen's jaw tightened. "I've never seen you wear this. It's—"

"I don't take it off," she admitted slowly. "I… I never really thought about it."

Vaelen turned to face her fully, brows drawn. "Why not?"

Elira reached up, her fingers brushing the cool metal. For the first time, it *tingled.* Not in the way her magic did. This was something else.

"I thought it was just… ceremonial. A mark of my position. Something he gave me when I was still his daughter."

Vaelen's eyes narrowed. "That doesn't feel like a gift, Elira. It feels like a leash."

Her heart stuttered.

And then—

A whisper.

A memory.

You belong to me.

Elira staggered back a step.

The collar *hummed.*

Not in magic.

But in *recognition.*

"I think…" she breathed, "I think he's still using it."

Vaelen's voice was low, sharp. "To track you?"

"To watch. To control. To *find* me if he needs to."

The realization hit her like cold water.

"This is how he'll try to bring me back."

Vaelen stepped forward. "Then we get it off."

"It's not that simple," she said. "If it's laced into the illusion, if it's tied to him—removing it could do more than weaken him. It could draw him straight to me."

"Then we do it carefully. And we don't do it alone."

Elira swallowed hard, her hand still resting against the metal. "If I destroy this… it might break the last of what binds me to him."

Vaelen nodded. "Then let's *shatter* it."

Elira's hand dropped from the collar, her fingers curling into a fist.

She hated the way it felt now — like it pulsed against her throat in rhythm with her breath. As if it had always been watching. Always waiting.

Vaelen hadn't moved.

But his gaze never left her.

When she finally met his eyes again, there was no fear left in hers.

Only fire.

"I want it off," she said.

Vaelen stepped closer, voice steady. "Then we'll find a way."

"I don't want him inside my head anymore," she whispered. "I don't want him *here.*"

Vaelen reached out, slowly — not for the collar, but for *her.*

His hand settled gently against her neck, fingers warm just beneath the chain, his thumb resting at the hollow of her throat. He didn't press. Didn't tug.

He just *held.*

Her breath hitched.

"I don't want to be a symbol of what he created," she said, barely audible. "I want to be who I'm choosing to become."

"You already are," he murmured.

Their eyes locked — and something passed between them.

Not like before.

This wasn't about protection or comfort.

This was tension.

Desire restrained.

It pulsed beneath the surface, sharp and sweet — a magnetic ache that drew her closer before either of them could stop it.

Vaelen's thumb brushed lightly against her skin. "When we do remove it… you'll feel it."

"How?" she asked, voice low.

"Like the last door unlocking inside you."

Her lips parted — not for words, but for breath she couldn't quite take in.

And in that space between words, between tension and stillness, something bloomed.

Want.

Heavy. Slow. Irrefutable.

He stepped back first, just enough to break the spell — but not the connection.

"Elira," he said gently, "when we get it off… I want to be the first thing you feel."

Her heart stuttered.

But she didn't look away.

She didn't retreat.

She nodded once — quiet, fierce.

"Then be ready," she whispered. "Because I think I'll burn."

Chapter 32:

The library in the southern wing of the stronghold was unlike the others.

It wasn't carved into wood or stone.

It was *grown.*

Vines laced the walls, runes shaped like leaves pulsing gently in hues of green and silver. The shelves themselves twisted upward from living roots, cradling ancient scrolls and rune-bound tomes like fruit. The air was thick with the scent of earth and candle smoke, and the hush that filled the space felt *sacred.*

Elira stood beside the central table, her fingers skimming over the cover of an old binding manual, her brow furrowed.

"Here," Solen said, appearing behind her with a thick, rune-sealed volume. "This one's older. Might be closer to the kind of collar he used."

She nodded, accepting it, her hand brushing his briefly. "Thank you. I don't want to risk tearing it off without knowing what it's made of."

"You shouldn't," Solen agreed. "If it's linked to your energy, or worse—to him directly—removing it the wrong way could sever your magic. Or worse."

Vaelen looked up sharply from his place near the far wall. "Then we *don't* do it the wrong way."

His eyes met Elira's, and for a moment, the rest of the room faded.

That lingering touch from the night before.

His fingers against her throat.

The way he'd said he wanted to be the first thing she felt…

She turned back to the book, hiding the heat in her cheeks behind pages.

⁂

The day passed in study.

Solen moved through texts like a storm, muttering to himself. Elira took notes, drew the diagrams of different Lirian-era bindings, their warding patterns intricate and shifting. Vaelen barely left her side.

He was quiet.

But his presence…

It hummed.

When she leaned closer to show him a passage, her shoulder brushed his. When she turned a page, their fingers met on the paper. Small things. But they lingered.

She caught him watching her once—eyes dark, thoughtful.

She didn't look away.

She *wanted* him to look.

By nightfall, Solen stood and stretched with a groan. "I need sleep. And stronger tea. I'll keep digging tomorrow."

Elira nodded. "Thank you."

He grinned. "You're not alone in this."

Then, a wink. "And neither is Vaelen."

Elira rolled her eyes. "Goodnight, Solen."

He disappeared with a dramatic sigh and a wave of his hand.

She and Vaelen were alone now.

The runes in the walls pulsed faintly with evening energy, soft and low.

Elira closed the book in front of her and exhaled.

"I think we'll need more than books," she said. "This collar… it feels alive."

"Then maybe it is," Vaelen said, voice quiet. "Maybe he tied it to you in a way no ink can undo."

"Then we'll find another way."

He stepped closer.

"Elira," he said, voice gentler now. "You don't have to be brave all the time."

She looked up at him.

Her chest ached with something she couldn't name — not fear, not hope. Something heavier. Something *older.*

"I'm tired of being bound," she whispered. "In my magic. In my skin. In my *story.* I want to burn it all away."

Vaelen reached for her hand, entwining their fingers.

"Then let's set the match together."

Chapter 33:

The path to the underground chamber was older than even the Lirians could trace. Twisting stone corridors carved long before the illusion. Before the veil. Before the King.

Elira walked in silence, her fingers grazing the moss-covered walls, the cool stone humming with runes too faded to read but not forgotten.

Vaelen followed close behind, steps quiet, presence steady.

Neither of them had spoken since Solen had directed them there.

They didn't need to.

The air between them spoke in its own language now.

At the end of the corridor, they found the door.

Carved from obsidian, inlaid with silver leaf — the same silver that laced the collar at Elira's throat. The runes on the surface pulsed faintly when she stepped near, and a soft hum echoed through the air like a breath held too long.

Vaelen reached for her wrist gently. "Are you ready?"

She nodded.

But her voice betrayed her.

"I'm afraid."

He didn't let go.

"You're allowed to be."

Inside, the room was circular, domed with vines and carved symbols. A soft green glow lit the space from the roots above. At the center, a pedestal carved from tree-bone and crystal — a place for offerings. A place for truths.

Elira stepped toward it, slowly unfastening the clasp of her cloak. Her fingers shook as she reached for the collar, letting it rest fully in the open.

The moment she did, the runes around the room flared.

Magic *recognized* her.

Not because of her power.

But because of her *bind.*

Vaelen moved in behind her — not close enough to touch, but close enough to *feel.*

She swallowed. "It doesn't want to be removed."

"Then we make it *want* to," he said, voice low. "Not with force. With intent."

Elira closed her eyes.

She reached out—not with her hands, but her heart.

Not trying to *rip* the collar off… but trying to *understand* it.

And in the quiet, she heard it.

A whisper.

Not from the King.

But from *herself.*

A part of her still afraid.

A part still waiting to be claimed.

Her breath caught.

And behind her, Vaelen stepped closer. His hands found her shoulders, his presence grounding her like roots. She leaned into it, trembling.

"I don't know who I am without this," she said.

"Yes, you do," he murmured. "You've always known. You're just starting to believe it."

She turned to him then — slowly.

And something passed between them.

More than tension. More than want.

Readiness.

He reached for her cheek, and she leaned in.

The kiss was soft — not urgent, not wild — but deep.

Like a promise.

Like the breath before the flame.

Chapter 34:

The chamber glowed faintly, the runes in the walls pulsing in sync with Elira's breath.

She stood in the center, the collar still around her neck like a ghost of a past she hadn't chosen. But tonight… it didn't feel like it owned her anymore.

Not with him here.

Not with this fire between them.

Vaelen hadn't moved since she turned to him — since she kissed him like she already knew what came next.

And now, he stepped forward.

No rush.

No question.

Just *certainty*.

His fingers brushed the edge of the silver chain, not tugging — *asking*.

Elira nodded once.

He slid it aside, just enough to bare her collarbone. His lips followed a moment later, warm and reverent, pressing softly to the place where the metal met her skin.

She shivered — not from fear.

From release.

She reached for him then, palms against his chest, drawing him closer.

When they kissed again, it was slower. Deeper. Every movement deliberate.

Hands exploring but not demanding.

Breath catching in quiet places.

Clothes fell away between touches, between pauses, between the space where words might have lived but weren't needed.

They moved together in the center of the chamber — two heartbeats syncing, two bodies finding rhythm not from lust, but from *knowing.*

Vaelen was careful.

Elira was bold.

Not because she wasn't afraid — but because she *trusted.*

The way he held her as they sank to the moss-covered floor.

The way he looked at her, even now, like she was something sacred.

When he entered her, it was with a slowness that broke her open all over again.

She gasped.

Not from the stretch.

But from the feeling.

Of being *filled.*

Of being *seen.*

Vaelen's hands found hers, fingers twining above her head, grounding her even as she arched beneath him.

They moved like a prayer.

Like a memory she hadn't yet lived.

And when release came, it was not loud.

It was *quiet.*

Shattering.

Her body trembled. His did too.

He buried his face into the crook of her neck, breath heavy, hands tight around her like he couldn't quite believe she was real.

And when the silence returned, it wasn't empty.

It was full.

Of them.

They lay in the moss after, skin to skin, breath still catching.

It was Elira who spoke first.

"Before I met you," she whispered, "I thought love was weakness. That wanting something meant giving someone a way to break you."

Vaelen's hand slid up her back, slow and grounding. "It does."

She blinked, surprised.

"But the right person," he added, "doesn't break you. They hold the broken parts until you can put them back yourself."

Elira's throat tightened. "What if I never feel whole?"

"Then I'll love the fragments," he said. "Every single one."

She turned to him, eyes shining.

"I think…" she began. "I think the collar isn't just a chain. It's a scar. And I'm afraid of what happens when it's gone."

"Then let me be there when you let it go."

She nodded, tears slipping silently down her cheek.

And Vaelen reached up, brushing one away with his thumb.

"You're not what he made you," he said. "You're what you *choose* to be next."

The quiet between them lingered like a breath held too long.

Elira lay against Vaelen's chest, her skin flushed, still humming from the release she hadn't known she needed. He held her close, one hand tracing slow, absent-minded circles across her back.

"You're quiet," she murmured.

He tilted his head down to look at her, eyes darker than before — not unreadable, but *burning* with something new.

"I wanted to be gentler this time," he said softly. "Make sure I didn't… push you."

"You didn't," she whispered. "You were perfect."

A beat of silence.

Then he exhaled, rougher this time — a breath that trembled with restraint.

"Good," he said, voice dipping low. "Because now I want you again."

Elira's eyes widened, but her breath hitched in anticipation.

He rolled her gently beneath him, one hand braced at her side, the other sliding down her thigh, slow and possessive.

"I want to show you," he murmured, mouth grazing her jaw, "just how powerful you are when you let go."

Her breath caught. "Vaelen—"

"Shhh," he whispered, voice velvet and heat. "Let me love you the way *you* deserve."

He kissed her again — deeper this time, rougher, lips dragging across hers like he was starving for the taste of her.

His hand slipped between her thighs, fingers parting her slowly, reverently.

And then—

Inside.

Just one at first. Then another.

She gasped, back arching off the mossy floor, her body already slick and ready from the fire he'd stoked before.

"Gods," she breathed. "That feels…"

"So good," he finished for her, his voice like gravel and silk. "You don't even know what you do to me."

He curled his fingers just right — slow, then quick, teasing and relentless — watching her with unblinking intensity. Her hips bucked against his hand, her moans growing needier with each stroke.

"I want you to fall apart just like this," he said, voice rough with want. "For *you.* Not for me. Not for anyone else. Just you."

And she did.

With a cry that echoed off the rune-walls, her body clenching around his hand as she shattered again — harder, fuller, more *herself* than ever before.

He didn't stop kissing her.

Didn't stop whispering.

"Beautiful," he said against her throat. "*Mine.*"

When she was still trembling, still panting, he pulled his hand away and kissed the space where her collar met skin — and then the center of her chest, like a vow.

"I want to feel you again," he said. "All of you."

She reached for him, fingers digging into his arms, her body aching in the *best* way.

"I want to feel you, too."

And when he entered her again this time — there was no hesitation.

No restraint.

His thrusts were deeper. Stronger. Their bodies slamming together with rhythmic certainty. She moaned his name like a prayer, and he groaned hers like a promise.

"I kind of like the thought," he panted into her ear, "of you being at least a little sore after."

Elira gasped, half-laughing, half-melting.

"Vaelen—"

"I want you to feel me," he whispered, "even when I'm not inside you."

She came again at those words — trembling, crying out, completely undone.

And he followed, teeth clenched, growling her name like it *meant something holy.*

They collapsed together afterward, a mess of breath and skin and heat.

But this time?

This time, Elira didn't feel unraveled.

She felt claimed.

Not by Vaelen.

By *herself.*

tr

Chapter 35:

The chamber was still, save for the slow, steady rise and fall of Elira's breath.

She stood at the pedestal, bare from the waist up, the silver collar resting like a brand against her skin. It had never looked heavier.

Vaelen stood just behind her, shirtless, quiet, steady — not guiding this time, but *witnessing*.

The heat of their bodies still lingered in the air.

But the fire in Elira's eyes now… was different.

This was not the fire of want.

This was the fire of *freedom*.

She reached for the rune blade Solen had left — not to cut, but to *channel*. The tip glowed softly with binding sigils, etched in patterns meant to separate magic from soul.

Elira pressed the flat of the blade to the collar, her other hand braced against the pedestal.

And she whispered.

A name.

Not her own.

His.

"Aurik."

The moment the name left her lips, the collar *screamed*.

Not aloud.

But in *her mind*.

A shriek of resistance, of rage, of command.

Her knees buckled — but Vaelen caught her from behind, hands firm at her waist.

"Hold on," he whispered.

"I am," she gritted through her teeth. "I'm not letting him win."

The collar flared silver — then black.

The runes in the chamber pulsed violently, reacting to the unraveling bond.

Pain lanced through her chest — not from the metal, but from the *memories.* The lies the King had fed her. The voice she'd once trusted.

You were never enough.

You were never meant to awaken.

You are mine.

"NO," Elira cried out, voice sharp as lightning. "I am NOT YOURS!"

The collar split.

A jagged tear of metal and magic — and the moment it broke, a shockwave of energy blasted outward, knocking Vaelen back and flaring every rune in the chamber into blinding white light.

Elira collapsed to her knees, chest heaving, hands trembling as the broken pieces clattered to the stone floor beside her.

It was done.

She was free.

Above, in the palace, the King fell to his knees.

Blood dripped from his nose.

His illusion flickered.

Paintings warped.

Windows shattered inward.

And for the first time in decades…

He *felt pain.*

He screamed.

Back in the chamber, Vaelen was already at Elira's side, cradling her gently.

Her skin was hot.

Her eyes wild.

But she was smiling.

A little.

Soft.

Shaky.

Free.

"You did it," he whispered.

"No," she breathed. "*We* did."

And in her hands?

Nothing but silver dust.

The silver dust still shimmered across Elira's palms, but her breath had begun to even out. The magic had stilled. The runes dimmed. And the collar—the thing that had caged her since childhood—was *gone.*

But it wasn't relief that bloomed first.

It was fear.

She turned sharply. "Vaelen."

He was sitting against the far wall, one hand braced behind him, the other pressed to his ribs. His hair was mussed, shirt still discarded, and there was a streak of ash across his cheek.

But he was *smiling.*

"Elira," he said with a hoarse laugh, "you *exploded* magic. You could've warned me."

She scrambled toward him, dropping to her knees at his side. "You got knocked back. I didn't know it would—are you hurt?"

"Only my pride," he said with a smirk. "And maybe my elbow."

"That's not funny."

"Didn't say it was."

She ran her fingers over his arm gently, checking for any serious injury. "You shouldn't have been that close."

"I wasn't going to let you do it alone."

"You *could've*—"

He caught her hand.

"Elira."

She stilled.

"I would've stood between you and the collar if I thought it would help. I'd stand between you and *anything* that tries to take you back."

She searched his face.

"You know what this means," she said softly. "Now that it's gone… I'm more of a threat than ever. He'll come for me. He'll *send* things."

"I know."

"You'll be in danger just by being with me."

"I know that too."

She looked down. "I wouldn't blame you if you stepped back now."

Vaelen leaned in, his forehead brushing hers.

"I won't."

Her breath caught.

"I've faced wars, monsters, and things that crawl out of shadows," he whispered. "But nothing scares me more than the thought of you going through this without someone to fight for you."

"You don't have to protect me."

"I know," he said. "But I *will.*"

His thumb brushed over her cheek. "And if anything tries to hurt you again… I'll throw myself in front of it before it gets the chance."

She exhaled, shaky but stronger than before. "You're insane."

"I'm in love."

She stilled.

Vaelen froze.

The words had slipped out like breath.

But he didn't take them back.

Didn't flinch.

Didn't run.

"I mean it," he said, voice steady. "I love you."

And this time—

She didn't break.

She bloomed.

Chapter 36:

The morning light filtering through the forest canopy felt different now.

Brighter, somehow.

Sharper.

Elira walked barefoot along the moss-covered path just beyond the stronghold, the remnants of rune-light flickering in her skin like tiny pulses of starlight. The collar was gone — nothing but dust, swept away by the wind.

But she still felt it.

Not as a presence.

As an *absence.*

A space once occupied by fear now thrummed with something she didn't yet know how to name.

Power, maybe.

Or something more dangerous.

Possibility.

Behind her, the soft crunch of footfalls drew her attention.

Vaelen.

He joined her without a word, matching her pace, fingers brushing against hers as they walked.

"You're different today," he said after a moment.

She glanced at him. "I feel it."

"Stronger?"

"Lighter."

He nodded slowly. "The forest feels it too."

She stopped at the edge of a small clearing — one she didn't remember ever seeing before. Wildflowers bloomed in a ring around a fallen tree, the air thick with the scent of cedar and something older.

"I think it opened for you," Vaelen said softly.

Elira took a step forward, her fingertips grazing a vine-wrapped branch. The plant responded — curling upward to meet her skin, glowing faintly.

"She's awakening," came a voice from behind them.

Solen.

He stood at the edge of the clearing, arms crossed, watching her like she was something rare.

"No more chains," he said. "No more anchors. You're unbound now."

"That scares me," Elira admitted.

"It should," Solen said with a smile. "But it should scare *him* more."

Back in the stronghold, the Lirians moved differently around her now.

Not with fear.

With *reverence.*

Maerys bowed her head when Elira passed in the corridor. Riven, the stone-skinned sentry, murmured something like "She walks free now" under his breath.

And at the council table, the oldest among them—Aelrin, the whispering archivist—spoke aloud for the first time in decades.

"The girl who unbound herself," he said, voice thin and rusted with time. "She is no longer dreaming."

Elira tried not to shrink under the weight of it.

But it was hard.

Not because she didn't believe them.

But because she didn't yet believe *herself.*

That night, she sat with Vaelen on the balcony above the glowing grove.

No more armor between them.

No more questions between silences.

She leaned into him, her head resting against his shoulder.

"I feel like I've stepped off the edge of something," she murmured. "And now I'm just… falling."

"You're not falling," Vaelen said. "You're flying. You just haven't realized it yet."

They sat like that for a while.

Quiet.

Whole.

And beneath them, the forest *watched.*

Not waiting.

Welcoming.

The moon hung low above the treetops, casting the grove in soft silver light.

Elira leaned into Vaelen's warmth on the balcony, the air cool against her bare arms. For a while, they said nothing — content in the quiet, in the knowing.

Then Vaelen's voice broke the stillness.

"You're stronger than you know."

She smiled faintly. "People keep telling me that."

"They're right."

He turned toward her, his arm sliding behind her back, his voice low and certain.

"Elira… I've fought in more battles than I care to remember. Seen what fear does to people. What illusion does to *hope*. I've watched warriors twice your size crumble under pressure you've walked through like fire."

She blinked, surprised. "You think I've walked through this?"

"I think," he said, "you're leading the way."

She looked down at her hands, her fingers curling slightly.

"I didn't ask to be that."

"I know," he said softly. "That's what makes it real."

She turned to face him more fully now, studying the sharpness in his jaw, the way the moonlight softened him.

"Why are you here?" she asked. "Really? With me, with the Lirians?"

He didn't answer at first.

Then: "Because illusion took everything from me too."

Her breath stilled.

"I was born in the outer provinces," he said. "Small place. Quiet. My father was a protector of the forest lines — the old sacred grounds that the King claimed belonged to the crown. My mother was a song weaver. She used to hum while she worked. Said the world listened when you sang to it."

Elira felt something tighten in her chest.

"She stopped singing the day they came," he said. "The King's guard. They accused my father of harboring magic. Said he'd been seen helping a Lirian cross through the eastern gate. They burned our home."

Elira's hand slid into his instinctively.

"What happened?"

"My mother was taken. My father disappeared. I survived. Barely."

He paused, voice roughening.

"And for years, I didn't care about anyone or anything. I just wanted to fight. To make someone *pay*. I didn't even believe in the Lirians when I first found them. I just needed something to aim at."

"And now?" she whispered.

"Now I believe in *you*."

Elira's throat closed, eyes brimming.

"You're not just fighting for yourself," he said. "You're fighting for the ones who didn't get the chance. People like my mother. Like your mother. Like the ones still waiting to wake up."

He reached up, brushing his thumb against her cheek.

"You're not just brave. You're *hopeful*. That's rarer than any magic."

Elira leaned into his hand; her voice small but sure.

"Then I'm glad I found you."

He smiled faintly. "I think I was always meant to find you."

Chapter 37:

The air beyond the Veil was wrong.

Not broken.

But *warped.*

Towns that once felt like dreams now felt hollow — people moved like shadows in sunlight, their steps too smooth, their smiles too still.

But behind their eyes?

Something was beginning to *flicker.*

In the capital city of Aerithal, a servant girl named Talia paused outside the mirrored corridor of the royal wing. She was carrying wine — the same path she'd walked a hundred times.

But tonight, the mirror didn't reflect her tray.

It reflected a *memory.*

A woman — younger, wild-eyed, with silver hair and a collar at her throat.

She dropped the tray.

Glass shattered.

And for a moment, the reflection *smiled.*

In the Eastern provinces, a former soldier woke up screaming.

He clutched his chest, sweat-soaked and breathless, muttering a name he didn't recognize.

"Elira."

His wife tried to calm him.

But he didn't hear her.

Because the dream had felt *real.*

Because her name made his bones hum.

In the far north, a child stood at the edge of the cliffs and sang.

A song she had never learned.

A lullaby in a language no one had taught her.

And the sea answered.

In the heart of the palace, the King stood before the largest mirror in the throne chamber.

The glass rippled faintly.

Then cracked.

Hairline.

Barely visible.

But enough.

He turned to his advisors with a snarl.

"She's bleeding into them," he growled.

"Who?" one dared to ask.

"The one I erased."

Back in the stronghold, Elira sat with Solen and Vaelen around the flickering rune-pit fire.

Maerys entered quietly, scroll in hand.

"Something's happening beyond the borders," she said. "Reports are coming in. People seeing things. Hearing things. Remembering things that should have been forgotten."

Solen leaned forward. "The illusion is unraveling."

Elira's stomach turned.

"I didn't mean to—"

"You didn't break it," Maerys said. "You *shook* it. And now the world remembers it was dreaming."

Elira's fingers curled into the blanket around her.

"What happens when it breaks completely?"

Maerys met her eyes.

"Then the King loses everything."

Chapter 38:

The night air was thick with something unseen.

Not cold. Not warm.

Just... charged.

Elira stood just outside the stronghold, alone, arms crossed over her chest as the forest whispered around her. She couldn't sleep. Couldn't rest.

Not with this *hum* under her skin.

It wasn't fear.

It wasn't power.

It was a *tug*.

Like invisible threads winding through her ribs, pulling her toward something she couldn't name.

She'd felt it since sunset.

A flicker in her pulse.

A strange pressure in her chest.

Not pain — but presence.

As though something was *trying* to reach her.

But it wasn't a voice.

It was a memory.

That wasn't hers.

Vaelen found her standing at the grove's edge.

"Elira," he said softly. "It's nearly dawn."

"I know."

"You feel it, don't you?"

She didn't ask what he meant.

Because she *did.*

"I thought it would stop after the collar was gone," she whispered. "But it's louder now. Not in my ears. In my *bones.*"

Vaelen stepped beside her, his expression unreadable. "Solen says some people born of strong magic can feel the Veil shifting. That it sings through their blood."

"Is that what this is?"

"I think this is *you,*" he said. "Becoming who you were meant to be."

Elira turned her face up to the stars, her throat tight.

"I don't know what to do with it."

"You don't have to do anything," he said. "Not yet."

She looked at him, eyes searching.

"But I *want* to."

Later that night, she dreamt of a woman with silver hair and violet eyes.

The woman stood on a cliff, arms outstretched, singing in a language Elira didn't know — but *understood.*

She woke with the melody still in her chest.

And a word echoing in her mind:

Elarion.

Elira sat in the grove long after the stars began to fade.

The strange hum inside her had quieted, replaced by something warmer. A memory. A longing.

She closed her eyes—and the world shifted.

When she opened them again, she was standing in the Hollow.

Only… it wasn't twisted or dark.

It was *peaceful.*

Soft violet light pulsed from the roots.

And Ashira stood before her.

Smiling.

"Ashira," Elira breathed.

Her best friend tilted her head, arms crossed in that familiar, amused way. "You didn't think I'd stay gone, did you?"

Elira's throat tightened. "I missed you."

"I know."

They stood in silence for a moment.

Then Elira asked, "Can you feel it, too?"

Ashira nodded. "The Veil is thinning. You're waking the world."

"I don't know if I'm ready."

"You don't have to be ready," Ashira said gently. "You just have to keep *being.*"

Elira hesitated. "It's not just the magic. It's… Vaelen."

Ashira smiled wider. "Ah. *That's* what this is about."

"I'm falling for him."

"I know."

Elira glanced away. "Do you think it's foolish? With everything happening?"

"I think," Ashira said, "you deserve something that doesn't ask you to suffer first. I think he makes you *breathe.* And I think that scares you more than anything."

Elira laughed softly, wiping a tear from her cheek.

Then, quieter: "Do you think she's still out there?"

Ashira's voice gentled. "Your mother?"

Elira nodded.

"I think she's waiting. Just like you. And when the Veil falls, I think the two of you will find each other."

Elira's chest ached.

"I want to know her."

Ashira stepped forward, pressing her palm to Elira's heart. "You already do. You carry her voice in your magic."

When Elira opened her eyes again, she was back in the grove.

But she could still feel Ashira's presence like a whisper against her skin.

And for the first time in a long while…

She didn't feel alone.

Chapter 39:

The name echoed in her chest all morning.

The Wellspring.

She didn't know how she knew it.

Only that she *did.*

Like a song she had never learned but could hum by heart.

By the time the sun rose fully over the stronghold, Elira was already in the map room.

Solen stood nearby, flipping through a scroll with ink-stained fingers. Vaelen leaned against the doorway, arms crossed, watching her with an unreadable expression.

"There's no record of it," Solen said finally. "Not in any of the known provinces. Not in old kingdom archives. Not even in the Lirian scrolls."

"That doesn't mean it doesn't exist," Elira said. "Just that it doesn't *want* to be found."

Solen tilted his head. "You think it's hidden?"

"I *know* it is," she said. "And I think… I think it's calling me."

Vaelen finally stepped forward. "Then we follow it."

Elira met his gaze. "You'd go with me? Even if we don't know where we're going?"

"I've already followed you into fire and ruin," he said with a crooked smile. "Might as well add mystery and prophecy."

They left by dusk.

No fanfare. No council votes. Just Elira, Vaelen, Solen, and Maerys — the four who understood that some things can't be found by maps alone.

The forest shifted as they passed.

Not closing.

Opening.

Paths curved in ways they hadn't before. Trees bent ever so slightly, guiding them eastward, deeper into wild magic.

Elira felt it with every step — the way the world leaned toward her now. Not as a ruler. Not as a threat.

As a *key.*

⁂

They camped near a ring of standing stones the second night.

As the fire flickered low, Elira sat beside Vaelen, her back against his chest, his arms wrapped around her middle.

"You feel it, don't you?" she asked softly.

He rested his chin against her shoulder. "You hum like something waking up."

"I think it's where I was born."

"The Wellsrping?"

She nodded. "Or at least… where my *magic* was born. Maybe where my mother once lived."

Vaelen didn't speak for a moment.

Then: "Do you think she's alive?"

Elira closed her eyes.

"I have to believe she is."

He held her a little tighter.

"Then we'll find her."

In the distance, the wind shifted.

And somewhere, deep within the wilds ahead, something *heard* her coming.

Something old.

Something waiting.

Chapter 40:

The forest changed the farther they traveled.

Not in obvious ways. The trees still towered, the path still curved beneath moss and moonlight. But there was a *watchfulness* now. An awareness in the hush.

The closer they drew to The Wellspring, the more the land seemed to breathe around them.

Even the air buzzed with it — not with danger, but with memory.

As if the ground itself *remembered* her.

Elira walked a few paces ahead of the others, letting the quiet settle over her shoulders. Her skin still hummed faintly from last night's dream… from Ashira's voice… from the pull that kept growing in her chest.

But even with all of that—her magic, her fear, her mission—her thoughts kept drifting back to *him.*

To Vaelen.

To the warmth of his hands. The feel of his breath against her neck.

And the look he'd given her that morning when she'd caught him watching her braid her hair.

"Something on your mind?" he asked now, voice low as he stepped beside her.

She didn't look at him. "Just the forest."

"Mm." He matched her pace easily. "It's not the forest that made you blush."

She narrowed her eyes at him.

"I wasn't blushing."

"You were pink."

"It was the light."

He leaned a little closer. "You're pink *now.*"

Her pulse jumped.

She glared at the path ahead. "You're annoying."

"You like it."

She said nothing.

But the corner of her mouth betrayed her.

Later, when they stopped to rest, Elira sat with her back against a twisted root, legs pulled up, arms wrapped around her knees.

Vaelen joined her silently.

They didn't speak.

But she leaned into his side without hesitation.

His arm slid behind her shoulders.

And for a while, she just *breathed.*

She didn't have to ask him to stay.

He already was.

That night, as they lay beside the low fire, wrapped in furs beneath the open sky, she felt his hand brush hers beneath the blanket.

Fingertips barely touching.

She didn't pull away.

Instead, she twined her fingers with his, slow and sure.

"I don't think I can do this without you," she whispered, just for him.

"You won't have to," he murmured. "Not now. Not ever."

Chapter 41:

The path ahead narrowed as they wove deeper into the forest.

Twisting trees cast silver shadows, and the air grew thick with runes that flickered just out of sight. The Wellspring was close. Elira could feel it — humming in her chest like a pulse not her own.

But her focus?

It kept slipping.

To the man beside her.

To the tension that had been building like a storm all day.

Vaelen's presence was steady as always — quiet strength, measured steps, alert gaze — but beneath it, she could *feel* him coiled like a loaded bowstring.

And she couldn't help herself.

"Something wrong?" she asked innocently as they stopped for water. She leaned against a mossy tree, arms folded, one brow raised.

Vaelen didn't look up from the edge of the stream. "No."

"You're tense."

"Because I'm focused."

She stepped closer. "Focused on *what*, exactly?"

He glanced up, eyes narrowing slightly. "You."

A beat.

She smirked. "What about me?"

"Don't push me, Elira."

"Why not?"

He stood, slowly. "Because if you keep teasing me like that, I'm going to stop being nice about it."

Her breath hitched.

Then she stepped even closer — brushing past him just enough to let her fingertips graze his stomach.

"I'm not scared of you."

"You should be."

She looked up at him through her lashes. "I think I like seeing what I do to you."

His jaw flexed.

"Elira."

"Mm?"

"If you keep talking like that, I *will* show you."

"Promise?"

That did it.

They barely made it back to camp before it snapped.

Elira was tugged into the shadows behind a boulder, Vaelen's mouth crashing down onto hers before she could say another word. It wasn't gentle. It was hungry. Desperate.

His hands roamed without hesitation, gripping her hips hard enough to bruise, then spinning her around to press her against the cool stone wall.

She gasped as his teeth grazed her shoulder — then bit, just enough to make her gasp again.

He growled her name like it was all he knew.

"Still not scared?" he asked, breath ragged.

"No," she whispered, voice trembling — not from fear, but from *want.*

"Good."

He took her right there — rough, unrelenting, every thrust making her legs shake, his hands holding her like she might disappear. And still, she wanted more.

She moaned his name until it echoed through the trees.

And when he finally came, he collapsed against her back, breath shaking, arms trembling.

But then… he stilled.

And everything shifted.

They lay tangled in blankets later, sweat cooling on skin, the fire burning low.

Elira was quiet.

Vaelen's fingers brushed along the curve of her thigh — but gentler now. Reverent.

"You're not saying anything," he murmured.

"I'm fine," she said softly.

He turned toward her fully, eyes scanning her face.

"Elira."

She met his gaze, searching.

"I liked it," she said. "I *wanted* it. But… I'm sore."

His expression crumpled a little.

"I'm sorry."

She blinked. "What?"

"I didn't mean to lose control like that. I—" He exhaled sharply. "There are emotions I still don't know how to carry. Rage. Lust. They… burn. Sometimes too hot. And I never want to hurt you."

"You didn't hurt me," she said gently, reaching up to touch his face. "You made me feel wanted. Consumed. I just…

want you to know you don't have to be so *strong* with me all the time."

His eyes softened. "I don't know how to be anything else."

She smiled. "Then I'll teach you."

He leaned in, brushing his lips to her forehead.

And for the first time, the fire between them felt like something more than heat.

It felt like *healing*.

Chapter 42:

They reached it just after dusk.

The trees parted in a wide circle, like a breath drawn in silence. At the center: a pool, glowing with faint silver light, its surface impossibly still. Ancient stone pillars curved around it in a crescent — each etched with runes Elira couldn't read but *understood.*

The air shifted the moment she stepped forward.

Warmer.

Denser.

Watching.

"This is it," Solen whispered. "The Wellspring."

Even he sounded reverent.

Elira stepped closer, her boots crunching softly on the moss.

The pool shimmered.

And something inside her responded — her pulse skipping, her magic stretching beneath her skin like it *recognized* this place.

She fell to her knees.

Not from pain.

From memory.

Flashes. A lullaby she never learned. A woman's hands, glowing gold. A name she couldn't quite grasp—

"Elira!"

Vaelen's voice. His arms around her.

She gasped, trembling.

"I'm okay," she whispered. "I think… it's showing me something."

Solen moved carefully toward the stone arch nearest the pool. "This isn't just water," he said. "This is a *mirror*. The Wellspring shows what's buried. It *tests* those who seek it."

Elira looked back toward the still surface.

It was reflecting her face.

But not just her.

In the pool… she saw herself *as a child*.

Wide-eyed. Alone. Crying for someone who never came.

Her throat tightened.

She didn't move.

Didn't blink.

Then the image changed — she saw the collar being fastened around her neck.

But this time, her eyes *fought back*.

And in the water, the child-Elira stood.

Strong.

Unbroken.

Chosen.

She reached for the surface — and it rippled beneath her fingers.

Magic pulsed out like a ring of light.

And the runes on the stones lit up *all at once*.

Maerys gasped. Solen stepped back. Even Vaelen flinched.

Because the Wellspring was no longer waiting.

It was *welcoming*.

Elira rose slowly.

The water had not wet her skin.

But she felt changed.

More *herself* than she had ever been.

"What did it show you?" Vaelen asked as they stepped back from the circle.

She turned toward him, eyes shining.

"Who I was. Who I am. And who I need to become."

Chapter 43:

They didn't speak for a long time after leaving the Wellspring.

Even Solen stayed quiet — no theories, no history lessons. Just the sound of their footsteps pressing into the softened earth.

The forest around them had changed.

It wasn't darker.

But it *was* deeper — like the trees had shifted to make room for something more sacred.

For *her.*

They made camp just before the ridge line, under a natural canopy of branches that glowed faintly with ancient runes. The ground itself seemed to hum beneath their bodies — the rhythm of something old and alive.

Elira sat apart from the others, knees drawn to her chest, firelight flickering across her skin.

She didn't feel scared.

She felt… still.

Like the world inside her had gone quiet for the first time in years.

Vaelen approached slowly, a blanket draped over one shoulder. He didn't speak until he was beside her.

"You look like your magic is dreaming."

She glanced at him. "Maybe it is."

He knelt, brushing her hair away from her face, letting his hand linger.

"I saw what the Wellspring did to you."

"What do you mean?"

"You carry yourself differently now."

Elira smiled faintly. "I feel like I just saw every version of myself in the same breath. And none of them were afraid."

"You were never afraid," he said. "You just hadn't *remembered* yet."

She turned toward him, the firelight catching in her eyes. "You always say the right thing."

He leaned in just a little. "That's because you make me want to."

They sat like that for a while.

Close.

Quiet.

But the tension between them *simmered* — a whisper beneath every breath.

She brushed her fingers along his thigh, innocent enough to be deniable.

He tensed.

"Elira," he said, voice low.

She looked up at him with feigned innocence. "Yes?"

"You don't get to tease me right now."

"Why not?"

"Because if you do," he said, eyes darkening, "I'm not going to be gentle."

She tilted her head. "Who says I want you to be?"

His jaw clenched.

"I do," he growled, voice thick. "Because the next time I touch you… I'm going to *show* you what gentle feels like."

Her breath caught.

"And after that?"

"After that," he whispered, leaning closer, "you're not walking straight for days."

She swallowed, skin tingling.

But instead of answering, she leaned in, kissed his cheek, and whispered in his ear:

"Then you better *earn it.*"

Chapter 44:

The forest was asleep.

But Elira was wide awake.

She lay beneath the furs, eyes open, heartbeat steady — but *strange.* It was as though her body wasn't quite done echoing what the Wellspring had poured into her.

She sat up quietly, slipping out from the camp's edge, letting the moonlight guide her.

Back to the pool.

Back to the heart of it all.

The water shimmered as she approached, still glowing, still humming like a song only she could hear.

This time, when she knelt beside it, it *greeted* her — with a vision not of herself…

But of a woman.

Hair dark as night. Eyes like hers.

The woman was weeping, but strong — not broken.

And when she spoke, it wasn't out loud.

It was *inside* Elira.

"You survived."

Elira's throat closed.

"Are you her?" she whispered. "Are you my mother?"

The vision only nodded — then pressed a hand to her chest.

"You were never meant to be used. You were meant to awaken."

Tears spilled down Elira's cheeks.

"I want to find you."

"You will. When the Veil is broken, I'll be waiting."

And then… the vision faded.

But the warmth it left behind didn't.

She turned, expecting silence.

But Vaelen was there.

Barefoot. Shirtless. Standing beneath the arch of glowing runes like he *belonged* in that sacred place with her.

"I didn't want to interrupt," he said softly.

"You didn't."

They just stood for a moment — two shadows surrounded by ancient light.

And then Elira stepped into him.

No words.

Just arms.

Just breath.

Just *need.*

He held her tightly, one hand at her back, the other at her waist — grounding her as the last of her shaking left her body.

"You found something," he said.

She nodded against his chest. "I think I found *her.*"

He pressed a kiss to her hair.

"I'm proud of you."

Elira looked up, heart thudding. "Can I ask you something?"

"Anything."

"Will you stay with me tonight? Just… hold me?"

A pause.

"Always."

They lay curled together beneath the stars — skin to skin, breath to breath — and though nothing passed between them but warmth and steady hands…

The tension beneath it all thrummed like an unstruck chord.

Waiting.

Wanting.

Chapter 45:

Elira woke to the sound of shifting fabric and the steady hush of night winds outside the tent.

Vaelen sat a few feet away, his back to her, shirtless, head bowed, muscles rigid with tension. The moonlight painted silver lines down his spine — but there was something in his posture that made her heart ache.

Quiet. Still.

Like a man unraveling without a sound.

She rose carefully and crossed to him, wrapping the blanket around her shoulders before kneeling at his side.

"Vaelen?" she asked softly.

He didn't look at her.

"I'm sorry."

Her brow furrowed. "For what?"

"For… the other night."

He exhaled sharply; jaw clenched.

"I told myself I'd never lose control like that. Not with you. And when you told me you were sore… I tried to brush it off. Pretend it was nothing. But it's not."

He finally looked at her.

And his eyes were wet.

Elira's breath caught.

"I hurt you," he said. "And I swore I never would."

Her hand found his. "Vaelen—"

"I felt like a monster," he whispered, voice breaking. "Like I became exactly what I promised you I wasn't. And it's not just you… it's the way it made me feel after. Like I was out of my body. Like I could've gone too far. Like I might not have stopped."

He dropped his gaze.

"I hate that part of me. The one that doesn't know when to let go. The one the King tried to shape into a weapon. I've buried it for so long… and I let it slip."

Elira moved in front of him, cradling his face in her hands.

"You didn't hurt me," she said firmly. "You *held* me. You worshipped me. Even when it was rough… it was still you. You never scared me. Not for one second."

His lip trembled.

"You felt too good to stop," she said with a small smile. "And I didn't *want* you to."

"But I made you sore."

"Because you wanted *all* of me. And that made me feel powerful."

Vaelen stared at her.

And then — slowly — tears slid down his cheeks.

She leaned in and kissed them away.

"You are not a monster," she whispered. "You're a man with more feeling than he knows what to do with. And that's what I love about you."

They lay down after that, wrapped in each other beneath the blanket.

His head tucked beneath her chin.

Her hand combing slowly through his hair.

And for a long while… there was nothing but silence.

The kind that heals.

But when she felt his breath warm against her neck, something shifted.

Not rushed.

Not demanding.

Just… *present.*

And full of fire.

"Elira," he said, voice gravel soft. "Let me show you. Let me show you everything I didn't get to before."

She turned to him.

Eyes wide. Heart open.

"Yes."

His touch was *softer* than she'd ever known.

He undressed her like she was sacred — slow, reverent, every inch of skin met with lips or fingers or whispered praise.

"Beautiful."

"Strong."

"Mine."

And when she lay back against the bedroll, trembling in anticipation, he didn't climb on top of her.

He knelt between her legs and kissed her thighs first.

Whispered against her skin.

"Relax for me, Elira."

She exhaled slowly.

He kissed higher.

"I want you to just *feel.* Nothing else."

She whimpered, head falling back.

And then his hand slid between her legs — slow, coaxing, teasing. Two fingers inside her, shallow at first… then deeper.

She cried out softly, breath breaking.

He curled them just right.

And her body *shattered.*

Her orgasm came in waves — full-body, soul-deep.

She sobbed his name into the darkness.

He waited until she caught her breath.

Until her hands reached for him, hungry and certain.

Then — only then — did he take her.

Slow. Deep. Intentional.

Like every thrust was a promise.

And when she clenched around him, he praised her between gasps.

"Good girl…"

"So perfect…"

"All mine…"

When he came, it was with her name on his lips and a tear trailing down his cheek.

And when it was over, they didn't move.

They just *breathed* — chests rising together. Hearts synced.

No shame.

No pain.

Only *peace.*

Elira lay tangled in Vaelen's arms, her body still trembling with the aftershocks of what he'd just given her.

It had been soft.

It had been deep.

And it had *wrecked* her.

Not from the intensity — but from the *care.*

No one had ever touched her like that. No one had ever *seen* her like that. Every part of her had been held, cherished, worshipped — not for what she could do, but for who she *was.*

And that broke something open inside her.

A soft sob slipped past her lips before she could stop it.

Vaelen stirred instantly, rising on one elbow, his hand cupping her cheek.

"Elira? Did I hurt you?"

She shook her head, tears slipping down.

"No. No, … you didn't hurt me."

"Then what is it?"

She tried to speak.

Tried again.

And finally: "You… you keep putting me first."

His brow furrowed, but his thumb brushed gently under her eyes, catching the tears as they fell.

"No one's ever done that," she whispered. "Not like you do. Not just in bed. But everywhere. Every time. You *see* me. You protect me. You believe in me before I believe in myself."

"Elira—"

She sat up, sobs shaking her now.

"You give and give and give. Even when you're hurting. Even when you're scared. You let me see your worst and then you… *hold me* like I'm worth everything."

Her words hit him hard. He blinked rapidly, his own eyes welling again.

"Elira," he breathed, voice raw. "You *are* everything."

And then he kissed her.

Not with urgency.

Not with hunger.

But with *reverence.*

Like he was tasting something holy.

Their mouths moved together, slow and deep, her hands fisting in his hair, his arms wrapped tight around her. Every breath, every whisper, every tear between them melted into that kiss.

And then he pulled back — just enough to look at her, his thumb sliding between her thighs again.

"I want to give you more," he said. "Just you. For you."

"Vaelen—"

"Let me," he whispered.

And when he touched her again, it was with nothing but devotion.

Slow.

Focused.

His eyes never left hers.

He circled her with care, coaxing her open, deeper, deeper — until she came again with a cry muffled against his shoulder, tears spilling as pleasure rippled through her like a song.

When it was over, he held her.

And neither of them said a word.

Because none were needed.

Chapter 46:

Morning came slow and golden.

Sunlight slipped through the branches above the tent, painting lazy patterns across the fabric and the blankets they'd tangled themselves in. Birds sang softly in the distance. The camp beyond them was quiet.

But Elira was already awake.

Warmth radiated against her back — Vaelen's chest pressed to her spine, his arm heavy across her waist. His fingers were tangled in hers, as if even in sleep he refused to let go.

And she didn't want him to.

Not ever.

She shifted slightly, turning in his arms to face him.

He stirred.

Eyes still closed.

But his fingers moved to her hip.

His voice came rough with sleep. "You, okay?"

She smiled softly. "Better than okay."

He opened his eyes, sleep-blurred and dark with something that still simmered beneath the surface.

"You feel it too, don't you?" she whispered.

"The need?"

She nodded.

"It never left," he murmured. "Just… waited."

He leaned in and kissed her slowly — no urgency, no teasing. Just warmth. Heat. A whisper of everything he hadn't said.

She pulled back slightly, resting her hand on his chest. "Do you want me?"

He blinked at her like the question stunned him.

"I always want you."

"Then take me."

He hesitated.

And then — softly — "Not today."

She frowned. "What?"

"I mean… I'll take you. But I'm not going to finish."

Her heart stuttered.

"You're not—?"

He kissed her nose. "Not this time."

"But why?"

His gaze was steady. Tender.

"Because this is for *you*. I want you to feel *worshipped*. I want to leave you shaking and full and breathless — not because I needed it, but because *you* deserve it."

Her breath caught.

She tried to argue — but he silenced her with a look.

And then…

He moved.

He settled her beneath him slowly, gently — kissing every inch of her as if re-learning her body by memory alone.

Her shoulders.

Her ribs.

Her hips.

Her thighs.

He didn't tease this time.

He *honored*.

When he slid into her, he did it achingly slow — watching her face, memorizing every twitch, every moan, every flutter of lashes.

She arched into him, nails digging into his arms, breath breaking.

"Please," she whispered.

"I've got you," he breathed. "Let go."

He thrust gently, deeply, holding himself back with sheer will.

And when she started to beg — "Please, Vaelen, I need—" — he only kissed her deeper.

"No, love," he whispered. "This time, I need you to take. Let me give."

She came with his name on her lips again.

Soft. Sweet. Shattering.

And when she tried to pull him closer, to coax him into taking more—

He shook his head.

"Not today," he said again. "Today is just for you."

They curled back into the furs afterward, limbs tangled, skin glowing with sweat and morning light.

Elira rested her head on his chest.

And for the first time since the collar broke, since the Wellspring… since *everything*…

She felt safe.

Not just *free.*

Loved.

Chapter 47:

The wind carried whispers now.

Not words.

Just *knowing*.

The kind of quiet that made the hairs on the back of Elira's neck rise, even as she walked together with Vaelen back toward the camp.

The Wellspring had done more than offer clarity.

It had *shifted* something.

In her.

In him.

In *everything*.

Solen stood waiting for them when they returned — arms crossed, his brow furrowed in that thoughtful, unsettled way Elira had learned to read.

"What is it?" she asked, voice steady despite the tension that licked at the edge of her spine.

"We've received word," he said. "From the western sentries. Something's coming."

Elira stiffened. "The King's men?"

"Not just men," Solen said. "Something darker. Shadow-bound."

Maerys stepped forward from behind him, holding a parchment. "Illusion magic—twisted. Carried by beasts with no names. They're not just patrolling."

"They're *searching*," Vaelen growled.

Solen nodded. "They've felt the crack. They know something is changing."

"They're hunting *me*," Elira said.

No one answered.

Because everyone already knew.

That night, around the fire, Elira traced the edge of the silver pendant around her neck — a charm Maerys had given her after the Wellspring. It wasn't for protection, not really.

It was a reminder.

Of whom she was.

Who she was becoming.

Vaelen sat beside her, silent, but *present.* His hand resting lightly on her thigh. A constant.

The others spoke in low voices about strategy, about escape routes, about how soon they might need to move again.

But Elira just stared at the fire.

And whispered to it.

"Let them come."

Vaelen crouched beside her — not pressing, not speaking. Just there.

Her anchor.

His fingers brushed lightly along hers. Silent reassurance.

But Elira's thoughts were a whirlwind.

How much longer could they run?

How many more would the King send?

How many would bleed just for knowing her name?

She stood slowly and wandered toward the grove's edge, letting the night press against her skin.

She could still feel the echo of the Wellspring in her bones — not burning, not heavy. Just… *there.*

Awake.

And with that awakening came a choice.

She turned to face the stars above the trees.

"I didn't ask for this," she whispered.

"But I won't run anymore."

Vaelen's voice came from behind her, quiet. "You shouldn't have to fight alone."

She looked back at him — and in his face, she didn't see fear.

She saw *faith.*

"I won't let you," she said.

⁂

That night, sleep came late.

And with it, dreams of silver chains, broken mirrors, and a rising tide of blood that reached for her with clawed hands.

But when she woke, bathed in sweat and moonlight…

Vaelen's arms were already around her.

And she breathed.

Chapter 48:

The wind changed on the third day.

It wasn't stronger.

But it carried the scent of something wrong.

Burned ash. Frozen soil. Magic that didn't belong to the land.

Elira stood near the watch post at dawn, eyes fixed on the far ridge where the fog had thickened. She hadn't spoken much since the Wellspring. But something in her posture had changed.

She didn't seem afraid.

She seemed *ready*.

Vaelen watched her from a short distance, arms crossed, jaw set. He didn't need to ask what she was thinking — he already knew.

This wasn't just a threat.

It was a *summons*.

And she was answering it.

Maerys and Solen joined them an hour later with updates.

"The scouts haven't returned from the southern loop," Maerys said. "We're assuming they've either gone to ground or—"

"Or worse," Solen finished grimly. "There's movement along the river bend. It's not natural."

"What do we know?" Elira asked, voice steady.

"They don't move like soldiers," Solen replied. "Too quiet. Too coordinated."

"Controlled," Vaelen muttered. "Like puppets."

"Or predators," Maerys added.

Elira's gaze darkened. "Then we stop running."

⁂

Back in the clearing, Elira unrolled a weathered map of the forest and traced her fingers along the edges.

"This is where they'll come through," she said, tapping a narrow pass between two ridges. "It funnels them right into us."

"And us into them," Vaelen pointed out.

She met his gaze. "Exactly."

"You want to trap them?"

"No," she said. "I want them to see me. And I want to break whatever the King sent them here to do."

⁂

Preparations began before nightfall.

The others set up wards, laid enchanted markers, prepared the clearing for what could be their first real confrontation.

Elira moved quietly through it all — not just watching but guiding. Instructing. Protecting.

She stopped once at the center of the clearing, eyes closed, hand pressed to the earth.

The forest pulsed beneath her palm.

And for a moment… she felt something.

Not fear.

Not darkness.

But *power.*

Not the kind she wielded.

The kind that *waited.*

⁂

That night, she sat with Vaelen at the edge of the fire, their hands entwined beneath a shared blanket.

"You're quiet," he said softly.

"Thinking."

"About the fight?"

She shook her head. "About the others. About what happens after."

"After what?"

"After we win."

Vaelen turned to her, brows raised.

"Confident."

"I have to be."

He smiled. "Then let them come."

She leaned into him, resting her head on his shoulder.

"Stay close to me tomorrow," she whispered.

"Always."

Chapter 49:

The wind had teeth by morning.

It tore through the trees with a shriek, bending branches that hadn't moved in years. The fog was thicker now — curling, creeping, alive with something unnatural.

They came just after sunrise.

Not with horns.

Not with banners.

But with silence.

And a hunger that made the birds flee before the first step hit the clearing.

Elira stood in the center of the stone-marked field, her palms open at her sides, runes glowing faintly across her skin — a gift from the Wellspring, or a warning. She wasn't sure.

The ground vibrated beneath her boots.

And then they broke through the trees.

Not men.

Not fully.

Shadow-bound figures, faces twisted by illusion, eyes glowing with the King's false light. Some walked on two legs. Some crawled. Some had too many limbs.

All of them moved as if they were one.

Elira took a step forward.

And they *paused.*

Almost… confused.

She felt her magic respond — a hum beneath her ribs.

Vaelen stepped beside her, sword already drawn, jaw clenched. Maerys and Solen flanked her from behind.

"Now," Elira whispered.

And the forest *erupted.*

The first wave came fast — shrieking, distorted things that clawed at the edges of the clearing. Arrows flew. Blades met bone. Light magic cracked across the field like lightning.

Elira lifted her hands — and the runes on her arms flared gold.

She sent a pulse through the earth, blasting one of the creatures back with a scream of cracking stone. Another came from her left — only for Vaelen to intercept it mid-leap, blade slicing through the illusion with brutal force.

They fought side by side — seamless, instinctual, like they were carved from the same flame.

But the creatures didn't stop.

Didn't slow.

And then—

A sharp cry.

Maerys stumbled.

Solen caught her.

And more poured through the trees.

One of them broke through the line.

Too fast.

Too quiet.

Elira turned just in time to see the shadow-bound creature slam into her — claws raking across her side, teeth bared.

She screamed.

Blood bloomed down her ribs.

She dropped to one knee, vision swimming.

"*ELIRA!*"

Vaelen's voice tore through the clearing.

And then he was *gone* from her side.

What happened next was a blur of rage and steel.

Vaelen exploded through the line of creatures with a fury Elira had never seen. His blade struck like fire. His fists, his boots, his *rage* — it was unstoppable.

He didn't call her name again.

He didn't speak at all.

He *destroyed.*

And when the last of the creatures fell — when the fog thinned, and the forest stilled.

He dropped to his knees beside her.

"Elira," he whispered, voice breaking.

She was pale, trembling, blood soaking through her side.

"I'm okay," she whispered.

"Don't you lie to me."

She smiled weakly. "You came for me."

"Always."

He scooped her into his arms, holding her like she was made of glass, whispering something into her hair that she didn't quite catch — just the tremble in his voice, and the kiss he pressed to her temple.

And as the others regrouped, wounded and weary…

Vaelen carried her away from the blood-soaked field.

As if nothing else mattered.

Chapter 50:

The clearing had quieted.

The fog had lifted.

But Elira's blood still stained the ground.

Vaelen carried her like she weighed nothing — like she was more *precious* than anything he'd ever held. His jaw was set, eyes wild, rage barely restrained beneath the fear thrumming through every inch of him.

"I need her healed," he growled to Solen as they reached the edge of the Lirian grove.

Solen nodded. "Take her to Irienne."

Vaelen's gaze snapped to him. "She's still alive?"

"She won't take in just anyone. But she'll see you."

Irienne lived in a hollow of the grove, surrounded by glowing trees that pulsed with magic so old it made Elira's skin hum even through the pain. The healer stepped forward with silver-streaked hair, a narrow face, and eyes that seemed to see *through* you.

She took one look at Elira and said, "Put her down. Gently."

Vaelen obeyed.

Irienne's hands glowed as she hovered them over Elira's wound. Elira winced, breathing shallow. Irienne's fingers paused just above her ribcage, light sinking into flesh like warmth into water.

"Who is she to you?" Irienne asked softly, without looking up.

Vaelen didn't hesitate.

"She's mine."

Irienne finally glanced at him. "Yours?"

He stepped closer. Voice firm.

"She's, my partner. My other half. My reason."

A pause.

"She's *mine.*"

Irienne studied him for a moment… then nodded.

"That will help."

And she pressed her palms to Elira's side — and the healing began.

Later, after Elira was stable and sleeping in a bed of moss and rune-light, Vaelen sat nearby, head bowed, hands bloodied.

Solen approached, dropping to a seat beside him.

"She'll be alright," Solen said.

"I know," Vaelen answered. But his voice was hollow.

Solen was quiet for a moment.

Then: "Do you know why I brought her here?"

Vaelen looked up.

"She wasn't just the girl I saw in the ruins. She was *felt* by the grove. She woke something the moment her foot touched the forest. Something sacred."

Vaelen didn't speak.

Solen went on. "But even then, I didn't understand why the Wellspring stirred. Not until I saw the way you looked at her."

Vaelen's breath hitched.

"She isn't just a key to breaking the Veil," Solen said gently. "She's *yours*. And maybe… you were always meant to be hers."

A beat of silence.

Then Solen rose, brushing dirt from his hands.

"Love her well, Vaelen. Because she is changing the world. And you're the only one she lets see *how it's changing her*."

Vaelen returned to Elira's side, kneeling beside her.

She stirred, eyelids fluttering open.

"Hey," he whispered. "You're safe."

She smiled faintly. "You stayed."

"Always."

She reached for his hand — and he took it in both of his.

And without another word, he kissed the back of her fingers and rested them against his chest.

Where she belonged.

As Irienne finished wrapping a thin band of enchanted silk around Elira's waist — the wound already closing beneath her touch — she glanced toward Vaelen.

"You're bleeding too," she said calmly.

"I'm fine," Vaelen replied.

"You're not."

Solen stepped up beside him. "Go. I'll watch over her."

Vaelen hesitated, still kneeling beside Elira. She was awake now, eyes fluttering open, her fingers lightly curled around his wrist.

Solen placed a reassuring hand on Vaelen's shoulder. "I promise. She's in good hands."

Vaelen narrowed his eyes. "If anything happens to her—"

Solen chuckled. "You'll personally bury me in the woods. I know."

Vaelen smirked despite himself. He leaned in to kiss Elira's forehead, brushing a lock of hair from her face.

"I won't be long," he murmured.

She nodded. "I'll be right here."

With one last look — reluctant, protective — he stood and walked with Irienne toward the outer grove.

Solen settled beside Elira with a quiet breath, his usual sarcasm softened into something more reflective.

"You scared the life out of him, you know," he said gently. "I don't think I've ever seen him *run* before."

Elira gave a weak smile. "I didn't mean to."

"He would've fought the entire forest to get to you," Solen added. "And from what I saw… he nearly did."

He paused.

Then his voice dropped to something more honest.

"Vaelen wasn't always like this."

Elira turned to him slightly. "What was he like?"

"Closed off. Calculated. Fierce, yes, but cold. Like he'd forgotten how to feel anything but duty and fire. That's who he was when I met him."

He looked toward the trees, voice quieting.

"But then you came. And I watched him shift. In ways I didn't think were possible."

He met her gaze again, kind and clear.

"You bring light into him, Elira. You slow his rage. You give it purpose."

She swallowed. "He said I'm his."

Solen smiled. "He didn't just say it. He *meant* it. Every syllable. Every breath."

He touched her hand gently, as if passing her something unseen.

"Healing isn't just a body mending," he said. "It's the soul remembering how to feel again. That's what you're doing for him. Whether you know it or not."

Tears pricked Elira's eyes.

Solen leaned in closer, voice lowering just for her.

"Don't be afraid of how much he loves you. Or how much you love him. The world has been starving for something like that."

A few minutes later, Vaelen returned — freshly cleaned, bandaged, scowling about "annoying Lirian healers."

But the second his eyes met Elira's, that scowl melted.

She smiled weakly. "You came back."

He knelt and took her hand again. "Always."

Solen stood quietly, nodding once at Elira before turning away.

And for a few heartbeats, the only thing that existed was the way Vaelen looked at her.

Like she wasn't just his world.

She was the *reason* it still turned.

Chapter 51:

Elira's body healed faster than expected.

Whether it was Irienne's magic or the strength the Wellspring had left inside her, she wasn't sure — but after two days, the wound in her side was more scar than pain.

Still, Vaelen hovered like she might disappear if he blinked.

She didn't mind.

Every time she stirred, he was there — a steady shadow at her side. Helping her stand. Guiding her down forest paths to stretch her legs. Carrying her food before she even asked.

And at night… he wrapped himself around her like a second skin.

On the third morning, she woke before him.

Sunlight streamed in soft through the tent's folds. His arm draped across her waist, fingers resting just below her navel — familiar, tender.

She turned carefully, watching the way his hair spilled across the pillow, the relaxed curve of his lips, the slow rhythm of his breath.

And something in her *ached.*

Not from pain.

From *love.*

Later, they walked the grove together — slowly, hand-in-hand, the forest humming around them like it *knew.*

Solen met them near the outer edge, standing by a small grouping of Lirian guards and scouts. His expression was unusually serious.

"You're not going to like this," he said, by way of greeting.

Vaelen raised a brow. "Then don't say it."

Solen ignored him. "There's movement again. The King is testing new ground — northern ridges this time. Wider spread. Less controlled."

Elira frowned. "Looking for a new way in?"

"Or out," Solen said. "Either way, it's different."

Vaelen stepped forward. "He's unraveling."

Elira nodded slowly. "The Veil is cracking."

"And he knows it."

That evening, while others spoke of strategy and contingencies, Elira wandered back toward the Wellspring's path alone.

Not far.

Just far enough to feel the hum of magic under her boots.

She sat on a moss-covered stone, letting her fingers trace the bark of a nearby tree that pulsed faintly with light. The air was quieter here — older. Like it held secrets waiting to be spoken.

"Are you ready?" came a voice from behind her.

Vaelen.

She smiled softly. "I think I'm becoming ready."

He stepped beside her and offered a hand.

"No," she said. "Not yet."

He nodded, sitting beside her instead.

They didn't speak for a long while.

Just breathed.

Side by side.

"I don't want to keep running," she said finally.

"You won't."

"But I don't want to charge into fire either. Not if it'll cost more than I can bear."

He reached for her hand. "Then we'll find a way. Together."

She looked at him, head tilted.

"You said something earlier… about not believing in fate. Until me."

He glanced away, like he hadn't expected her to ask.

"Did you mean it?" she pressed.

He exhaled slowly. "Yes."

She leaned in, voice quiet. "Why?"

He was silent for a few moments.

Then—

"Because I never believed there was someone out there for *me*. Not in the way people talk about. A partner. A tether. A truth you can lean into when the world burns."

He paused.

"I didn't believe that kind of thing was meant for people like me."

Elira's brow furrowed. "What kind of people?"

"The ones who were trained to hold blades instead of hands. Who learned silence instead of softness. Who got used to hiding everything that hurt."

His voice faltered slightly — just enough that she noticed.

"I didn't know how to *want* more than the fight. Until I saw you standing in front of it."

She reached for his hand, threading her fingers through his.

"You gave me a reason to stay steady. Not because I had to. But because I *wanted to.* Because you made me want something beyond surviving."

Elira's throat tightened.

"I didn't think I deserved it," he said. "But when you look at me… I feel like I do."

She leaned into him then, pressing her forehead to his shoulder.

"You *do,*" she whispered.

"You make me feel like I could be something more than a weapon."

"You are."

He looked at her — really looked.

"You've always seen me, haven't you?"

She nodded. "Even before I understood why."

He touched her cheek gently, like she might vanish if he pressed too hard.

"And every time I let myself hope," he said, "you meet me there."

Elira blinked back sudden tears. "Then keep hoping."

"I will," he promised. "As long as you're with me."

The forest held them in silence.

Not watching.

Just *holding.*

And for the first time, Elira didn't feel like she was preparing to lose something.

She felt like she was learning how to keep it.

Chapter 52:

They walked the forest trails in the late afternoon, sunlight filtering through the branches above like golden threads.

Elira's steps were slow but steady, her strength returning day by day. Vaelen kept close — not hovering, just near enough that she could feel him. Like gravity.

They hadn't spoken much since their conversation beneath the trees the night before. But Elira's mind hadn't stopped spinning.

Not with questions.

Not with the weight of *everything she hadn't understood until now.*

She broke the silence first.

"Why did the King ban emotional intimacy?"

Vaelen looked over at her, brows drawn.

"I mean," she went on, "why make it so… monitored? Cold? I remember the way it was discussed — unions formed only for reproduction. Assigned partners. No privacy. No affection. Just obligation."

He was quiet for a moment before answering.

"Because the King is afraid."

"Of what?"

"Connection," Vaelen said. "Raw, unfiltered, *unchained* connection. The kind that could unravel everything."

He turned to her, voice lower now. "Because real love, real passion… it breeds emotion. And emotion is the one thing he can't fully control."

Elira's breath hitched.

"So, he trains people to suppress it. To fear it. And when that isn't enough…" Vaelen's jaw tensed. "He makes it a transaction. Removes the choice. Assigns partners, strips them of dignity, of autonomy. Especially those who show signs of resistance."

Elira felt sick. "You've seen it."

He nodded slowly. "I've witnessed it. The hollow expressions. The silent compliance. The way people retreat into themselves just to survive it."

"Did you ever—?"

"No," he said quickly. "I was kept for battle. For strategy. But I've seen others forced into it. Watched them break."

Her voice was soft. "Is that part of why… this—us—feels different to you?"

Vaelen looked at her then, something raw in his gaze.

"Yes. Because it's *yours*. It's *mine*. It's not forced. It's *allowed to exist*."

They paused by a stream, the light rippling across their joined hands.

Elira stared at their fingers for a long moment.

"There was someone," she said quietly. "Someone the King… assigned to me. It was never announced. But I met him."

Vaelen stilled.

"Who?"

"A man named Malric."

Vaelen's head snapped toward her. "The King's war advisor?"

She nodded. "He said it would be a good match. That our bloodlines were compatible. That we'd strengthen the illusion if we created heirs."

Disgust curled in Vaelen's gut. "And you agreed?"

"I was young. I didn't *agree*—I obeyed. I thought that was love. Malric was kind, I thought. At least, he pretended to be."

Vaelen was quiet for a long time.

Then: "He's still with the King."

Elira nodded. "Which means he knows I'm alive. And he'll come for me."

Vaelen's hand tightened in hers.

"Let him."

She blinked. "What?"

Vaelen stepped closer, his voice like steel wrapped in fire.

"Let him come. Let him try to touch what's *mine.* I swear to the stars, Elira—I'll end the King, and I'll *end him*, too."

She swallowed, heart pounding.

"I'm not saying that because I'm jealous," he said. "I'm saying it because you are *not* a prize to be assigned. You're not a pawn."

His hand came to her cheek.

"You are *mine.* Because *you chose me.* And because I would burn this entire kingdom to ash before I let him take you again."

The silence that followed was thick — not awkward, not fearful.

Just *true.*

Elira exhaled slowly, turning her face toward the canopy overhead. The sunlight flickered between the leaves, warm against her skin. It was so different from the cold stone walls she used to live in.

So different from *him.*

"There's more," she said, her voice tight.

Vaelen stilled.

She didn't look at him when she spoke again — she couldn't.

"Before the illusion cracked for me… before Ashira died, before I understood what I was really feeling… I started pulling away. From Malric. From the roles the King had set. I started *feeling* things I wasn't supposed to. Doubts. Dreams. Resistance."

She clenched her jaw.

"And the King noticed."

Vaelen's entire body tensed beside her.

"He ordered Malric to… make me compliant. However, he saw fit. Said I was a danger to the illusion if I believed in choice. Said I needed to be reminded that intimacy wasn't meant for love or connection. Only for control."

Now she turned to him — and her eyes were bright with unshed tears, but clear.

"He told Malric to break me."

Vaelen's hands were fists at his sides.

Elira went on, voice flat with remembered pain.

"One night… Malric asked me to join him for tea. Like always. Polite. Measured. And then, once the doors closed…"

She swallowed hard.

"He changed."

Vaelen's breath hitched, but he didn't interrupt.

"He told me it was time I accepted my place. That if I resisted again, he'd inform the King I was too unstable to remain unwed. That I'd be sent away. Or worse."

She looked down at her hands.

"He restrained me. Just to prove he could."

Vaelen's knuckles were white now, jaw locked.

"He said he'd show me what it would be like when we were 'bound' officially. What I could expect. What he would take from me."

Her voice cracked.

"He touched me."

Vaelen's heart dropped.

Elira pressed her hand against her sternum as if trying to hold the hurt in place.

"Not… fully. But enough. Enough to make me feel small. Afraid. Dirty. I was sore in a place I shouldn't have been. Not from pleasure. Not from love. Just pain."

She looked at him now, tears falling freely.

"And the first time you… when you were rough with me, I didn't realize why it hurt so much emotionally. I *wanted* you. I trusted you. But the soreness… it brought me back."

A pause.

"And yet, you listened. You *stopped*. You changed. You gave me softness."

Vaelen stared at her like his chest had been split open.

"Elira," he breathed. "I'm so sorry."

She reached for his hand, taking it into hers.

"You didn't hurt me the way he did. Not even close. But it helped me *remember*. And that was hard. But it also helped me *heal*. You didn't break me. You held me."

He moved then, cupping her face, gently pressing his forehead to hers.

"If I ever make you feel that way again… stop me. I need you to promise."

She nodded.

"I'll never take from you," he whispered. "Only give."

A few quiet heartbeats passed.

Then, gently, he brushed a kiss against her brow.

"You're not just mine, Elira. I'm yours too. And I would bleed before I let anyone take that from you again."

Chapter 53:

The next morning, the sky was heavy with low clouds — the kind that whispered of rain but never delivered it.

Elira stepped barefoot onto the moss outside their tent, the ground cool and soft beneath her toes. The trees swayed gently above, but there was a tension in the air she couldn't ignore.

Not fear.

Anticipation.

She stood still, listening.

To the wind.

To the earth.

To *herself.*

And for the first time since her awakening, she didn't feel lost in it.

She felt… rooted.

Vaelen watched her from a few steps back, arms folded, expression unreadable.

She turned to him, one brow lifting. "Are you just going to stare?"

"I thought you might float away," he murmured.

She smirked. "I'm not going anywhere."

His gaze softened.

"Good."

Later that day, the inner circle gathered again — Solen, Maerys, Vaelen, and two other Lirians Elira hadn't met before. Scouts, by the way they moved. Light on their feet, sharp-eyed.

"The King is mobilizing more than just shadows now," Solen said, unfurling a fresh map across the table. "He's drawing soldiers from deep within the capital. The ones who've been most affected by the illusion."

"The ones we can't reason with," Maerys added.

"They're hunting now," Solen said, "not just guarding. We think they've discovered a pattern in our movement."

"They're getting smarter," Vaelen muttered.

"No," Elira said, stepping forward. "They're getting *desperate*. The Veil is thinning. He's afraid."

The room quieted.

She laid her hand flat over the map.

"We need to move. Not away."

Solen blinked. "Toward him?"

"No," she said. "Toward the people still caught inside."

They all looked at her.

"We can't just run. We can't just hide. There are others — like me. Others who've felt the cracks. Others who are waiting for someone to *show them it's real*."

"You want to build a resistance," Solen said quietly.

She nodded.

"I want to *wake them up*."

That night, Elira and Vaelen sat by a small, quiet fire.

He was sharpening his blade.

She was holding her journal — a worn, leather-bound book filled with fragments of memories and dreams.

Neither spoke for a while.

Finally, Elira said, "Do you think it's foolish?"

He didn't look up. "What?"

"To think we can actually win."

He finished a stroke, then set the blade aside.

And turned to face her fully.

"I think you're the only one who can."

She stared at him, stunned by the certainty in his voice.

"I think every breath you take," he said, "is a threat to the King. And I think the more you believe in yourself… the more the world will believe in you, too."

She didn't realize she was crying until he reached up to catch the tear.

"I don't want to be their savior," she whispered.

"Then don't be."

He leaned in.

"Be *yours*. First."

The fire had burned low.

Embers glowed soft and gold, casting flickers across the lines of Elira's face.

Vaelen watched her for a long time. His eyes drifted to the worn leather journal resting in her lap — the same one he'd seen her carry every day, never letting it leave her side.

He tilted his head.

"What's in there?"

She blinked, pulled from her thoughts. "Hmm?"

"That book. You've kept it close since the ruins. You sleep beside it. I've seen the way your fingers tighten around it when you dream."

She looked down at it — then away.

"Nothing important."

He arched a brow. "Elira."

Her grip tightened slightly. "It's personal."

His voice softened. "I figured. But that doesn't mean I'm not curious."

She didn't answer.

Vaelen leaned closer. "Is it dangerous?"

A pause.

She gave a dry laugh. "Only to me."

Something in his gaze darkened.

"I want to know you," he said. "All of you. Even the parts you keep in ink."

Elira hesitated.

She couldn't find the words — couldn't *say* the things she'd written. But she could feel him waiting.

And she didn't want to lock him out anymore.

So, with trembling fingers, she held it out.

He took it gently. Looked at her once — questioning.

She nodded.

And he opened it.

He didn't speak as he flipped through the pages.

The handwriting shifted throughout. Some lines were shaking. Some furious. Others were barely legible — as though they'd been written through tears.

He read about her doubts.

Her dreams.

The illusion fracturing piece by piece.

He read the moment she began to fear she wasn't *wrong* — but that the world around her was.

And then he read about *him*.

Malric.

The night.

The hands on her skin.

The silence she kept afterward.

The shame.

The way she'd written — *Maybe I deserved it. Maybe I should have kept quiet. Maybe it's my fault.*

Something *snapped* inside him.

He stood abruptly, fists clenched, journal shaking in his hand.

"Elira."

His voice was sharp.

She looked up, startled. "Vaelen?"

"*He touched you.*"

Tears welled in her eyes. "Yes."

"And you thought it was *your fault?*"

He tossed the journal to the ground, hands trembling with fury.

"I'll kill him," he growled. "I'll kill them *both.* I'll burn every stronghold to the ground—"

"Vaelen—"

"No. *No.* You are *mine*, Elira. You are not a pawn. You are not a prize to be claimed or broken or restrained—"

He moved fast.

Too fast.

In one breath, he was over her — hands on either side of her thighs, caging her in without touching.

His eyes were wild. His body was *fire.*

And his mouth was already lowering to hers when—

She flinched.

Just slightly.

But enough.

He froze.

Time stilled.

Then he *backed away* like she'd struck him.

"Elira," he breathed, horrified. "I'm sorry. I didn't mean—"

"You promised," she whispered.

"I know. I know, I—" His voice broke. "I would never hurt you. I just… I saw what he did. What they tried to make you believe. And I lost control."

Her hands reached for him.

Pulled him back.

He looked stunned.

"I'm okay," she said softly. "You didn't hurt me. You stopped. That's what matters."

"Elira—"

"I want you," she said. "But I need to ask for it. I need to *want* it."

He searched her eyes.

And she gave him her heart in her next words.

"We're going to win this," she whispered. "I believe that. But in case we don't… I need a reminder. Of *us*. Of *me*. Of everything I'm fighting for."

She moved his hand to her chest, over her heart.

"I need *you*."

He didn't rush this time.

He kissed her slowly, reverently.

Like a man kneeling at the altar of something sacred.

Clothing was removed in quiet pieces. Fingers shook not from lust, but from *meaning*.

He took his time with her.

Every kiss was permission.

Every touch, a vow.

He pressed inside her with a breathless reverence — eyes locked on hers, searching for any sign of pain.

There was none.

Only trust.

Only need.

She came apart for him, and this time, when she trembled — it wasn't from fear.

It was from love.

Afterward, as he cradled her against his chest, breath still uneven, he whispered into her hair.

"You're teaching me to feel again. You're helping me control it. The rage. The desire. All the pieces I've buried."

He kissed the top of her head.

"I think you're the only one who ever could."

Chapter 54:

The sky cracked open just after sunrise.

Not with thunder.

But with *screams.*

The kind that didn't belong to birds or beasts.

The kind that meant war.

Elira shot upright, the sound dragging her from sleep before she even remembered where she was.

Vaelen was already out of bed, blade in hand, eyes dark with knowing.

"They found us," he said grimly.

"How?" she whispered, already reaching for her boots.

He hesitated — just long enough for her to notice.

"What is it?"

"They didn't track us," he said. "They *felt* you."

By the time they reached the edge of the grove, Solen and Maerys were already in motion, shouting orders, casting wards.

A pulse of darkness rolled through the trees like a second wind — foul, twisting, *unnatural.*

Lirian scouts fell back into defensive positions. Magic lit the treetops.

But the shadows didn't crawl in this time.

They *charged.*

Dozens of creatures — part-human, part-nightmare — tore through the trees like fire given form. Their eyes glowed with false light. Their mouths foamed. And in the center of them all…

A rider.

A man draped in silver and bone.

Vaelen's jaw clenched. "That's one of the King's prophets."

"Prophets?" Elira echoed.

"They speak for him. Or so they claim. They carry messages — and sometimes… *punishment.*"

The prophet didn't speak.

He didn't need to.

The air itself seemed to whisper the words into Elira's ears:

"You were warned."

The creatures surged forward.

And Elira lifted her hand.

The runes along her skin blazed gold — reacting before her thoughts could catch up. A blast of pure force exploded from her palm, hurling three of the creatures backward into the trees.

Vaelen was at her side in an instant, blades slicing with controlled fury.

Solen conjured light, Maerys unleashed a sonic wave that splintered bark and bone.

But they just kept coming.

"Behind you!" Vaelen roared.

Elira turned too late.

One of the twisted beasts was already mid-air, claws aimed for her throat.

A blast of lightning cracked through the air — not from her.

From *him.*

The prophet.

She ducked.

The bolt struck the ground near her feet, sending her sprawling.

The magic hit her ribs like fire.

"Elira!"

Vaelen was there — grabbing her, shielding her as more magic crackled across the sky.

But she could feel it.

The illusion.

Pressing against her mind.

Pushing her to *forget.*

To surrender.

To let the light go out.

She screamed — not in pain, but in defiance.

And the runes answered.

Her body glowed brighter than it ever had.

And when she stood again…

The illusion cracked.

Right in front of them.

The prophet flinched — just for a moment.

Then turned his horse and vanished into the trees.

The beasts fell still.

Collapsing like puppets cut from their strings.

Silence followed.

Then, slowly, Solen spoke.

"You're not just resisting anymore," he said, voice quiet. "You're *breaking* it."

Elira stood in the center of the destruction — bloodied, breathless.

But unbowed.

Vaelen moved to her side, touching her back gently.

"Are you alright?"

She didn't answer.

Because she wasn't sure.

But what she *was* sure of… was this:

The King had felt her power.

And now, there would be *no going back*.

Chapter 55:

The forest didn't settle after the attack.

It *waited.*

The kind of stillness that comes before another blow — the kind that hums beneath the skin.

Elira could feel it.

But something else stirred beneath it.

Her.

She walked the edges of the battlefield alone that evening, her fingertips brushing charred branches, blood-soaked leaves, and the still-warm blades left by fallen creatures.

But she didn't feel afraid.

She felt *close.*

Like the magic humming in her chest was pulling her toward something she hadn't quite remembered yet.

Not just the truth.

The *call.*

She heard it before she saw it.

A single, soft voice.

"Elira…"

She spun, heart clenching — because that voice was *impossible.*

But she saw her.

Ashira.

Standing at the edge of the smoke and trees, solid this time. Whole.

Her smile was faint — sorrowful, proud, *glowing.*

Elira's throat closed.

"Ashira?"

"I told you I'd find you again."

The others were frozen behind her. Vaelen stood protectively at Elira's side, eyes wide.

"She's… real," he whispered.

"I'm not alive," Ashira said, stepping forward. "But I'm not gone either."

She touched Elira's arm, and it didn't pass through.

"Elira, you've awakened more than the Wellspring. You're calling the voices that were *silenced.* And I was one of them."

The ground trembled again — not just in magic, but in warning.

Another group of shadow-bound beasts burst from the northern ridge.

Elira didn't wait for a signal.

She raised her hands.

And *Ashira raised hers with her.*

Twin bursts of golden light exploded from their palms.

The creatures screamed, recoiled, *dissolved.*

Elira blinked. "How—?"

"You're pulling open the seam," Ashira said. "You're reaching the ones he couldn't kill. The ones who were too powerful. Too emotional. Too *true.* He exiled them. Hid them in the cracks between worlds."

Elira's heartbeat faster. "Can I reach them?"

Ashira's gaze was fire and tears. "You already are."

Later that night, Elira sat by the fire, the others asleep or recovering nearby. Vaelen sat beside her, shoulder to shoulder, warm and steady.

"I want to find them," she said. "All of them. The ones the King cast out. The ones who couldn't be erased."

"Do you think they'll fight with us?"

She nodded slowly. "I think they've been waiting for someone to *ask*."

He watched her with quiet reverence.

"You're not just breaking the illusion anymore," he said. "You're undoing the erasure."

Within three days, they began the journey.

Solen had warned her it would be dangerous — the realm beyond the Veil was wild, layered with emotion-magic, some of it unstable.

But Elira was ready.

They crossed into the threshold near the southern cliff — a place that pulsed with forgotten power.

And what they found?

Was a world of *emotion incarnate.*

The first Lirian they met was born of *regret* — tall and cloaked, their magic like ripples of grief and memory.

Then came *wonder* — a small, luminous figure who spoke in stars.

Then *wrath.* Wild. Untamed. Nearly lost to itself — until Elira's touch calmed it.

There were more.

Emotions she hadn't even known had names.

Melancholy.

Longing.

Devotion.

Even one that called itself *Hope After Loss* — and shone with a fractured kind of light

These weren't just exiles.

They were *survivors.*

And they were waiting for *her.*

Not a queen.

Not a savior.

But someone who *felt* enough to fight with them.

And when Elira stood before them, voice shaking but sure, and asked—

"Will you help me take back what was stolen?"

They didn't hesitate.

The answer was one word.

"Yes."

Top of Form

Bottom of Form

Chapter 56:

The air in the in-between realm was different.

Not just thick with magic — but *alive* with it.

It pulsed beneath Elira's feet like breath. A slow, steady rhythm that matched the drumbeat of something stirring inside her.

The emotion-born Lirians had not returned to the world for centuries. Some had forgotten what sunlight felt like. Others refused to speak aloud, afraid that even their voices could be taken.

But Elira had changed that.

With each word she spoke.

Each memory she reclaimed.

Each *choice* she made.

She was doing what no one had dared in generations.

Undoing erasure.

Solen watched her from the edge of the circle as she stood before them all, light flickering across her skin.

"She's not just awakening," he murmured to Vaelen. "She's becoming."

Vaelen's arms were crossed, expression unreadable — but his eyes never left her.

"She was always meant to."

When Elira raised her hand and summoned a rune of pure light in midair — *without drawing it* — the entire grove gasped.

The Lirians nearest to her dropped to one knee.

Not out of obedience.

But recognition.

The girl who had been bound and silenced was now *calling back the lost.*

And the Veil… *shuddered.*

⁂

Far away, in the palace of mirrors and silence, the King jolted upright in his throne.

The illusion cracked across the southern edge.

He felt it like a blade to the chest.

A pull toward something *he couldn't see.*

Couldn't *control.*

He turned to his advisors — eyes flashing silver.

"Find her."

Malric stepped forward, lips curling in cold precision. "We already are."

Back in the realm beyond, Elira sat with one of the Lirians — a girl no older than fifteen in appearance, though her magic trembled with ageless sadness.

"What's your name?" Elira asked.

The girl tilted her head. "I was called Silence."

Elira reached out. "Then let's give you a new one."

The girl blinked — and then smiled, tears bright in her eyes.

"Hope," she whispered.

And the moment she said it…

The ground *glowed* beneath them.

Vaelen approached Elira later, finding her seated near the water's edge. The others were resting. Dreaming. Planning.

"You're building something," he said quietly.

She looked up. "I'm *remembering* something."

"What?"

"That we weren't meant to survive alone."

He knelt beside her, voice low.

"I've seen kingdoms rise and fall. Wars for power. Battles for thrones. But I've never seen anything like *you.*"

She smiled. "You don't have to flatter me, you know."

"I'm not," he said. "I'm telling you the truth."

He reached for her hand, threading their fingers together.

"And the King feels it now. You *shook him.*"

"I know," she said. "And we're not done yet."

That night, Elira dreamed again.

Not of ruins.

But of *flames.*

Not of fear.

But of *freedom.*

And when she woke, she whispered into the stars—

"We rise at dawn."

Chapter 57:

The camp stirred long before the light reached the trees.

It wasn't chaos.

It was purpose.

Elira stood at the edge of the grove, wrapped in a cloak woven by one of the emotion-born — threads that shimmered silver-blue in the dark. Not armor. But *presence.*

Around her, the Lirians moved like breath and shadow — ethereal, emotional, *ready*.

This wasn't an army in the traditional sense.

It was a force born of *feeling.*

Of everything the King had tried to stamp out.

And today… they would strike first

Solen spread a map across a flat stone, glowing softly with markings only the resistance could read.

"There's an old outpost near the river," he said. "It's used to channel energy through illusion runes. It's not heavily guarded — they think we're still licking our wounds."

"They'll expect us to stay hidden," Vaelen added, folding his arms. "To wait."

"They won't expect *her*," Solen said, nodding at Elira.

She studied the map. Then pointed to the ridge just behind the outpost.

"We don't go for the gates. We go *above.* We let the illusion feel us before they see us."

She looked up, eyes glowing with quiet command.

"We make them *afraid* of what they can't control."

By midday, they moved.

Lirians flanked the path — moving with unnatural grace.

Elira rode at the center, not on a steed, but on foot — her presence like a *beacon* pulsing outward.

When the ridge came into view, Vaelen touched her shoulder.

"This is it," he murmured.

She turned to him.

"Will you stand with me?"

"Always."

The first rune Elira cast pulsed from her palm and landed silently on the edge of the warding line. A moment later, the entire barrier *shivered.*

Then broke.

The illusion fell apart like mist — revealing the outpost, the guards, the runes anchoring the magic.

And Elira stepped forward.

They didn't have time to react.

Lirian magic swept through like a tide — not to kill, but to *expose*. Each blast dissolved the false light. Each blow *rattled* the illusion deeper.

The guards screamed — not from pain.

From *clarity.*

Some dropped their weapons. Others fled. A few fell to their knees, clutching their heads.

And then one looked up at Elira — blinking like he had just woken from a long sleep.

"Who… are you?"

She didn't answer with a name.

She raised her hand — and light poured from her.

And the man began to *weep.*

⁂

By nightfall, the outpost was theirs.

No casualties.

No bloodbath.

Just *truth.*

Elira stood at the center, hands trembling slightly as the magic faded from her fingertips.

Vaelen came up behind her, sliding an arm around her waist.

"You did it."

She exhaled slowly. "This was just the beginning."

He looked at her — not with surprise.

But *awe.*

"You're becoming the storm."

That night, she met with Solen and the emotion-born leaders.

They circled the fire, the flames dancing in rhythm with the pulse of the Veil above.

"What's next?" one asked.

Elira didn't hesitate.

"We find the next anchor point. We break it. Then the next."

She looked to Solen. "And we start finding *more* of the King's forgotten."

Her voice rose.

"Because we aren't just here to break his illusion. We're here to remind them all of *what's real.*"

⁂

Far away, the King screamed into a silent chamber — his hands bloodied from clawing at a mirror that no longer reflected him.

"She's *awakening them.*"

Malric stood calmly nearby.

"She's not just fighting, sire," he said.

"She's *winning.*"

Chapter 58:

Elira looked at him. The fire still burned in the outpost, but the night had quieted.

Too much.

Elira stood at the edge of the hill, cloak trailing behind her, watching the forest below like it might speak. Her body still buzzed with magic, but her soul felt *hollowed out* — like she'd given so much of herself to the light that there was barely anything left for the dark to grab.

She didn't speak when Vaelen approached. She didn't have to.

He stepped beside her, his silence a comfort rather than a void.

"They're scared," she whispered.

He nodded. "Good."

"They should be. But… they're also *watching*. Waiting. And the ones who haven't chosen sides yet… I don't know if this was enough."

"You moved the world today."

"But what if it moves back?"

Later, she walked through the encampment. The emotion-born were resting — some in small huddles, others scattered like starlight across the grove. Some didn't sleep at all. Their emotions kept them awake, glowing like embers in their skin.

Solen sat near the wellspring, weaving a new set of protective runes into the earth.

He looked up when she passed.

"You're not resting."

"I can't."

He nodded as if he understood — and he did.

"You've made them believe," he said. "That's not small."

"I'm afraid it's not enough."

"You lit the match, Elira," he murmured. "The fire is their choice now."

Morning broke with the scent of ash.

The outpost was still theirs, but something in the wind had *shifted.*

Elira noticed it first.

Not in her body.

In the silence.

The birds didn't sing.

The leaves didn't rustle.

Even the emotion-born looked up — eyes flicking toward the trees like they were *remembering* something they'd tried to forget.

Then it came.

A pulse.

Not of power.

Of *pain.*

It hit the wards first — cracking them like glass.

Then the sky.

A thunderous ripple that turned sunlight into smoke.

And then the voices.

Hundreds.

Screaming.

Elira ran.

By the time she reached the northern edge of the grove, half the trees had already *wilted.*

Not burned. Not slashed.

Withered.

Drained.

And in the center of it all…

A sigil.

Carved into the ground in blood.

The King's mark.

Vaelen grabbed her arm before she could step into the circle.

"Don't."

"What is it?"

"It's a message."

Elira stared at the curling lines — a spiral meant to disorient. A rune meant to unmake.

"It's not just a warning," she whispered. "It's a tether. He's *watching us.*"

Solen arrived, fury flashing in his eyes.

"This was meant to tell you something," he said. "You broke his hold on an outpost. Now he's reminding you how quickly he can touch the world around you."

Elira crouched near the mark.

And she *felt* it.

A whisper not from a voice, but from memory.

You cannot protect them all.

She stood.

"Maybe not," she said softly.

"But I'll die trying."

That night, they buried three of the younger emotion-born.

Not from battle.

From the mark.

The energy had drained them. The pain had reached too far.

Elira sat beside their graves until long after the sun had gone.

Vaelen found her there, his expression raw.

"He's escalating," he said.

"I know."

"You saw what that did. He's trying to make you hesitate. To question. To fear."

She turned toward him.

"I do fear."

He moved closer.

"But I also remember," she said. "Every time I let fear lead… I became smaller."

He touched her cheek. "You're not small anymore."

She leaned into him.

"I don't want to lose any more of them."

"Then let's fight harder."

That night, she didn't dream of light.

She dreamed of fire.

Of a throne crumbling into ruin.

And herself, standing before it — bleeding, burning, *alive.*

And when she woke, the whisper was not the King's.

It was *hers.*

"We keep going."

Chapter 59:

They left the withered grove behind just before dusk.

No ceremony.

No words.

Only silence and smoke.

Elira walked with her hood up, but her eyes scanned every tree, every shadow. Not for enemies — but for *signs*. Of weakening. Of vulnerability. Of where the next strike might land.

Vaelen kept pace beside her. His steps quiet, gaze sharper than usual.

But he hadn't spoken much since the burial.

Neither had she.

Their grief hung between them like fog.

But it wasn't distance.

It was weight.

And they carried it *together*.

When they made camp that night, Solen and Maerys left them alone by the fire. Most of the Lirians had learned by now that when the two of them sat close like this — knees touching, hands brushing occasionally — it wasn't just affection.

It was *armor*.

The kind that didn't clang like metal, but *held like light*.

Elira stared into the flames.

"He knew what that attack would do," she said quietly. "He didn't strike to win. He struck to *wound*. To remind me that I can't save them all."

Vaelen leaned forward, resting his forearms on his knees.

"You don't have to."

She looked over at him, brow furrowing.

"I know you want to," he added. "But you're not a god, Elira. You're still human. Still breaking. Still healing. You're doing more than any of us thought possible — and still, it's not enough for you."

Her throat tightened.

"Because if I stop… even for a moment…" She blinked back sudden tears. "I'm afraid I'll lose everything."

Vaelen reached for her hand, slow and sure.

"You won't."

"How do you know?"

He turned to her fully now, eyes steady.

"Because I won't let you."

They sat like that for a long time — just the crackling of fire between them.

Finally, Elira leaned her head against his shoulder.

"You've been quiet," she said.

"So have you."

She gave a soft huff. "You okay?"

He didn't answer right away.

Then—

"I hated seeing you grieve."

She looked up at him, surprised.

"You were so quiet. So strong. But I could feel it, Elira. You were barely holding it together. And I couldn't fix it."

"You don't have to fix everything."

He smiled faintly. "I've spent most of my life fighting battles with a sword. And then you came along… and reminded me some wounds can't be fought like that."

She smiled softly, resting her hand over his heart.

"I don't need you to fight *for* me," she said. "I just need you to stay."

His hand curled around hers.

"I'm not going anywhere."

That night, in the quiet of their shared tent, Elira curled into his side — not for heat.

For *comfort.*

For *closeness.*

Their fingers remained intertwined as they drifted off to sleep, her breath steadying in the cradle of his chest.

And as sleep took them both, something flickered in the air around them.

A thread.

Silver.

Soft.

And *unbreakable.*

The first physical sign of a bond deeper than either had ever known.

And the Veil?

It *shivered* again.

Chapter 60:

Elira rose before dawn.

The camp was still asleep, blanketed in mist and hush, but her body hummed with too much energy to stay still. It wasn't adrenaline. It wasn't fear.

It was *knowing.*

Something was coming.

She walked to the edge of the trees, fingers brushing the cool bark of the old sentinel oaks. Her runes pulsed softly beneath her skin — low, rhythmic, like a heartbeat echoing not just in her chest, but in the world itself.

She was part of something now.

And it was *moving.*

Vaelen found her just after first light, a cloak draped over one arm and two steaming mugs of something warm in the other.

He handed her one without a word.

She smiled, grateful.

"You always know where to find me."

"I stopped looking," he said. "I just go where the light is."

She rolled her eyes, but the smile lingered.

They stood together in silence, watching the pink-and-gold edge of morning stretch across the horizon.

It felt different today.

Not softer.

Just *clearer.*

Later, a meeting was called. Solen had returned from the southern scouts. His face was tight with tension.

"They're mobilizing again," he said. "This time, from the western reaches. We believe they're headed for the old sanctuary at Lyneth Hollow."

Elira frowned. "I thought it was abandoned."

"It is. But it still holds relics. Anchors. Traces of old Lirian blood. If the King corrupts it—"

"He weakens the rest of you," Vaelen finished.

Solen nodded.

"And the Veil?"

"It's weakening there too," Solen said. "You might be able to use it."

Elira looked up sharply. "Use it how?"

"Step through it," he said simply.

"To *where?*"

"To the places the King hasn't touched. *Can't* touch."

A chill ran through her.

"You want me to leave?"

"I want you to lead."

⁂

That night, Elira sat by the fire with her journal open on her knees.

She didn't write anything.

She just stared at the last page.

The one that used to say *I don't know who I am.*

Now, she knew.

Not everything. Not yet.

But enough to *fight.*

Enough to *believe.*

Vaelen joined her, sitting close, his fingers brushing her knee.

She looked at him — not as a protector. Not as a warrior.

But as a *constant.*

"You know this is getting bigger than us, right?" she asked softly.

He nodded.

"And I'm still with you."

She took a breath.

"Even if I have to step into something terrifying?"

He leaned in, forehead touching hers.

"I'll be waiting on the other side."

The wind picked up, whispering through the trees.

And far, far away, the King sat in silence — sensing something slip beyond his reach again.

Not just a girl.

Not just a rebel.

But a *force.*

A flame he could no longer smother.

Chapter 61:

The camp had gone quiet.

Not in fear. Not in tension.

But in *peace* – the rare kind that only settled when the mind and heart had been cracked open, and something healing had begun to bloom inside the wreckage.

Elira sat just beyond the firelight, he back against the roots of a sprawling tree, knees drawn to her chest. Her journal lay open in her lap, untouched. The pages no longer felt heavy – just waiting.

She didn't write.

She didn't have to.

Not tonight.

Vaelen approached without a word.

He didn't ask to sit.

He just *was* — a steady presence in a world that shifted with every breath she took.

After a long stretch of silence, he reached for her hand.

Fingers laced. Thumb trailing soft lines over her knuckles.

"You've been quiet," he said.

"So have you."

"I'm trying to make space."

She turned to him, eyes glowing faintly in the moonlight. "For what?"

"For whatever you need."

That almost broke her.

They sat in the hush together, the only sound the crackling of the fire and the wind threading through the leaves above them.

Elira finally looked at him — *really* looked at him.

The scar along his collarbone.

The faint bruise at his jaw from the last battle.

The silver thread of hair curling behind his ear that she hadn't noticed before.

"You always act like you're unbreakable," she whispered.

"I'm not."

"You don't flinch. You don't doubt. You just… stand there and take everything the world throws at you."

He smiled faintly. "Not everything."

Elira leaned in, pressing her forehead to his.

"You don't have to be strong all the time."

"I know," he said softly.

"Then let me be strong for you tonight."

His hand moved to her cheek, thumb brushing beneath her eye.

She didn't realize she'd been crying.

Not hard.

Just… letting go.

"I think you already are," he said.

"Why?"

"Because I've never known peace like this. And I've never *wanted* peace like this."

She leaned into him.

"It scares me sometimes," she whispered.

"What does?"

"This feeling. Like something good is finally mine. Like maybe… I'm allowed to have this."

Vaelen's eyes burned.

"You are."

She looked up. "Then promise me. When everything else falls apart… we don't."

"I swear it," he said. "By the stars. By the Veil. By everything I am."

They curled into each other, wrapped in silence and warmth, under a sky full of cracks and constellations.

A bond formed not through war, but through *witnessing*.

And far away, unseen, the Veil trembled.

Because something was stirring in the spaces between shadow and softness.

And its name…

Was *love*.

Chapter 62:

The morning came slower than usual.

Muted light spilled across the trees, as though the sun hesitated — unsure if it was welcome on this day of thresholds.

Elira stood near the edge of the glade, the wind toying with the edge of her cloak. Before her, a thin shimmer clung to the air — a ripple, a distortion, like a mirror made of breath.

The Veil.

But not the illusion this time.

The crossing point.

Solen had drawn it with the help of three emotion-born Lirians, all with trembling fingers and somber eyes. Even they didn't know what would be waiting on the other side.

"This passage," Solen said quietly, "hasn't been opened in decades. Maybe longer. Not since the last of the exiled faded."

Elira nodded, steady.

She wasn't afraid.

Not anymore.

Vaelen stood at her side, his arm brushing hers. He hadn't said much since they woke — just enough to let her know he'd follow her into whatever waited beyond.

"You don't have to be the first," he said, voice low.

"I think I do," she whispered.

As she stepped forward, the Veil shimmered around her.

She reached a hand out.

And the moment her fingers touched the shimmer, *everything changed.*

It wasn't painful.

It wasn't violent.

It was like being *remembered.*

The magic rushed through her like a long-lost breath — filling cracks she hadn't known were there. Her runes flared. Her heart raced.

And then…

She vanished.

The realm beyond wasn't dark.

It was *light* — too much of it. Blinding. Sharp. Not warmth, but clarity.

Shapes moved in the brightness — silhouettes of beings that hadn't touched the physical world in ages.

Emotion-born.

Thousands.

Elira fell to her knees, overwhelmed.

Her body didn't hurt — but her *soul* did. Like something was peeling open, layer by layer.

And then, a voice:

"You've come."

She looked up.

A figure stood before her, tall and androgynous, wrapped in glowing white and green threads. Neither man nor woman — *feeling made form.*

"You are the one who remembers," they said. "The one who breaks what should never have been built."

"I need your help," Elira said. Her voice shook.

"We know."

The figure held out a hand. "Come. There is more waiting for you."

On the other side of the Veil, Vaelen stepped through.

And as he did, his senses *screamed.*

Something was wrong.

He didn't feel Elira's presence.

Not immediately.

Instead, he felt…

Shadow.

Not of this place. Not born of emotion.

Born of control.

The King had followed.

Or worse…

He had *found a way through.*

Elira turned in the brightness — felt a flicker of fear pierce the light like a needle.

She didn't know what it was yet.

But it was *coming.*

Chapter 63:

The brightness fractured.

Elira felt the moment it happened – like a crack in a stained-glass window, splitting the light into something sharp and wrong.

The emotion-born around her flinched, some collapsing to the ground, others gasping like air had turned to fire.

The guide who had welcomed her – the one made of threads of light – dropped their hand and whispered, "He's here."

Elira's heart stilled.

"No," she breathed. "He shouldn't be able to - "

"He followed the bond," the guide said, stepping back. "He found your light… and wrapped his darkness around it."

On the edge of the clearing, the Veil *ripped.*

Vaelen burst through, sword already drawn.

And behind him… *shadows.*

Not beasts. Not prophets.

Worse.

Wraiths.

Constructs made of illusion and hatred. Born of the King's fear. Born of his need to control what he couldn't possess.

Elira rose, eyes glowing gold now, runes pulsing like wildfire across her skin.

The emotion-born scattered, instinctively avoiding the creatures, knowing they couldn't fight them – only she could.

Only *they* could.

Vaelen was already moving – cutting down the first wraith in a blur of silver and black. It shrieked and dissolved into smoke.

"Elira!" he called, turning toward her. "I told you I'd throw myself in front of anything that tried to touch you."

She didn't smile.

But the tears in her eyes spoke louder.

"I'm done hiding," she said.

And then her magic *unleashed.*

The first blast turned two wraiths into sparks of dust.

The second collapsed the twisted pathway behind them.

And the third?

The third wasn't cast from her hands.

It came from her *chest.*

From the place where her bond with Vaelen lived.

He looked up, stunned, as gold light seared through the center of the battlefield – tracing a line between them.

Elira realized it too late.

The king was using it.

The bond.

To find her.

To reach her.

He didn't come in body.

But in voice.

And it struck like cold iron:

"You may gather your lost ones. You may stitch your little truths. But emotion makes you vulnerable, child. And I will always use it."

Elira dropped to her knees, clutching her head, the voice crawling through her mind like rot.

Vaelen roared and surged forward, cutting down another wraith, then sliding beside her – wrapping his arms around her, shielding her from everything.

"Look at me," he said, his voice ragged. *"Look at me, Elira."*

Her eyes opened.

And in that moment, the voice faded.

Because *he* was stronger than the illusion.

They were.

The remaining wraiths began to retreat, hissing into the brightness like oil on water.

The Veil pulsed, trying to repair itself.

And the last shadow faded, silence fell.

Elira and Vaelen stayed wrapped together on the forest floor, her face buried in his chest, his arms locked around her like a promise.

"You're still here," she whispered.

"I always will be."

Later, the others regrouped, after Solen and the guide confirmed the damage was temporary – that Elira's bond hadn't broken but had been *exploited* – she sat alone with Vaelen in the edge of their tent.

Her hands were still shaking.

Not from fear.

From *needing to feel safe again.*

And as he cupped her face, as his forehead rested against hers…

She whispered, "I don't want to be alone tonight."

His voice cracked. "You're not."

She kissed him.

Once.

Twice.

And then again, until the taste of him reminded her she was still whole.

Chapter 64:

The fire outside their tent had burned low, casting only the faintest flickers of orange against the canvas. Inside, Elira sat curled at the edge of their bedding, knees pulled to her chest, fingers trembling. Her runes were dim. Not gone—just... quiet.

Vaelen had stepped out to give her space, but now he stood in the entry, waiting. Watching. Knowing.

He didn't speak until she looked up.

"Come in," she whispered.

He did.

She swallowed hard, her voice catching in her throat. "I've been thinking..."

Vaelen said nothing, but his gaze softened.

"I don't know if it's worth it," she admitted. "Putting all of this on the line. All of them. You."

He came closer, dropping to a knee before her. "Say what you mean."

Her eyes welled. "What if I went back? Did what the King wanted. Just to keep everyone safe. To keep *you* safe."

Something flickered across Vaelen's face—not anger, but hurt. Deep. Quiet. Unmoving.

He reached for her hand.

"If you did that," he said slowly, "I would tear through every illusion, every wall, every realm to get you back."

She blinked.

"I would rather die fighting for you than live in a world where you're bound and broken. Again."

He cupped her face, his voice a whisper now.

"I won't let you go back to that. Not to him. Not to *Malric*. Not to a world that thought it could take someone like you and twist her into silence."

His jaw clenched. "The thought of him touching you... of him *owning* what is *mine*... it makes me want to burn everything to the ground."

Elira let out a shaky breath.

"I don't know what I'm doing," she said, her voice barely audible. Vulnerable.

Vaelen leaned in, lips brushing hers. "Yes, you do," he murmured. "But I'll guide you."

He moved slowly at first, drawing her into his lap, letting her settle over him, her thighs on either side of his hips. Her breath hitched as his hands found her waist.

"You don't have to be certain," he whispered. "You just have to want it. Want me."

Her hands hesitated, fluttering across his chest, unsure. She kissed him softly, nervously, her lips brushing his like a question. He let her take her time, let her explore. His fingers stayed firm but gentle, guiding her hips as she pressed against him, tentative and curious.

When she pulled back slightly, cheeks flushed, he met her eyes. "You're doing so well. But now... let me show *you*."

With a sudden shift, he reversed their positions, pressing her gently onto the bedding, covering her body with his own. His kiss deepened—hungry, reverent, possessive. She gasped as his hands traced the length of her thighs, slow and purposeful.

"You're mine, Elira. No one else will ever touch you like this. No one else *deserves* to."

He kissed down her throat, across her collarbone, his hands never leaving her skin. He worshipped every inch of her with lips and fingers, coaxing pleasure from her with whispered praise and skill that bordered on reverence.

He brought her to the edge once—slow and sweet. Then again, harder, rougher. She writhed beneath him, her fingers tangled in his hair, her moans breaking in the quiet.

And still, he kept going.

"This is what I'll fight for," he growled against her skin. "This is what I'll protect with every breath."

She tried to catch her breath, trembling.

"Vaelen... I can't... I need..."

He kissed her again, deeply, grounding her. "You *can.* You will. One more. Just for me."

She came undone again, tears sliding down her cheeks. And only then—only when she lay boneless and breathless beneath him—did he slow.

He pulled her close, her body flush against his, his lips pressed to her temple.

"This is how far I'll go for you, Elira. To make sure you never doubt who you are, or what you mean to me."

She nestled against his chest, one hand still fisted in his tunic, the other resting over his heart.

They didn't speak for a long time.

They didn't have to.

Because in that quiet, in that closeness, in the way their bodies and hearts and magic had fused—they knew.

This was their truth.

And nothing would ever break it.

Later, when her breathing slowed and her limbs felt like mist, Elira shifted gently in his arms. Her voice was soft, teasing, breathy with exhaustion. "You sure you want the risk that being with me brings?"

Vaelen's eyes opened slowly, the silver still glowing faintly behind his irises. His voice rumbled low, dangerous and fond. "If that left you asking *that* question... maybe I didn't go far enough."

She let out a sleepy, quiet giggle, tilting her face toward his. "This might be my favorite emotion out of you."

He raised a brow. "What emotion?"

She dragged a finger down his chest, still playful. "That little edge of possessiveness... The way I get a rise out of you."

He smirked. "You like poking the wolf, do you?"

She grinned. "I like knowing I can. That I make you feel that much. That I can drive you mad with a single touch. Or sometimes..." she kissed his shoulder, tracing her hand lower, "with two."

Her hand slipped farther down, fingers curling around him gently, teasingly.

He inhaled sharply. "Elira..."

"Hmm?" she asked, far too innocent.

"What are you doing?"

"I don't know," she whispered, giggling again.

His hand caught her wrist, firm and slow. His tone dropped; heat laced in warning. "If you keep going, little light... I'm going to make sure you can't sit for a week."

She met his gaze, eyes wide and wicked. "Maybe I want that."

His groan was low and dangerous, and in one swift movement, he had her beneath him again, his mouth at her ear.

"Then don't say I didn't warn you."

He grabbed her thighs and pulled her to the edge of the bedding, flipping her effortlessly onto her stomach, then dragging her hips up until she was on her knees, bare and breathless for him. His hands were everywhere—rough and reverent, stroking, gripping, claiming.

When he entered her, it was deep. Intentional. Punishing in all the ways she craved.

She cried out, her hands gripping the bedding. Vaelen growled behind her, thrusting hard, slow at first, then deeper, harder, just like he said he would. Just like she'd begged for.

"This," he hissed, leaning over her, one hand threading into her hair, the other at her hip, anchoring her. "This is what happens when you tempt me. When you tease what's mine."

Elira moaned, her body shaking with every stroke, her skin burning where his hands held her. The stretch, the fullness, the pressure—it was too much. It was perfect.

He reached between her thighs and circled his fingers with maddening precision.

"Say it," he growled. "Say you're mine."

"I'm yours," she gasped, her body tightening around him.

"Again."

"I'm yours, Vaelen. Always."

That snapped something in him.

He growled her name like a prayer as she shattered again, and only then did he let himself go, collapsing forward to hold her close, their bodies locked, breath tangled.

He kissed the back of her neck. "You have no idea what you do to me."

She was trembling beneath him, raw and wrecked in the best way. And yet, when he moved to pull out, she reached back and stopped him.

"Stay," she whispered.

He did.

And they breathed there in the afterglow—a fire burned down to embers, but still burning.

Chapter 65:

Elira woke to warmth.

Not just from the blanket tangled around her waist, or the heat of Vaelen's body curled behind her — but something deeper.

A *peace* she hadn't known her bones could carry.

His arm draped across her waist, heavy and protective. His breath brushed her neck in slow, even waves. And his fingers… even in sleep, they curled against her like he couldn't bear to let her go.

She blinked up at the tent's roof, letting silence stretch between them.

And then, softly, she whispered, "You're still here."

Vaelen stirred, voice gravel-thick. "Where else would I be?"

She rolled to face him, her body aching in ways that made her smile.

"I meant… after everything. After last night."

His eyes opened, storm-gray and gentle. "You think I'd touch you like that and walk away?"

"I don't know what I think," she admitted. "It's just… I've never felt this."

He lifted a hand and tucked a piece of her hair behind her ear.

"Neither have I."

She took a slow breath, trying to find the right words. "You make me feel like I'm safe. Even when everything else is chaos. Like I could fall apart, and you'd just… hold me together."

Vaelen pressed his forehead to hers.

"That's what it means to choose someone, Elira."

"I didn't know it could be like this."

"Neither did I."

He ran his thumb across her cheek, watching her. "But I want it to stay like this. I want you to know… I'd never take from you. Never force. Never demand. But I *will* keep showing you what you deserve. Every time."

Her eyes stung again — not from pain this time, but from *recognition.*

Of herself.

Of him.

Of *them.*

After a long moment, she whispered, "Do you ever worry that what we're building… it might not last?"

He didn't flinch. "Every day."

She looked up, surprised.

"I worry because it *matters.* Because if something happened to you, I'd feel it. Not just in my heart. In my *magic.* In my soul. That's what this is now."

Elira slid her hand over his chest, right above his heart. "And if I fall?"

"I'll catch you."

"And if I break?"

"I'll hold the pieces."

She leaned in and kissed him softly. "I'm scared of how much I need you."

Vaelen's voice was low. "I'm scared of how much I love needing you back."

They lay there, wrapped in each other and words not yet spoken.

Not promises.

Not vows.

But something older.

A bond that said: *I see you. And I stay.*

A quiet moment passed. Then another. Elira blinked, and tears slipped from her eyes before she could stop them.

Vaelen's hand immediately cupped her cheek, alarmed. "Elira—did I hurt you?"

"No," she said quickly, shaking her head. "No, not at all."

He leaned over her, brushing a thumb across her temple. "Then what is it?"

She swallowed hard, her voice thick. "I'm just… thinking."

"About what?"

Her eyes searched his. "About what it must be like—for those who don't get this. Who don't know that this—*us*—is how it should feel. Who were told that intimacy is a task. A duty. Something to be endured instead of desired."

Vaelen stilled, his expression darkening slightly. Listening.

Elira's voice cracked. "That was almost me."

She looked away, then back, fierce and soft all at once. "It *could* have been me. And I wouldn't have even known the difference. I would've accepted it. Lived with it. Survived it."

"But now that I know?" She met his eyes, tears trailing down her cheeks. "Now that I've felt this? *You?* I'll fight so no one else ever has to wonder. I'll fight so they all know—this is what it's *supposed* to be. Not clinical. Not forced. Not stolen."

Vaelen leaned in, resting his forehead against hers again, his voice a quiet vow. "Then I'll fight beside you. Every step. Every strike. Every breath."

She smiled, broken and beautiful. "I don't think I'll ever stop loving you for this."

He kissed her, softly, reverently. "Then don't."

And for the first time in her life, Elira believed that loving someone didn't have to come with pain.

It could come with *power.*

Chapter 66:

The morning air was cooler than usual, laced with something different — not danger, but movement. Change.

Elira stepped out of the tent, wrapped in one of Vaelen's cloaks. Her body still hummed with the memory of him, but her mind had sharpened. There was no fog. No confusion.

She was still sore. Still tender.

But *stronger.*

Behind her, Vaelen stirred — half-dressed, still resting, but alert in that way he always was. His gaze followed her, calm and steady, like a tether she could always reach back for.

Solen stood near the perimeter, runes glowing faintly around his palms. He glanced over as she approached and smiled — not wide, but warm. Knowing.

"You look… different," he said quietly.

"I feel different."

"Good different?"

Elira nodded. "Like something settled. Something I'd been holding back."

Solen's gaze dropped to the marks on her skin — the faint shimmer of runes that hadn't fully faded from the night before.

"Not all power comes in battle," he said. "Sometimes the most dangerous magic is the kind that makes you *want* to stay alive."

Elira looked toward the trees, where the Veil shimmered softly in the distance. "We're not done, are we?"

"No," Solen said. "But we're not alone anymore, either."

Later that morning, as the group regrouped for strategy, a ripple of tension passed through the Lirians. Word had spread — through whispers and runes and flickers of shared emotion — that something had shifted in the Veil.

Ashira's presence had been seen again, not just by Elira… but by another.

A younger emotion-born named Kallen had claimed to see her at the outer edge of the Wellspring, surrounded by threads of light that pulsed with memory and grief.

"She didn't speak," he said. "But she looked… proud."

Elira's chest tightened.

Maybe Ashira *knew.* Maybe she *felt* the bond. The growth. The healing.

And maybe… she was preparing the way for what came next.

That night, after plans were drawn and rest began to settle again, Vaelen joined Elira by the fire. He said nothing for a long while.

Then, with quiet conviction, he murmured, "I used to think the only thing that could change this world was war."

Elira turned toward him.

"And now?"

He reached for her hand.

"Now I think it might be *you.*"

Chapter 67:

The Veil shimmered unnaturally.

Not from power.

Not from healing.

From *strain.*

Solen's runes pulsed red this time — a color Elira had never seen from him before. He stood at the edge of the clearing, brows furrowed, lips moving in incantation as he traced glowing lines through the air.

"What is it?" she asked, stepping closer.

He didn't look at her at first. Just whispered, "It's stretching too far. Too fast."

Elira's pulse quickened. "What does that mean?"

"It means we're not the only ones awakening it anymore."

She felt it in her bones — a vibration in the center of her chest. The Veil wasn't just reacting to *her* anymore. It was starting to fracture in response to the King's movements, too. A reaction. A warping. A *race.*

That night, the scouts returned with word of a gathering not far from the outer edge of the Veil. Not hostile — curious.

Emotion-born.

From the exile.

Dozens of them.

Elira and Vaelen met the group just before dusk, where broken stone pillars rose like teeth from the earth. They were quiet at first — watching, unsure.

Then one stepped forward. A woman with ash-gray skin and hair like coiled vines.

"We felt something," she said. "A pull. Not from pain. Not from rage. From *hope*."

Elira's throat tightened. "Then we welcome you. All of you."

The emotion-born bowed.

And for the first time, the movement felt *real*.

⁂

But peace didn't last.

Later that night, a crack split the air — not in sound, but in sensation.

A rune flared across the camp, drawn in burning silver light, too elegant to be anything but *intentional*.

Solen rushed forward, trying to dissipate it, but it was already forming.

And then

A figure stepped forward in smoke and shadow, half-real, half-illusion.

Malric.

Elira's body froze.

His voice slid through the air like oil.

"How far you've come, little girl. And still, you are tethered by the weakest part of yourself… your *heart*."

Vaelen stepped beside her, blade in hand, but Elira raised a hand. "Let it speak."

Malric's projection moved closer. Not to attack. To taunt.

"He's watching, Elira. Every flicker of your soul, every inch of your skin you give to that Lirian filth. He sees you. He knows you. And he will *end* you the moment you believe yourself safe."

Elira clenched her fists, the runes in her skin sparking gold.

Malric smiled.

"But he offers you a gift. Return. Submit. And we will spare those who stand beside you."

A pause.

"Vaelen included."

Vaelen growled low, stepping forward.

Elira reached for his arm. "No."

Malric's smile grew wider. **"Think on it. Or don't. Either way… we'll see you soon."**

And then he vanished.

--

Silence blanketed the camp.

Solen whispered, "It was a message… and a threat. But also, a *test.*"

Vaelen looked at Elira, eyes dark. "You don't believe a word of it, do you?"

Elira's jaw tightened. "No. But I believe what it *means.* He's getting desperate. Which means he's also getting more dangerous."

Vaelen nodded. "Then it's time we give him a reason to be afraid."

Chapter 68:

Elira didn't sleep that night.

She sat alone by the dying fire, the rune mark where Malric's illusion had appeared still faintly burned into the dirt before her.

The message echoed in her head on a loop — not the threat. The *offer.*

"Return. Submit. And we will spare those who stand beside you."

And the worst part?

A small part of her believed he meant it.

Vaelen found her just before dawn, cloaked in shadow and silence. He didn't say a word at first. Just sat beside her, hands resting open, waiting for her to speak.

She didn't.

So, he did.

"He's good at it, isn't he?" he murmured. "The King. Malric. All of them. They don't just strike where it hurts… they strike where it *feels.*"

She nodded. "It would be easier… if it didn't sound like something I wanted."

Vaelen's head turned sharply, but she held up a hand.

"I don't mean I want to surrender. I mean… I want everyone to be safe. I want to stop seeing you bleed. Stop worrying that every night might be our last. That someone else I care about might vanish. I want peace. And that's the hook he used."

She clenched her jaw.

"He offered peace. And he knew exactly how to make it sound *beautiful*."

The fire crackled low between them.

Vaelen was quiet for a long time. Then, softly:

"Elira… I need you to hear something."

She looked at him.

"I don't need peace if it means I lose you. I don't need safety if it's a cage. I don't want a world where your fire is quiet just so everyone else can sleep easy."

His voice dropped, rough with emotion.

"You are the reason we fight. Not a threat. Not a burden. Not a price. *The reason*."

She blinked against the sudden sting in her eyes.

He leaned in, pressing his forehead to hers. "He doesn't offer peace. He offers *silence*. And you've already broken that."

Later, as morning burned off the mist, Solen approached with news.

Two more clusters of emotion-born had arrived — pulled by the ripples of power, of magic, of *Elira*. Some were hesitant. Some nearly feral with volatile emotion. But all were drawn to the same pulse.

The *crack*.

The *change*.

The *call*.

One of them, a tall Lirian with gold-streaked hair and hollowed cheeks, bowed low before Elira.

"You are the one who remembers," he said. "The one who *feels*."

She met his gaze. "Then help me make the others feel, too."

He smiled faintly. "We already are."

That night, another message came.

This one not through illusion, but in dream.

Elira found herself in a place of mirrors and silence. A world without color, without sound — only *reflections.* Her own face, a hundred times over, staring back at her.

And in the center… the King.

Not fully formed. Not physical. Just *present.*

"You cannot hold them all together," he said softly. "They will turn on you when your emotions break you. They will suffer because you feel too much. They will die in your name."

Elira trembled.

But her voice stayed clear.

"Then I'll teach them to live in mine instead."

The mirrors shattered.

She woke with fire in her chest.

Chapter 69:

The Veil shimmered again — not in warning, but in *welcome.*

Elira stood near the edge of the valley where the air felt thinner, the trees older, their trunks etched with runes that pulsed when she came close. Her presence no longer just stirred emotion. It *called it forward.*

Solen called it a "resonance."

Vaelen called it *power.*

Elira didn't know what to call it — only that more and more Lirians were answering it.

They came from the hollows. From the ruins. From places not mapped, but remembered.

And they came for *her.*

⁂

That morning, a scout brought back word of another group — but this time, it wasn't a peaceful arrival.

"They're fractured," the scout had said. "Wild with rage. They don't even speak."

Elira nodded. "We'll go to them."

Vaelen didn't even blink at the danger. He simply asked, "How far?"

The journey was short but tense. They moved through the deeper part of the forest, where light filtered in like a whispered promise. Elira could feel it in her skin — not pain. Not danger.

Grief.

That's what they were walking into.

Not rage.

Grief that had *festered.*

The group they found wasn't large — maybe twelve — but every single one pulsed with an unstable magic that made the air heavy. One of them let out a low, fractured scream the moment they saw Elira. Another fell to their knees, sobbing without reason.

Solen whispered, "They were born from loss that never healed. They've never known grounding."

Elira stepped forward.

Vaelen reached for her arm.

"Elira—"

"I have to," she said.

And then she opened her arms.

They came to her slowly, unsure, trembling. One brushed against her fingers and *stilled.* Another collapsed into her, wailing as if every death they'd ever witnessed poured from their mouth at once.

She held them.

Not with words.

Not with commands.

With *feeling.*

And one by one, they *began to breathe.*

Later, after the group settled — not entirely healed, but quieter — Vaelen pulled Elira aside.

"You keep doing that," he said softly.

"Doing what?"

"Turning pain into loyalty. Into light. Into something the King can't control."

She looked down at her hands. "Because I know what it's like to be buried by it."

He tucked a piece of hair behind her ear. "And you're proving there's a way out."

That night, as the camp settled, Solen approached with a folded scroll in his hand — sealed in silver wax.

Elira's stomach dropped.

"It appeared in the center of the rune circle," he said. "We didn't summon it."

Vaelen was already at her side, but Elira reached out and took it before he could object.

The wax melted in her palm.

Inside was one line, scrawled in the King's hand:

You are gathering the forgotten, but I remember every one of them. And I will take them back.

Elira folded the note and tossed it into the fire.

"No," she whispered.

Then louder, to the flames: "They're *mine* now."

Chapter 70:

The camp had settled for the night, but the air was far from still.

The Veil shimmered gently above the treetops, as if breathing. Not cracking this time. Not fighting. Just *changing.*

Elira stood at the edge of camp, her fingers brushing a silver-threaded leaf that hadn't been there the night before. New growth. From nowhere.

The forest was *waking up.*

Footsteps approached quietly behind her — light, uncertain.

"Are you Elira?"

She turned.

The woman who stood there looked young but worn. Her long silver hair was braided back, and her hands trembled at her sides. But it wasn't fear. It was something deeper. Fragile. Hopeful.

"I am," Elira said gently. "And you are?"

The woman's eyes brimmed. "A mistake, or a miracle. I don't know which."

Vaelen appeared at Elira's side instantly, not aggressive — just *present.*

The woman took a slow breath and placed a hand over her belly.

"I'm pregnant."

The words hit like thunder — not loud, but *shattering.*

Elira stepped forward. "I… didn't know that was possible here."

"It wasn't," the woman whispered. "Not like this."

She looked down at her stomach, tears falling freely now.

"My people… we were taught that conception came by assignment. That love was a luxury. That pleasure was a *risk*. But this…"

Her voice cracked.

"This child was born of love. Of *choice*. Not orders. Not surveillance. And no one has ever seen it happen this way."

Solen appeared then, breath catching as he felt the ripple in the air. His voice dropped to a whisper.

"The Veil is breaking."

Elira stepped forward, tears rising in her own throat. "Do you know what this means?"

The woman nodded. "It means the King will hunt me."

"Not if I can help it," Vaelen growled.

Elira stepped close, placing her hand over the woman's. "What's your name?"

"Alari."

Elira nodded. "Alari, I swear to you — you and this child will be protected. No matter what."

Vaelen placed a hand on Elira's shoulder. "And if he tries to take her… he'll have to get through *both* of us."

The emotion-born around them stirred.

The ripple traveled through the roots.

The forest responded.

The Veil *quivered*.

Later that night, Solen pulled Elira aside.

"There's something you should know," he said softly.

She looked at him, tense.

"That child… it's not just life. It's a *manifestation*. An echo of the bond that created it. That child could grow to break the illusion entirely — to undo everything the King has spent lifetimes twisting."

Elira's heart thudded. "You're saying this baby could end him?"

Solen smiled faintly. "Or start the world again."

Chapter 71:

It started with a whisper.

Not from the Veil.

From Solen's runes.

He stood at the edge of camp, fingers hovering over the cracked remnants of a message that had burned itself into the ground — one of the ancient codes only high seers knew.

And when Elira approached, his face was pale.

"We've been played," he said quietly.

Elira stood motionless as Solen spoke.

"The child… wasn't just a sign of the Veil breaking. It was *bait.*"

Her stomach dropped.

"He *let* it happen?" she whispered.

Solen nodded. "The King's magic is still embedded deep in places we've barely uncovered. It's possible he *encouraged* the bond between Alari and her mate… knowing what it would create. Knowing it would draw *you.*"

Vaelen's fists clenched at his sides. "He's using an unborn child to manipulate her."

"To *trap* her," Solen said. "To anchor her in compassion — because he knows that's what makes her powerful. But also… vulnerable."

Elira stared into the trees, her voice low and burning.

"He thinks he can make me choose."

When Elira found Alari by the quiet stream near camp, the woman looked up, already sensing something had changed.

"I feel him," she said. "In the air. In the water. I thought it was fear… but it's something else."

Elira crouched beside her, gently taking her hand.

"It wasn't a mistake," Elira said. "But it wasn't an accident either."

Alari's eyes widened.

"The King… he allowed this. Knowing it would draw attention. Knowing it would pull me in."

Alari swallowed. "So, I'm just another pawn?"

"No," Elira said firmly. "You're *proof* that he's losing."

Later that evening, a figure appeared at the edge of the camp — shrouded, eyes down, silent as the wind.

It was one of the King's messengers.

He held no weapon. Only a scroll.

Vaelen and Solen intercepted him, but he only asked for one thing: to deliver the words aloud.

He unrolled the scroll, voice shaking with forced reverence.

"To the girl who believes she can birth revolution from broken hearts — I offer you one chance. Return to the Hollow. Alone. No armies. No blades. Bring the mother. And I will spare the child."

Elira stood tall as he spoke, her jaw locked.

"Refuse, and the burden of her death — and that of her unborn — will belong to *you*."

The messenger dropped the scroll and vanished in smoke.

Silence crushed the camp.

Vaelen turned to Elira, rage written across his face. "You're not going."

She looked up, eyes glassy. "You know I have to."

"Not alone."

"No," Solen cut in. "This is what he wants. Emotion. Desperation. And now he's making it a *clock*."

Elira stepped away from them both, staring into the night sky.

Her heart ached. Not with fear.

With *fire.*

"I'll go," she said softly. "But I'll bring more than a mother."

Her eyes flared gold.

"I'll bring a reckoning."

Chapter 72:

The camp stirred with tension — not loud, not frantic. Just *tight.*

Every movement was measured.

Every glance lingered too long.

They all knew what was coming.

Elira stood at the map table, her fingers tracing the contour of the Hollow — the place where the King demanded her return. Alone. Unarmed. With Alari at her side.

Solen paced nearby, muttering under his breath as new runes bled across parchment. Vaelen sat on the far edge of the tent, eyes dark, blade across his lap.

"I hate this," he said for the third time.

"I know," Elira whispered.

"I *don't* trust it."

"You're not supposed to."

Alari entered then — shoulders squared, one hand protectively over her belly. She looked stronger today. Not fearless. But *braver.*

"I'll go with you," she said simply.

Elira turned to her. "You don't have to."

"I know," she replied. "But I'm not the same woman I was when I found you. You showed me that this child isn't just a trap… it's a sign."

Elira's throat tightened. "We'll protect it."

"Not just with swords," Alari said, her voice quiet but fierce. "With *truth.*"

The plan was simple on paper.

But heavy in reality.

Elira would go to the Hollow.

Alari at her side.

No army. No overt defense.

But Solen would plant a veil of protective runes that would activate at Elira's signal — giving her a narrow window to escape or strike.

Vaelen, however, refused to stay behind.

"I'll be close," he said. "Not visible. But near enough to kill anything that touches you."

Elira didn't argue.

Because in truth — she needed him there.

That night, as the camp settled, Elira and Vaelen lay awake under the stars. No words for a long time. Just heartbeats.

Then finally:

"I'm not afraid to face him," she whispered.

Vaelen turned to her. "I know."

"I'm afraid of what I'll feel. Of what he'll *twist*."

Vaelen leaned in, his lips brushing her temple. "He can't twist what you've already claimed."

She looked at him, searching his eyes. "You think I can win this?"

"I think you already are."

Just before dawn, Elira and Alari stepped beyond the edge of the trees, cloaked in shadow, magic threaded beneath their feet. The Hollow loomed ahead — dark, vast, cold.

And waiting.

Elira paused at the threshold, her fingers tightening around the charm Solen had given her.

Vaelen's voice whispered behind her from the trees:

"I'll be watching."

And Elira stepped forward.

Straight into the King's trap.

Not to surrender.

To *shatter* it.

Chapter 73:

The Hollow was colder than Elira remembered.

The stillness was unnatural — like the air itself was holding its breath.

She walked forward, Alari just behind her, steps cautious, her hand occasionally brushing over her belly. They were alone. Visibly.

But Elira could feel them — the Veil-born waiting just beyond the trees. Vaelen's presence like a steady hum in her bones. Solen's magic coiled like a spring in the earth beneath her feet.

Still… the tension made her skin crawl.

And then—

They came.

The King's guard moved like shadows — silent and quick. Too many for a message. Too many for a meeting.

Elira turned, just in time to see them surround Alari.

"No!" she shouted, rushing toward her.

But steel came between them.

One of the guards raised a blade, holding it near Alari's neck. She didn't scream — but her eyes found Elira's, wide with fear.

A voice echoed through the Hollow, calm and cruel.

"You gave me your heart, girl. You just didn't realize I'd use it to *end you.*"

The King stepped from the fog, cloaked in black, eyes lit with twisted power.

"You'll watch this hope die," he said. "And then you'll follow it."

Elira's hands shook as she reached for the rune charm at her side.

Not yet.

Not yet.

Then the blade shifted—pressing closer to Alari's throat.

And Elira whispered the signal: *"Now."*

The world *erupted.*

Solen's runes detonated in a flash of silver fire, blinding the guards and sending shockwaves through the stone.

From the trees, emotion-born poured in — fury and grief and *love* made manifest.

Vaelen was a blur of shadow and steel, moving through the chaos with a singular purpose.

"*Elira!*" he roared, cutting down a guard and lunging for Alari.

Solen stepped into the center of the storm, his body glowing with dangerous, ancient light.

"*Look at me!*" he shouted, drawing the guard's attention — his entire form flaring like a beacon.

And in that blinding moment, Vaelen *took her* — Alari into his arms, his body protecting hers as he vanished into the cover of trees.

Elira turned to find Solen—

Just in time to see a blade pierce his side.

"No!" she screamed.

He staggered, falling to one knee, blood blooming across his robes.

But he smiled through it. "Get her *out.*"

Elira turned as Vaelen returned — breathless, furious, *safe.*

"She's hidden. Protected."

He drew his blade, stepping beside Elira.

"Now," he growled, "let's finish this."

The King watched from a distance, his gaze sweeping across the resistance — the emotion-born, the fire, the fury rising around him.

His eyes locked with Elira's.

And he smiled.

"I'll be back."

Then he vanished — not defeated.

But *rattled*.

Elira dropped to Solen's side, helping him lie back gently. He winced but grinned.

"Still here."

"You shouldn't have—"

"I *had* to," he said. "Because you… you're the real distraction."

Chapter 74:

The camp was quiet.

Not from peace.

But from exhaustion.

Smoke curled from the edges of burned cloth. Healing salves scented the air. The ground was still warm from the runes that had flared in defense.

Elira moved among her people — no longer just the girl who resisted.

Now, she was the one they *watched.* The one they *waited for.*

The one who *lived,* when so many would've broken.

Solen lay beneath a tree wrapped in linen, his breathing slow but steady. Elira knelt beside him, pressing a warm cloth to his brow.

"I told you not to draw that much power," she said softly.

"You also told me to survive," he rasped. "So… I did."

She laughed — barely — and squeezed his hand. "Thank you."

His smile was faint but knowing. "You're not just fighting anymore, Elira. You're *leading.*"

Later, Elira found Vaelen near the fire, sharpening his blade — more out of habit than need. His eyes tracked her as she approached, and something in them softened immediately.

"She's safe," he said before she could ask. "Alari and the baby. They're under protection now. Deep in the grove."

Elira nodded, relief washing through her in a visible shiver.

Vaelen stood, stepping closer. "You did what he never expected."

"Took a stand?"

He shook his head. "Chose *hope*. Over rage. Over fear. That's what makes you dangerous to him."

She leaned against his chest, and he wrapped her in his arms.

"He wanted to scare me into silence," she whispered.

"You roared instead."

That night, as the moon rose and the Veil shimmered above them in hues of green and violet, the emotion-born gathered.

Not in chaos.

In unity.

A new flame had caught.

And it wore Elira's name.

Solen, weak but lucid, sat beside the fire with a journal in his lap, scribbling slowly with shaking hands.

When Elira asked what he was doing, he said:

"Writing it down. The moment the Veil cracked wider. When they couldn't deny it anymore."

He looked up at her.

"When they realized *you* were the beginning of the end."

Chapter 75:

Solen's hand trembled as he turned the page.

The journal in his lap was older than any Elira had ever seen — its cover cracked, its runes faded with time and memory.

Vaelen hovered nearby, arms crossed, gaze sharp. Every time Solen paused to cough or grimace in pain, he clenched his fists.

But the moment Solen's eyes widened, Elira felt it — the shift.

He looked up slowly. "I remember something."

They gathered in the tent, low candlelight casting flickering shadows on the walls. Solen laid the journal between them, open to a page with runes so worn they were barely visible.

"I read this once, a long time ago. Before I ever met you," he said. "It spoke of a realm beyond even the Veil. A hidden space sealed off when the illusion was first formed. When the King rose."

Elira leaned in. "Why?"

"Because it held something dangerous," Solen said. "A memory too pure to be controlled. A source of emotion untouched by the King's design."

Vaelen's jaw tightened. "A weapon?"

Solen hesitated. "Maybe. Or maybe just the *truth* the King couldn't bury."

He turned the page, revealing a symbol scrawled in gold ink — a spiral within a flame, circled by stars.

"It's called *The Vault of Origins.*" Solen's voice was barely a whisper now. "A place where the first emotions were captured. Recorded. Preserved."

Elira stared. "And it still exists?"

"It has to," he said. "The Veil's cracking fast enough now. If we find it, you might be able to unlock what the King sealed away."

"Then let's go," she said immediately.

Vaelen's hand touched her arm. "It won't be that easy."

Solen nodded. "It's buried in the Forgotten Wastes. A realm corrupted by silence. Nothing grows there. Nothing speaks."

"Then I'll bring the noise," Elira said, fire catching in her voice.

Vaelen smirked. "That's my girl."

Solen added gently, "If the Vault is real, it will test you. It wasn't made for mortals to access. Only those *fully awakened* could enter."

Elira didn't flinch. "Then I'll awaken."

Later that night, as the camp slept and the fire crackled low, Elira stood with her hand over the runed journal. She could feel it — something deep in her blood responding.

Memories.

Emotions that weren't just hers.

Truths trying to return.

She turned her head as Vaelen approached, wrapping his arms around her waist.

"You really believe it's out there?" he murmured.

"I think it's waiting for someone to be *ready.*"

His mouth brushed her ear. "Then we better get ready."

Chapter 76:

They left just before sunrise.

The light filtered through the trees like silk, soft and hesitant — as if even the sky was unsure about where they were going.

The Forgotten Wastes were not a place marked on any map. Even Solen's journals had little more than sketches and fractured memories. But the pull was real.

The moment Elira stepped beyond the grove's edge, something shifted.

The wind stopped.

The color bled from the trees.

Even the runes on her skin dimmed — not from fear, but reverence.

They had arrived at the boundary of silence.

Vaelen walked just behind her, quiet, watchful.

Solen moved slower, still weak but insistent on being with them. "This place…" he murmured, "it's where the King buried more than history. He buried *emotion* itself."

Elira nodded, eyes forward. "Then we'll dig it up."

The landscape changed quickly.

Trees faded to stone. The ground cracked and pale, littered with half-buried relics — fragments of runes, broken charms, the remains of old wards long since erased.

There were no sounds. No birds. No wind. Even footsteps were muffled.

The silence wasn't just absence.

It was *forced.*

Vaelen reached out and squeezed Elira's hand.

"I don't like this," he said under his breath.

"I don't either," she replied.

But still — they pressed on.

By midday, they reached a ridge that dropped off into what looked like a sea of ash.

Beneath it, half-sunken, stood a structure — more temple than ruin. Its spires curved toward the sky, carved from black stone veined with gold.

The air vibrated faintly.

The Vault.

Elira's knees buckled for a second. Not from pain.

From *recognition.*

This place *knew* her.

Solen whispered, "Only those awakened in truth can open it."

Elira stepped forward.

And the world responded.

The gold-veined stone shimmered.

A pulse of energy rippled outward — not loud, but deep. Elira's runes flared white-hot, matching the heartbeat she didn't know was hers… or someone else's.

The door opened.

Not outward.

Inward.

Inside, the Vault wasn't dark. It was *alive* with light — threads of memory suspended in the air, voices like echoes caught in crystal. Emotion hummed through the space — raw, untamed, pure.

Elira walked slowly among the threads. Each one called to something different in her — grief, joy, rage, longing.

And then — she touched one.

And her vision shattered.

A woman stood before her.

Golden-eyed. Fierce. Familiar.

She wore armor etched with runes Elira didn't recognize, but her face…

It looked like *hers*.

"You are the piece I left behind," the vision whispered. "The one he could never erase. You are *remembrance*. You are *rebirth*. And the final thread is already in motion."

Elira reached for her — but the vision dissolved.

And suddenly, she *remembered something* she was never meant to know.

Chapter 77:

The Vault pulsed with memory.

Each glowing strand floated like silk suspended in water, gently drifting, waiting to be claimed.

Elira stood in the center of the chamber, breath shallow, eyes locked on the one thread that shimmered differently from the rest — not silver, not gold.

Lirian blue.

Her fingers hovered just above it, trembling.

She didn't know how she knew — but she *knew.*

This one was *hers.*

No… not just hers.

Her mother's.

When her skin touched the thread, the room fell away.

She stood on a high cliff, wind racing through her hair. Below, a sea of silver mist. And beside her—

A woman with fire in her eyes.

Armor carved from moonstone. Tattoos lining her arms — the same swirling patterns that danced over Elira's skin now, only older. Deeper.

And the resemblance was unmistakable.

"Hello, daughter," the woman said.

Elira's knees buckled. "Mother…?"

"I am Ilyana," she said. "And you are my second chance."

Images flooded her — not in sequence, but emotion.

Ilyana walking the halls of the King's palace, cloaked in charm and seduction, her eyes sharp behind every smile.

The Lirians whispering, trusting her to be the inside blade — to gather what no scout could.

The moment the King *fell for her.*

The moment he discovered the truth.

The moment he took *Elira* as punishment.

Ilyana screaming as guards dragged her away.

The betrayal. The exile. The silence.

And still — the mission burned in her.

"You were never supposed to be part of the plan," Ilyana's voice said. "But you became the entire purpose."

Elira couldn't breathe. "You tried to end it before."

"I tried to *understand* it," Ilyana said. "To find the root. But once you were taken… I had no choice but to vanish. To hide. And wait."

The wind shifted.

"But you've done what I couldn't. You've cracked it."

"And now… you must finish it."

The vision shimmered.

Elira reached out, desperate to stay.

"Where are you now?"

"I am where he cannot reach me. But not forever."

Tears spilled from Elira's eyes. "I need you."

"I'm in you," Ilyana whispered. "In every breath. Every emotion. You are stronger than I ever was. And soon… we will finish this *together.*"

The Vault dissolved around her, and she collapsed to her knees.

Vaelen was there in a breath, arms catching her, grounding her.

"Elira—what happened? Are you—?"

She clutched his tunic, gasping. "It was her. My mother. She's alive."

Solen stared, eyes wide.

"She's the key," Elira whispered. "She always was. And I'm following her path."

Vaelen's voice was steady but shaken. "Then we find her."

Elira looked up at the ceiling of the Vault.

"I think… she wants to be found."

Chapter 78:

The Vault's doors closed behind them without a sound.

But the silence that followed didn't feel like loss.

It felt like a *promise.*

Elira stood outside the ancient structure, her skin still glowing faintly with residual energy. Her heart was thundering in her chest — not from fear, but from something deeper.

Knowing.

She turned to Vaelen and Solen, both waiting.

"She's alive," Elira said, voice steady. "My mother. Ilyana."

Solen's breath caught. "That name hasn't been spoken in generations."

"I saw her. In the vision. She was beautiful. Strong. She's in hiding — but not gone. And she wants to be found."

They camped on the edge of the Wastes that night. No fire. Just stars.

Elira sat wrapped in a blanket of quiet and thought.

"She's the reason this started," she murmured to Vaelen beside her. "She tried to bring it all down. Seduced the King, gathered information from the inside. And when he found out… he took me. Used me to silence her. To punish her."

Vaelen's hand brushed hers. "And yet… here you are."

She looked over at him, eyes bright with unshed tears. "I'm finishing what she began."

"No," he said gently. "You're *becoming* what she hoped for."

Solen joined them just before dawn, scrolls in hand, face tight with thought.

"There's a place," he said. "A sanctuary, lost after the exile. Lirians who refused to bend or break. Ilyana may have gone there."

Elira straightened. "Where?"

"A pocket realm — veiled from the Veil itself. Emotion-born weren't just exiled, some vanished into the seams of the world. If she went anywhere, it would be there."

Vaelen nodded. "Then that's where we go."

As they packed, the winds shifted. The Veil shimmered above them — brighter. Cracked. But glowing.

Solen watched the sky with wonder. "She's stirring more than magic. She's stirring *memory*."

Elira glanced back toward the Vault.

Toward where her mother's presence still lingered like the echo of a heartbeat.

Then turned to the path ahead.

"Mother," she whispered, "I'm coming."

Chapter 79:

The path to the sanctuary was not marked by roads.

It was felt.

Pulled from a place deeper than memory — a tug in the chest, a pressure behind the ribs. The more Elira focused, the more the world around her seemed to blur.

The Veil didn't part for her.

It *opened.*

Like it had been waiting.

They arrived in silence.

A hidden clearing, encased by a barrier of starlight and runes far older than Solen could name. The moment Elira stepped through it, her runes flared so brightly it brought Vaelen to a full stop beside her.

"Elira," he said, voice reverent. "You're glowing."

"It knows me," she whispered.

They knew her.

Because they had been waiting.

Figures emerged from the trees — cautious, cloaked, magic humming at their fingertips.

Not soldiers.

Guardians.

A woman stepped forward — long white braids, skin like carved obsidian, silver dust in her lashes.

"You carry her blood," the woman said.

Solen raised a brow. "She knows who Elira is?"

The woman didn't answer.

Instead, she turned and gestured. "Come. Your mother waits."

They followed in silence, deeper into the sanctuary. The realm pulsed with gentle emotion — not chaos, not rage. Just presence. And power.

Then — a doorway carved into stone; vines laced through the frame.

The woman paused at the entrance. "Before you enter… there's something you should know."

Elira turned, breath catching.

The woman met her gaze with sympathy.

"You weren't the only one she left behind."

Inside, the chamber was glowing — a soft blue light rising from crystal sconces along the walls. And in the center…

A woman with silver hair stood tall, runes across her back, emotion flickering like wildfire in her eyes.

Elira's breath left her body.

"Mother…"

Ilyana turned slowly, and the moment their eyes met, the room felt too small to contain the weight of it.

"You found me," Ilyana whispered.

Elira nodded, voice cracking. "I remembered."

But just before Ilyana reached her — two shadows stepped into view from behind her.

One with fiery red curls.

The other with piercing storm-gray eyes not unlike Vaelen's.

Twins.

Emotion-born.

Old enough to stand with power of their own.

Ilyana said quietly, "And now you'll remember what else I couldn't tell you."

Elira blinked.

"Wait—"

The red-haired one stepped forward with a small, warm smile.

"I'm Auren."

The other gave a short nod. "And I'm Kael."

Elira could barely breathe. "You're—?"

"Your siblings," Ilyana said softly.

"Born of hope. Hidden by sacrifice."

Chapter 80:

The room pulsed with quiet power.

Not from danger.

From *recognition.*

Elira stood frozen; eyes locked on her siblings. Auren — soft fire in her smile, warmth radiating from every movement. Kael — storm-eyed, quiet, intense. Like Vaelen, if he had been born on the other side of the Veil.

And Ilyana, standing between them, not as a weapon.

As a *mother.*

"You hid them," Elira whispered, still trying to breathe.

"I had to," Ilyana said. "After the King took you, I realized how deep his reach had become. If he knew I carried more children — *emotion-born* children — he would've hunted them. And used them like he used you."

Vaelen stepped forward slowly. "He doesn't know?"

"Not a whisper," Ilyana said. "They've been protected since birth — cloaked in runes passed down from the first Lirians. Only now, as the Veil cracks… are those runes beginning to lift."

Solen stared in awe. "Which means their magic is *waking.*"

Elira looked back to her siblings, eyes wide. "Do you… remember me?"

Kael shrugged. "We were told stories."

Auren smiled. "But we didn't believe them. Not really. Until you stepped into this realm."

Kael stepped closer. "You lit everything up the moment you arrived. It was like we'd always been waiting for you."

They trained for hours that night — not with swords, but with *soulwork.*

Emotions twisted through their hands like light made real.

Elira's fire — sudden and wild.

Auren's healing — laced with warmth and a powerful, protective surge.

Kael's control — a quiet force of suppression and amplification, able to bend magic around others like a shield or blade.

And Ilyana — graceful and devastating. Her power was like a chorus of emotion, blending and magnifying whatever surrounded her.

They weren't just powerful.

They were *balanced.*

Solen watched in disbelief.

"It's like… they fill the space around each other. Where Elira's control falters, Kael centers her. Where Kael's focus breaks, Auren softens it. And Ilyana ties it together with precision I've never seen."

Vaelen crossed his arms. "The King has no idea what's coming."

Solen nodded. "He thinks he's breaking one thread. He doesn't know he's about to face a *weave.*"

Later that evening, Elira sat beside Ilyana on a small ledge overlooking the glowing forest. Below, Auren and Kael sparred — light against shadow.

"You built something incredible here," Elira said.

Ilyana nodded. "I built it hoping one day… it would meet *you.*"

Elira leaned her head against her mother's shoulder, voice soft.

"I still don't know if I'm strong enough."

"You don't have to be everything," Ilyana said. "You just have to be *you.* That's all the Veil needed."

Elira turned her face to the sky.

For the first time in her life, she felt *whole.*

Chapter 81:

Far beyond the sanctuary, in the shadowed depths of the King's palace, something *shifted.*

Not in the stone.

Not in the air.

In the *magic.*

The runes etched into the palace walls flickered — erratic. For the first time in decades.

A pulse that didn't come from him.

The King stood still in the center of his chamber, his fingers curling around the edges of his throne.

"She's found something," he said aloud to no one.

The shadows around him stirred uneasily.

"No… not something."

His eyes flared with unnatural silver.

"*Someone.*"

Back in the sanctuary, Elira breathed in the stillness of evening.

The trees whispered above, laced with threads of glowing moss that shimmered with power. Auren and Kael sparred nearby, laughing between spells. For the first time, Elira felt like she wasn't just preparing for a battle — she was *living.*

She smiled and leaned back on the hill, her head resting against Vaelen's shoulder.

And then Ilyana approached.

Her voice was soft, full of grace. "Mind if I borrow you both for a moment?"

They joined her near the edge of the overlook. Ilyana folded her hands, her gaze flicking between them.

"I haven't said thank you," she told Vaelen, "for how you've… protected her. Loved her."

Vaelen bowed his head. "I don't do it for thanks."

"I know," Ilyana said, smiling faintly. "But you deserve it anyway."

She turned to Elira. "I see how you soften around him. That's not weakness, Elira. That's *growth.*"

Elira blinked back sudden emotion. "You really think so?"

Ilyana touched her cheek. "I do. I think your magic has changed more than just the Veil. It's changed *him,* too."

Vaelen smiled at Elira, and she stepped away — called over by Auren, laughing and waving her over.

As Elira left them, Ilyana turned to Vaelen.

"I know that look," she said.

He looked startled. "What look?"

"The one that says you've already made a vow… even if you haven't spoken it."

He hesitated. Then, voice low, "I want to marry her. Once this is over. I want… everything. A life. Peace. With her."

Ilyana said nothing for a long moment.

Then: "Don't wait."

Vaelen's brows lifted.

"You think you need to survive the war to make it matter. But love is power, Vaelen. Not a reward. A *force.* Your bond — sealed fully — could be another crack in the Veil. Another fire the King can't extinguish."

Vaelen swallowed hard.

"I'm not saying rush her," Ilyana said. "I'm saying… don't hold back if she's ready."

She placed a hand over his heart. "You're already hers. And she's already yours. Make it *known*."

⁂

That night, Vaelen sat alone, the stars above echoing Ilyana's words.

Don't wait.

The idea took root.

And in the distance, a soft breeze whispered across the trees — carrying the faintest tremor through the Veil.

The King flinched as it brushed against him.

And he *knew*.

He hadn't just lost Elira.

He'd lost *her heart*.

Chapter 82:

Elira sat beside Ilyana under the silver-glow tree, the light pooling like moon water around their feet.

The forest around them was hushed, the air thick with a tension that didn't feel like danger — it felt like history waiting to be *spoken.*

Ilyana stared ahead for a long time, as if the words needed permission to rise.

Then:

"You know he wasn't always a King."

Elira turned. "What do you mean?"

"He was one of us. A Lirian. Once."

The silence cracked like glass.

Ilyana's voice was slow, deliberate — peeling open old wounds, old truths.

"He was called Dareth. He wasn't born cruel. He was born *frightened.* Overwhelmed by the depth of what we felt, what we could do. Where most of us found freedom in emotion, he saw only chaos."

Elira sat still, listening, heart thudding.

"He was powerful. Immensely. But he was terrified of what our kind could become. He believed emotion would destroy us — make us volatile. Unruly. Dangerous."

"So, he created the illusion," Elira whispered.

"No. *He became it.*" Ilyana's voice dropped lower. "He stole knowledge from the Vaults, twisted the runes, silenced the oldest magic. And when he couldn't suppress us entirely, he fabricated a new truth. A new world. One without connection."

Elira's stomach turned. "But why?"

"Because love made him *feel.* And what he felt, he couldn't control. He thought erasing feeling would give him order."

Ilyana turned her eyes on Elira — soft and ancient.

"And then he met me."

Elira's breath caught.

"I was assigned to him by the resistance," Ilyana said. "To get close. To infiltrate. But it… wasn't all an act. I saw the broken thing inside him. I pitied it. I tried to offer him something real — not as a weapon. As a *warning.*"

"And what happened?"

"He called it betrayal," she said. "Because it meant I loved something *other than him.* And then he took you."

Elira's hands curled in her lap.

"I tried to come for you," Ilyana whispered. "But by then, the illusion was sealed. I couldn't reach you… until the day you cracked it yourself."

Elira's voice trembled. "So, everything I've done… has already been tried."

"No," Ilyana said, "everything you've done has *gone farther.* You aren't just part of a legacy. You *are* the continuation of what love refused to let die."

At that moment, the forest shimmered — a flicker in the distance. Elira turned her head and caught a shadow, just at the edge of vision.

Kael approached from the trees. "We have something."

Vaelen followed, holding a piece of broken rune crystal.

"It's reacting to you," he told Elira. "We think it's tied to the *origin* of the illusion. Maybe even to *him.*"

Solen came up beside them, eyes wide. "If it's what I think it is… it could lead us to the core of his magic. The *source.*"

Ilyana stood, the wind wrapping around her like silk.

"Then it's time," she said. "To unmake what he made."

Elira met her mother's gaze, heart full, power burning beneath her skin.

"We end this," she said. "Together."

Chapter 83:

The rune fragment pulsed in Vaelen's hand like a heartbeat.

It hadn't stopped since Elira touched it.

Solen had spent hours decoding its threads, tracing the ancient glyphs carved into its center. Now, the group gathered in the center of the sanctuary, torches flickering low, magic coiling in the air like fog.

"This is from one of the original Sealing Stones," Solen said, eyes glinting. "The King built his illusion on seven. We've never found one still intact. But this—"

He held up the piece.

"This still remembers what it was."

Elira stepped closer, her fingers hovering above the rune. "What can we do with it?"

"It's a tether," Ilyana said quietly. "A thread that can lead us to the foundation — the core of the illusion. He didn't scatter the power across the realms. He buried it. One place. One ruin. Deep. Forgotten."

Kael tilted his head. "And if we go there?"

"We weaken him," Solen answered. "Not destroy — but disturb. Shake his magic. Fracture the silence."

"Get close enough," Ilyana added, "and Elira might even hear the original spell."

Vaelen stiffened. "You mean… rewrite it?"

Ilyana nodded. "Or unwrite it."

They set out the next morning — Elira, Vaelen, Solen, Ilyana, and the twins. The sanctuary faded behind them as mist swallowed the trees. The forest changed fast — trees curling inward, light dimming unnaturally.

They were entering the *Graywood.*

Where emotion couldn't root.

Where the Veil pulsed strongest.

Elira felt it first.

Not fear.

Suppression.

Her thoughts slowed. Her chest tightened. It felt like forgetting herself.

Vaelen was immediately at her side. "Elira."

"I'm fine," she whispered. "It's just… cold."

Auren reached out, touching her shoulder. Warmth pulsed through her.

Kael muttered, "It's feeding on connection. Trying to *mute* us."

Solen's runes flared. "Then we keep talking. Feeling. Holding each other in the sound of our voices."

Hours passed like days.

They reached the heart of the Graywood by dusk — a basin of cracked stone and silent trees. The rune fragment pulsed violently now, drawn to a ring of stone set deep into the earth.

A Sealing Site.

The glyphs were familiar — twisted versions of the ones Elira had seen in the Vault. But older. Angrier.

She stepped closer and the ground trembled.

And then… a *voice.*

"You're not supposed to be here."

Everyone froze.

The voice wasn't from above.

It came from the *stone.*

Elira reached down, brushing her hand across it.

A flicker of memory flashed through her mind — the King, younger, on his knees before a circle of Lirians. Runes branding his arms. His face contorted with grief and fear.

"Bind me if you must. But take away the *feeling.*"

She gasped.

He didn't just create the illusion.

He *begged* for it.

Her knees buckled and Ilyana caught her.

"He *wanted* to forget," Elira whispered. "He asked them to seal it all away."

Solen's voice was barely audible. "He was the first to be broken by emotion."

"And now he's trying to break *everyone* else."

The ground cracked beneath them — runes igniting in a spiral.

The King had felt her.

And he was coming.

Not in person.

In *force.*

Ilyana pulled Elira back. "This is only the edge. If we go deeper, we'll find the original site."

Vaelen was already drawing his blade. "Then we need to move. *Now.*"

Chapter 84:

The trees thinned as they descended into the hollow.

The rune shard in Elira's pack vibrated harder with every step, humming like it was alive — or afraid. The ground darkened, veins of silver and violet pulsing just beneath the surface.

No birds. No wind. Just the breath of magic wrapped too tight around itself.

Vaelen stayed at Elira's side, hand on the hilt of his blade. Auren whispered a small warmth spell at their backs, while Kael kept a perimeter of shielding pulsing around the group.

Then Ilyana stopped.

"This is it."

The chamber was carved into stone, half-sunken beneath the roots of an ancient, hollowed tree. The air inside didn't just feel stale — it felt *forgotten.*

In the center, a pillar of obsidian jutted from the ground, wrapped in threads of gold and crystalized ash. It was cracked, but still pulsing.

And in its center — a mark.

The same one Elira bore on her spine.

Solen sucked in a breath. "It's attuned to your bloodline."

Ilyana nodded slowly. "This was sealed with my hand. And now, it's calling for *yours.*"

Elira approached.

The air buzzed.

Vaelen reached for her arm. "Are you sure?"

"No," she whispered. "But it's time."

She placed her hand over the mark.

And the world *split.*

Not with sound.

With *memory.*

Elira's body jerked as visions crashed through her — not hers. Not even Ilyana's.

The King's.

A boy kneeling in the rain, screaming as emotion ripped through him — love, rage, loss — until he begged the elders to *take it away.*

A spell born not of power, but *grief.*

Runes carved into his skin as he wept — not because he wanted power.

Because he wanted to *feel nothing.*

Elira ripped her hand away, stumbling back.

Tears streamed down her cheeks. Not because of sympathy — but because of *recognition.*

"He *made* the illusion to protect himself," she gasped. "He was scared of what he felt. Of what we *all* feel."

Solen nodded slowly. "Then the first Seal wasn't a command."

Kael's eyes widened. "It was a *plea.*"

The pillar cracked deeper, light spilling from the inside.

Power rushed out — not in chaos, but in *clarity.*

Elira's runes lit up like a star map.

Auren cried out as her hands glowed with healing magic.

Kael sank to one knee, shielding flaring into new shapes.

And Ilyana… *smiled.*

"Do you feel that?" she said.

Vaelen gripped Elira's hand. "That wasn't just memory."

"No," Elira whispered.

"That was a *release*."

Above them, the Veil rippled.

Far away, in the King's palace, every crystal cracked at once.

And his scream echoed through both realms.

Chapter 85:

The sky broke.

It wasn't thunder.

It wasn't storm.

It was *war.*

By the time the group returned to the edge of the Graywood, the air was thick with smoke — *not theirs.* Not natural.

The King's scent was on it.

A foul twist of shadow and rot. A warning.

Solen staggered to a stop, eyes wide. "He didn't just feel the Seal break."

"He *watched* it happen," Ilyana said, her tone cold.

Elira's runes pulsed harder, lighting the way back toward the sanctuary.

They weren't going to make it back before he struck.

They crested the ridge.

And there they were.

Shadows across the trees.

Figures in black armor, faces hidden beneath mirrored masks. Veilguard — soldiers sculpted from broken emotion. Not dead. Not alive. Puppets — empty vessels the King had molded with one purpose.

To *silence.*

Elira's breath caught.

Vaelen drew his blade.

Kael whispered, "He's not testing us anymore."

"He's *purging.*" Auren's voice trembled.

Elira stepped forward.

And screamed.

Not in fear.

In *magic.*

Light exploded from her chest, catching the first wave of Veilguard mid-step. The ground cracked, vines erupting from the soil — emotion-born defenses rising with her.

The army crashed toward them.

Solen raised both hands, runes tearing into the air.

Auren touched the earth, healing pulses spreading like wildfire.

Kael stepped in front of Elira, shielding flaring.

And Vaelen—

Vaelen *moved.*

Not as a warrior.

As her *shadow.*

Everywhere she faltered, he struck. Every moment her magic surged, he followed — fierce, loyal, *furious.*

They were a storm.

And the King *felt it.*

At the center of the battle, Elira reached for more — the memory of the Seal, of the boy who begged to forget.

"I'm not him," she said aloud. "I *remember.* And I choose to *feel.*"

Power shot from her core.

And the first rank of Veilguard *crumbled.*

But they kept coming.

More than they'd ever faced.

And then—

A flare.

A distant cry.

From the ridge behind.

Reinforcements.

The emotion-born army had *heard* her.

Sparks and fire and lightning crashed down as allies stormed into the clearing.

And at their front—

Alari.

Alive. Fierce. No longer afraid.

By the end, the forest was scorched, the Veil flickering wildly above. The King hadn't come himself.

But his *voice* did.

From a nearby tree, burning with unnatural light.

"You've pushed too far."

Elira stepped forward, runes blazing.

"You should've buried us deeper."

A beat of silence.

Then:

"You've only woken the worst of me."

And then the tree split in two — a final echo.

A final *threat.*

They won that battle.

But no one mistook it for a *victory*.

They knew what was coming next.

The King himself.

Chapter 86:

The battle had passed, but its echoes still lingered in the trees.

The sanctuary was quiet again. Not silent — just *breathing.* Like the land itself was recovering alongside them.

Elira sat near the riverbank, hands clasped around a warm cup, watching the water curl past the stones. She was exhausted, body still humming with the magic she'd unleashed. Her muscles ached, her bones felt hollow.

But her heart?

Full.

Vaelen approached quietly, the way he always did when his emotions were too big for his usual stride. He dropped beside her, close but not quite touching.

"I saw your siblings earlier," he said, voice low. "They were training. Kael nearly leveled the sparring ring."

Elira smiled, faintly. "He's like you. Focused. Calm on the outside. Chaotic in a fight."

Vaelen chuckled once. "I like him."

Then a beat.

"I like all of them. And your mother..."

He paused.

"She's the strongest person I've ever met — besides you."

They sat in silence for a while, watching the ripples.

Then Elira turned to him, voice soft. "Do you miss yours?"

It took him a moment to answer. "Every day."

She looked over.

Vaelen's eyes were trained on the water now. "They lived in one of the mountain provinces. Quiet people. Not fighters. I left them when the Veil began to twist everything. To fight. I thought I'd be gone a year. Maybe two."

His jaw tightened. "It's been a decade."

Elira reached for his hand, fingers curling around his.

"You think they're still out there?"

"I don't know," he whispered. "But I still see my mother's face every time I put myself between you and a blade."

Elira blinked back a sudden sting of tears.

Vaelen turned to her fully, eyes locked to hers.

"I'm not saying this because I think the war will take me," he said. "I'm saying it because I've *already decided.*"

She tilted her head slightly.

"I want to marry you, Elira."

The words hit her like a second heartbeat.

"Not later. Not when it's over. *Soon.* I want to stand beside you not just as a warrior, or a shadow — but as yours. In name. In vow. In front of every Lirian and emotion-born who ever thought love wasn't worth it."

Elira swallowed; her throat suddenly tight. "Vaelen…"

He brushed her cheek.

"I don't want to wait for peace to live."

She leaned into him, lips brushing his, heart racing. Not from heat.

From *hope.*

He held her there, forehead pressed to hers.

"I love you," he said.

And this time, she didn't flinch.

"I love you too."

She didn't say *yes* yet.
But the promise was already forming in her bones.
In the way her fingers curled into his shirt.
In the way her lips found his again, softer this time.
In the way her whole body leaned toward him.
Because something else had cracked wide open.
Her future.
And she saw him in it.

Chapter 87:

The sanctuary had grown quiet again — but not like before.

Now, it was the kind of silence that held *weight.*

Elira moved through the grove, her fingertips brushing rune-lit trees, eyes catching every wary glance, every half-whispered word between her people.

The fear wasn't loud.

It was *creeping.*

And it had a name.

The King knows where we are.

Kael sat with Solen, studying damage to the wards. "He didn't strike to win," he muttered. "He struck to shake us. And it's working."

"He got into the minds of a few emotion-born," Auren added quietly. "They're questioning things. Their loyalty. Their *feelings.*"

Elira overheard this from the edge of camp.

It sent a chill up her spine.

This wasn't physical warfare anymore.

It was emotional sabotage.

That night, she found Ilyana alone, arms crossed, eyes on the stars.

"Did you feel it?" Elira asked.

"I felt *him,*" Ilyana answered. "He's not throwing fire anymore. He's whispering poison."

She turned to Elira, voice low. "That's how he breaks people. Not by force — by doubt. By making them wonder if the pain they carry… is their fault."

Elira clenched her fists. "He's trying to turn my gift into a weakness."

"No," Ilyana said. "He's trying to *convince you* it's a weakness. Don't let him."

Later, Elira curled up near the fire, and Vaelen settled in beside her.

He didn't speak at first. Just held her.

Then:

"I heard what Auren said."

Elira nodded. "I think he's slipping into the minds of those most vulnerable. The ones who don't know what to believe in yet."

"And that's why you *have* to keep believing," Vaelen said. "Even when they can't. Even when *I* can't. You have to be our center, Elira."

She turned to him, surprised.

"You really think I'm that strong?"

"I think you're stronger than all of us," he said. "Even when you fall apart."

The moment stretched between them, quiet and warm. Elira rested her head against his chest, heart slowing to match his.

And in the glow of the fire, her voice slipped out:

"If we lose… I want you to know I've never felt more alive than I do *right now.*"

Vaelen kissed her temple. "We're not going to lose."

And she believed him — not because of his strength. Because of *his certainty.*

Chapter 88:

It began in sleep.

Not a dream.

A *summons.*

Elira's body stilled beneath the blanket of moss, but her mind was already drifting — not upward, not inward.

Sideways.

Dragged.

The world around her fell into shadows and smoke. Familiar shapes twisted into things she couldn't name. The Veil shimmered above her like oil on water — too still. Too silent.

And then — she saw him.

The King.

Not cloaked in armor or rage.

Alone.

He stood in a wide hall of black stone, his back to her, hands clenched so tightly they trembled. Silver runes crawled up his arms like vines made of light.

He was… *screaming.*

But not with sound.

With *feeling.*

Elira stepped closer — or maybe she was being pulled. Her own magic thrummed against the vision, like it didn't belong here.

And then he turned.

His eyes weren't hollow.

They were *terrified.*

Not of her.

Of what he *couldn't stop.*

"She's remembering," he said, voice low and shaking. "They're *awakening*. I thought the Seal would hold…"

He staggered back, like something inside him had struck him hard.

"It wasn't supposed to last this long."

Elira felt her hands curl into fists.

He didn't know she could see this. He didn't know she'd slipped into *his* unraveling.

And he didn't know what to do.

A shadow passed behind him — massive, grotesque, *older* than him.

Something buried deeper than even the illusion.

It whispered in a voice like cracked stone:

"You promised to keep them silent."

"You failed."

Elira gasped as pain shot through her chest — not hers.

His.

She collapsed to her knees in the vision, clutching her ribs.

The King fell with her — mirror images, both caught in the aftermath of the unraveling.

His eyes met hers.

For a breath, they just stared.

And she saw it.

Not power.

Not dominance.

Guilt.

Then — the world shattered.

She woke screaming.

Vaelen was beside her instantly, grabbing her shoulders, anchoring her.

"Elira!"

She blinked up at him, heart racing, vision spinning.

"I saw him."

Vaelen's face stilled. "The King?"

Elira nodded slowly, breath ragged. "He's *cracking*, Vaelen. Worse than any Veil."

She looked toward the trees.

"He's afraid."

Later that night, Elira told Ilyana and Solen everything — the vision, the shadow, the whispers. Solen sat still for a long time.

"That shadow," he finally said. "It wasn't his magic."

"No," Ilyana agreed. "It was something deeper. Something *older*."

"A force he bound himself to," Solen murmured. "To create the illusion. He didn't just rewrite the world, Elira… he *traded something* for it."

Elira swallowed hard.

"What if breaking the illusion doesn't end everything?" she asked.

"What if it *unleashes* something worse?"

Chapter 89:

The library beneath the sanctuary wasn't made of stone.

It was carved from root and rune.

The walls glowed with soft blue script, pulsing in rhythm with the breath of the land itself. Shelves lined with scrolls, etched crystal slates, fragments of forgotten prophecy. Some of it written in languages Elira didn't recognize.

But when she touched them?

They *responded.*

Her magic made them *wake up.*

Solen held up a fractured slate, brushing dust away to reveal spiraling runes.

"This predates the King," he said, voice hushed. "Ilyana… this is older than any Vault memory. Older than the first Seal."

Ilyana ran her hand across it, eyes narrowing.

"It's the foundation text," she murmured. "The theory of the illusion… before it was ever created."

Auren read softly from a separate scroll:

"When the mind cannot bear the truth of feeling, it makes a cage and calls it mercy."

Kael frowned. "So, it wasn't his idea. Just… his execution."

Elira felt her heart twist. "He just became the *face* of it."

Vaelen lingered nearby, quiet. Watching.

Always watching her.

She felt him even before he stepped close — the way the heat of his body wrapped around her back, just a breath away.

"You okay?" he asked, his voice low enough for only her.

She didn't answer with words.

Just leaned into him.

Let his presence fill the places her fears had crept in.

He brushed a kiss to her temple — subtle, private — but it burned in the best way.

"I've got you," he murmured. "Always."

Ilyana handed Elira a small metal disk etched with interlocking symbols. "This was hidden at the bottom of the archives. It's not just language. It's a lock."

Elira ran her finger along the rim.

The runes flared — not red or blue. But *silver.*

The same shimmer that lived in her collar.

"It's tied to *that,*" she whispered. "To the part of me he could still use."

Kael cursed. "So if we unlock this—"

Solen nodded. "We may unlock *him.*"

The group exchanged tense glances.

"We need more than magic," Ilyana said. "We need *memory.* And you, Elira…"

She placed the disk in Elira's hand.

"…are the last living key."

That night, in the quiet of the sanctuary, Elira sat by the window of the high alcove, the metal disk glowing faintly in her palm.

Vaelen came to her silently, settling beside her.

"You feel it too, don't you?" she whispered. "That we're getting close. Too close."

He took the disk from her hand, set it aside, and pulled her gently into his lap.

"I feel you," he said simply.

Her eyes met his — soft, open, full.

The way his thumb brushed the bare skin just above her hip told her everything.

The fire between them hadn't gone out.

It had only deepened.

Waiting for the right moment to rise again.

Chapter 90:

The silver disk glowed faintly in Elira's hand as the others slept.

It pulsed not like magic…

…but like a *heartbeat.*

A matching rhythm. Not of time.

Of pain.

Elira sat near the center of the sanctuary's great tree, where the roots curled in a quiet spiral, forming a natural alcove lined with moss and memory. Vaelen had offered to stay, but she told him to rest. And yet… she felt his presence just nearby. As if he knew she needed space — but not *distance.*

The runes on her skin began to flicker without her calling them.

The disk pulsed again.

And then — *whispers.*

Not in the air.

In her.

A voice she didn't remember.

"Don't speak. It'll hurt more if you do."

Her body stiffened.

The moss beneath her hands went cold.

She saw flickers.

Not full visions.

Not yet.

Just flashes of a room. A gloved hand on her shoulder. Her own breath, shallow and ragged. The scent of iron and oil. Her fingers pressed into cold stone as someone held her down—

Elira flinched back.

No.

The memory snapped like a branch underfoot.

Her breathing was too fast.

But it had started.

The door had cracked.

And now it was waiting to be opened — fully.

Footsteps padded across the floor.

Vaelen.

He sat beside her without a word, just studying her face.

After a long silence: "You felt something, didn't you?"

She nodded slowly. "Not fully. Just… the edge of it."

He took the disk from her hand and set it aside.

"You don't have to rush this."

"I do," she whispered.

"Why?"

"Because I think… the illusion isn't the only thing that's locked. *I am.*"

She looked up at him, and her voice cracked as the words slipped free.

"What if the rest of my magic is buried under what he — what *they* — did to me? What if… I have to *remember* everything to fully awaken?"

Vaelen's jaw tensed. His hands curled into fists on his knees.

"Elira…"

She reached for his hand. "I don't know what I'll find. What I've blocked out. But if it's the key to breaking this… I have to try."

He looked like he wanted to argue.

But then, he said:

"I'll be there."

Elira blinked. "Even if—"

"*Especially* if."

He pulled her into his arms, holding her tightly against his chest.

"You don't go into that memory alone."

The disk pulsed once on the ground beside them.

Not just a lock anymore.

A *summon.*

And Elira was about to answer it.

Chapter 91:

They returned to the sanctuary's root-chamber before sunrise.

The others were still asleep.

Only the soft sound of the wind through the trees and the low flicker of the ward light kept them company.

Elira stood in the center; the silver disk clutched to her chest. Her hands were shaking. Not from fear — but from *knowing*.

This wasn't just about power.

This was *surgery*.

Spiritual. Emotional. Real.

Vaelen didn't speak as he followed her in. He carried no weapons. Wore no armor.

He knew this wasn't a battle he could fight *for* her.

But he could *stand beside her*.

He could *hold her through it*.

He sat on the floor, legs crossed, calm and still — the eye of a storm that hadn't begun yet.

Elira looked over her shoulder at him.

"I don't know how bad this will be," she whispered.

He held her gaze.

"Then I'll hold you through every second of it."

She knelt before the disk.

Closed her eyes.

And whispered:

"I remember."

The pulse hit her like a wave.

Not pain.

Not yet.

Just *displacement.*

Like falling into her own bones.

She was in the palace again.

Cold stone beneath her knees. Her collar weighing heavy around her neck.

She couldn't move.

Couldn't speak.

She was *aware* — that was the worst part.

The spell the King had forced on her kept her obedient.

Silent.

Compliant.

Even as Malric stepped into the room.

Even as the door locked behind him.

Even as he smiled like she was a *prize.*

Elira gasped in the real world, clutching at her chest.

Vaelen's arms were around her in an instant, murmuring something into her hair, grounding her with the warmth of his body and the strength of his voice.

But she wasn't *here.*

Not fully.

She was remembering the pressure of Malric's hand on her wrist.

The way he tilted her chin like she was something *his.*

How his breath touched her throat.

The whispers.

"This is what's meant to be, Elira. We were chosen."

"You'll learn to like it."

"You'll thank me for making you ready."

Tears streamed down her face.

In the real world, her breath came in stutters, and Vaelen just held her tighter.

"You're safe," he whispered again and again. "You're here. With me."

But she couldn't stop shaking.

Because she hadn't even reached the worst of it yet.

She *knew*.

The vision faded slowly.

Elira collapsed forward, trembling in his arms.

He laid them down gently, letting her cry into his chest, his hand on the back of her head, his heart breaking with every sound she made.

He didn't tell her to stop.

Didn't tell her to breathe.

He just held her while she *remembered.*

And when her sobs quieted into silence, and her body went limp with exhaustion…

He kissed her temple and whispered:

"I'm not letting them keep this part of you."

"You're taking it back."

Chapter 92:

Elira didn't sleep.

Even after the vision faded and her body stopped trembling, she couldn't close her eyes. Every time her lids fluttered shut, Malric's shadow lingered behind them.

Vaelen didn't speak. He held her close all night. His warmth wrapped around her like armor — his presence the only reason she hadn't completely shattered.

But the disk still pulsed beside them.

Calling.

Waiting.

At dawn, Elira stood again.

She didn't feel strong.

She felt *emptied*.

But she stepped back into the root circle with trembling legs and burning resolve.

"I need to go deeper," she said.

Vaelen rose to meet her. "I'm with you."

This time, when the memory pulled her under, it didn't come in flashes.

It came as a *flood*.

She was in the King's throne room.

Not the grand, cold version dressed for court.

The one behind it. Smaller. Private.

She stood still, dressed in white — the ceremonial color of obedience.

Her collar glowed.

And she *felt nothing*.

That was the horror of it — the *illusion* blocked her emotions, muted them.

So, when Malric stepped in, rougher than before, voice colder, eyes full of ownership instead of admiration…

She didn't cry.

She didn't fight.

She just *froze*.

She remembered the restraints.

The bite of metal against her wrists.

How her legs were forced apart.

How he whispered promises of how the King wanted her broken. Willing.

How this was "necessary."

How she would "learn."

She remembered the pressure. The weight.

Not just of Malric's hands…

…but of *helplessness*.

Elira sobbed aloud — body jerking in the sanctuary.

Vaelen caught her again, arms wrapping tight around her as she writhed.

His voice cracked now. "I'm here, I'm here, I'm here—"

She remembered his fingers.

In her.

Violating.

She remembered thinking it was her fault.

That she had *invited* it somehow.

She remembered wishing someone would hear.

But no one did.

Because no one *was allowed* to.

And then the memory showed her something new.

The King.

Watching.

Saying nothing.

Allowing it.

Elira screamed — in the vision and in the real world.

The runes on her skin flared violently, gold bleeding into red.

Vaelen's hands were gentle, cradling her, even as she flailed and broke.

He didn't let go.

Even when his own tears fell freely.

Even when his rage shook him.

He stayed.

And finally, the memory *released* her.

Elira collapsed.

Gasping.

Burning.

Shattered.

But *awake.*

It was hours before she could speak again.

And when she did, it was hoarse.

"He watched."

Vaelen nodded, jaw locked tight. "I saw it."

"I remembered."

He kissed her forehead. "You took it back."

She looked at him through swollen eyes.

"I'm so broken."

"You're *not.*" His voice was sharp now. Fierce. "You're becoming *whole.*"

He cupped her face, brushing her tear-dampened cheeks.

"You are everything they couldn't destroy."

And somewhere deep in her chest…

Where memory once buried her…

Elira felt the first flicker of something *new.*

Freedom.

Chapter 93:

The next morning came slowly.

Elira didn't wake with a jolt or a scream.

She just *opened her eyes.*

And for the first time in a long while, she felt something *other* than fear.

Relief.

She sat wrapped in one of Vaelen's cloaks, curled in the curve of his arms, her head on his chest. He was still asleep — or pretending to be.

His heartbeat was steady beneath her cheek.

And it was hers now.

Not because she'd claimed it.

But because *he'd given it.*

Elira shifted slightly, just enough to feel the ache in her bones — but it wasn't pain.

It was weight.

The kind that said: *you survived this.*

She glanced up at him, took in the relaxed line of his jaw, the lashes resting against his cheeks, the strength in the arms that had held her through the night.

He didn't try to fix her.

He didn't flinch at her screams.

He *stayed.*

When he opened his eyes, he didn't speak.

He just cupped her cheek and let his thumb brush across the side of her face like he was memorizing her *again.*

"You didn't sleep," he said softly.

"I didn't need to," she whispered. "I just needed… this."

They didn't get dressed.

Didn't rush to rejoin the others.

Elira stayed wrapped in his arms, and Vaelen let her trace her fingers along his chest in slow, steady patterns. Her body was hers again — not a weapon, not a prison, not a puppet the King had pulled strings on.

Hers.

And Vaelen treated it like it was sacred.

Like *she* was sacred.

"I used to feel shame," she said after a long while. "About what happened. About what I let happen."

Vaelen didn't correct her.

He just looked at her.

And said: "You don't owe anyone that shame anymore."

She blinked hard. "Even you?"

"*Especially* not me."

He kissed her gently — no hunger, no rush.

Just *presence.*

Elira melted into it. Not because she needed it to forget.

But because she finally felt safe enough to *remember everything…*

…and *still want more.*

Chapter 94:

Elira walked into the morning light with bare feet and steady breath.

Her runes shimmered gently under her skin — not flaring. Not demanding.

Just *there.*

Her steps through the sanctuary felt different now.

Like the land could *feel* the change in her.

She didn't walk as someone haunted.

She walked as someone who had *come back.*

Solen was waiting by the outer ward line.

He straightened when he saw her, his eyes scanning her carefully.

Then: a slow, reverent smile.

"You're different," he said.

"I remembered more," she answered. "And I survived it."

Solen gave a soft bow of his head. "That's what makes you the threat."

As they approached the gathering space, Ilyana met them halfway, urgency in her steps.

"We have a situation," she said. "Three of the emotion-born from the outer reaches. They came back from the Graywood…"

A pause.

"…but they didn't come back *whole.*"

The clearing was quiet, tense.

Two men and a woman stood in the center, surrounded by runes that flickered between containment and chaos. Their bodies trembled with restrained magic — but it wasn't normal.

It *spilled.*

Uncontrolled. Toxic.

Pain.

Elira stepped closer, and her breath caught.

She didn't sense rage. Or hunger. Or darkness.

She sensed *grief.*

They were drowning in it.

"I know what this is," Elira said quietly.

Solen looked over. "You do?"

"They've remembered something they can't hold," she said. "Something that didn't just hurt them… it *defined* them."

Her hand hovered near the rune circle. "I know that feeling."

Ilyana frowned. "They're dangerous, Elira. If they unleash that magic without control—"

"They don't need a prison," Elira cut in. "They need *a hand.*"

Vaelen's voice came from behind her. "Yours?"

She nodded. "Who else?"

The ward fell away.

And Elira stepped into the storm.

The closest of the three — a woman with hollowed eyes and silver-flared veins — looked at her like prey.

But Elira didn't flinch.

She moved closer.

And whispered:

"I've screamed in silence too."

The woman's magic flickered.

The second man fell to his knees.

The third began to sob — and with it, his power *eased.*

Elira placed a hand over the woman's heart.

Not to suppress.

To *share.*

And something passed between them.

Not just energy.

But *understanding.*

When she stepped back, all three were breathing evenly.

Their runes dimmed.

And the silence that followed… was full of awe.

Solen whispered, "She didn't just calm them."

Vaelen stepped forward. "She *brought them back.*"

Ilyana's eyes burned.

"She's the beginning of the end," she said softly.

"The Veil is afraid of her."

Chapter 95:

They were alone again — deep inside the sanctuary's quiet alcove, the others having drifted off to rest or train.

The glow from the rune stones was low and golden, flickering like the last breath of twilight. Elira sat curled in the corner of the room, watching the flames in silence, her runes dimly lit along her arms.

Vaelen sat nearby.

Close.

But not touching.

He hadn't touched her since she stepped in front of the emotion-born.

She'd shone brighter than fire that day — and he hadn't known how to follow something so fierce without extinguishing it.

But tonight… the fire returned to *her eyes.*

And it was *directed at him.*

"I've been thinking," she said softly.

Her voice was calm.

But her fingers were shaking.

"I've been thinking about how they took something from me. Not just my body. But my *choice.* The way I move. The way I want."

Vaelen turned to face her, cautious, listening.

She met his eyes. "I don't want it to belong to them anymore."

He stilled. "Elira—"

"I want to reclaim it," she said. "All of it."

She swallowed, voice trembling. "Even… that."

His breath caught.

"You're sure?"

She nodded, slowly. "But I can't do it without you."

He stood, walked over to her — slow, measured.

He didn't touch her.

Not yet.

"Then tell me what you want," he whispered.

She reached for his hand and placed it gently against her collarbone.

"Everything."

He leaned down, kissed her softly.

"Then I'll give you everything," he said. "But only if you *take it.*"

She blinked. "Take it?"

He brushed his lips along the side of her neck, slow, reverent. "You lead this time. All of it. Until you say otherwise."

Her pulse fluttered beneath his mouth.

And so, she did.

Elira stood and walked toward the middle of the room, shedding her outer cloak, exposing the glowing runes that traced her spine. She turned to him — bare, vulnerable, and *unafraid.*

Vaelen followed, unfastening his shirt, revealing the lines of strength and scar across his chest.

When she reached for him, her hands didn't tremble.

They *claimed.*

He let her push him down against the soft woven mat, straddling him slowly, her thighs tight around his hips. Her hands traced along his jaw, her lips brushing his neck, her body grinding against his with increasing heat.

Vaelen groaned under her breath. "Elira…"

"Shhh," she whispered. "Let me."

But as her movements deepened, and his hands began to explore her curves again — her strength, her power — she began to falter.

She felt it.

That lingering trace of fear.

The ghost of *him.*

She stilled — breathing heavy, eyes distant.

Vaelen froze instantly. "Elira."

"I'm okay," she said, voice shaky.

He cupped her cheeks, made her look at him.

"You're not doing this for me. You're doing it for *you.*"

"I know," she whispered.

And then she added:

"But I *need* you to help me."

His expression changed — darkened with the kind of love that burned, not soothed.

"Then I'll show you what it means to feel this again."

He stood with her in his arms, turned her gently.

And laid her down.

"Tell me if anything feels wrong," he whispered against her ear.

She nodded.

And he began.

He kissed every place that had once felt like a prison — her wrists, her ribs, her thighs — and whispered something beautiful against each one.

"This doesn't belong to him."

"This is yours."

"This… is *mine* because you *chose* to give it."

When he finally entered her, it was with reverence.

But there was strength in it too.

Intention.

Elira gasped, her legs wrapping around him — not in fear, but in *possession.*

Her fingers dug into his back, and he moved inside her with a rhythm that was *hers*, matching every sound she made, every need her body had been afraid to speak.

And when she cried out?

It wasn't pain.

It was *power.*

Afterwards, he held her, trembling himself now.

And whispered into her skin:

"He made you think submission was weakness."

"But what you did tonight… was the strongest thing I've ever seen."

She smiled faintly, eyes misted.

"And you… Vaelen, you made me feel human again."

And deep in the shadow of the Veil…

The King *felt it.*

And he *raged.*

Because what was meant to silence her had become a *song.*

And she wasn't done singing yet.

Chapter 96:

The wind shifted that morning.

Not with power.

With *intent.*

The Veil rippled like fabric tugged from below. Trees leaned subtly, their leaves whispering secrets only the old magic could hear.

Elira stood on the ridge above the sanctuary, eyes narrowed, runes glowing faintly beneath her skin.

Vaelen came up behind her, silent as always. He didn't speak — he didn't have to.

She already felt it.

Something was coming.

And it wasn't subtle.

They gathered near the central grove as the distortion grew — visible now. A flickering tear in the edge of the world.

And then it *opened.*

A portal of fractured light. Like a scar in the sky.

And through it walked **Malric**.

Dressed in silver and black. Unarmed.

Smiling.

Kael stepped forward, hand on his blade. "I'll kill him where he stands."

"No," Elira said softly. "He's not here for a fight."

Malric bowed with a mockery of grace. "Always so clever, Elira."

Vaelen stood behind her — *still*, but every muscle was coiled.

Elira met Malric's gaze without flinching.

"What lie are you here to tell me this time?"

Malric stepped closer — too close — until Kael's blade gleamed in warning.

But Elira didn't move.

He smiled again, voice calm.

"I'm here with an *offer*."

She didn't answer.

So, he continued.

"The King has seen the unraveling. He knows what you're building. Who you're becoming. And he's willing to make… *allowances*."

Elira laughed bitterly. "Allowances?"

Malric nodded. "You want peace. Freedom. For your people. Your mother. Your siblings. Even for *him*"—he gestured toward Vaelen—"and what he is to you."

He took another step.

"We'll give it. You come back. You stop this rebellion. You take your rightful place. And no one else must suffer."

Vaelen growled low, his voice like thunder: "Don't listen to him."

Malric's eyes flicked to him with practiced indifference. "Your part in this, warrior, is temporary. She's not of your world."

Elira's hands trembled, but not with fear.

With fury.

"And what would that place be?" she asked coldly. "Back in chains? With your hands on me? With the King watching every time I breathe?"

Malric's smile faltered — only for a second.

"You'd be *untouched*. Safe. Respected. Powerful."

"But not *free.*"

The silence cracked.

Vaelen stepped beside her now, shoulder to shoulder.

Elira didn't need his words.

But she wanted his presence.

"Go back," she said. "Tell the King he should have buried me deeper."

Malric tilted his head. "Then everyone you love will burn."

Elira took one step forward.

Her runes flared.

And her voice dropped to a whisper.

"Then he'd better come with a fire big enough to swallow *everything.*"

Malric stared at her — and for a brief moment, something *uncertain* passed across his face.

Then he stepped back into the portal.

And vanished.

The grove stayed quiet long after.

Until Elira turned into Vaelen's chest and whispered,

"He's afraid."

Vaelen wrapped his arms around her.

"No," he murmured. "He's *desperate.*"

Chapter 97:

They left the grove in silence.

The air behind them still shimmered faintly where Malric had vanished. But it wasn't just the echo of his presence Elira felt.

It was the way the *Veil twitched.*

Like it knew its threads were unraveling… and didn't know how to stop it.

That night, the sanctuary was quiet again. The kind of stillness that settles *after* something important — and *before* something worse.

Elira and Vaelen stood by the reflecting pool, the stars mirrored in its surface, too still to feel real.

She dipped her hand into the water, watching the ripples warp her reflection.

"I think the worst part," she whispered, "is knowing he really thought I'd take that offer."

Vaelen stepped closer, his voice tight. "He never saw you as a threat. Only as a tool. That was his mistake."

She looked at him. "And you?"

"I saw you as a choice," he said. "One I'd make again. Every damn day."

The space between them shrank.

There wasn't fire.

Not yet.

Just gravity.

And the soft curl of something that meant safety.

They walked back together through the tree-lit corridor, brushing shoulders, fingers occasionally grazing, every look full of unspoken words.

Vaelen opened the door to her chamber but didn't follow.

Until she turned.

"I don't want to be alone tonight," she said softly.

He didn't ask questions.

He just stepped inside.

And shut the door.

They didn't undress fast.

They didn't leap into fire.

They moved slowly. Reverently. Like they knew their time was ticking, but refused to let it make them rush.

When they lay down, Elira curled against his chest, her fingers tracing the curve of his jaw.

"I hate how he still thinks he owns pieces of me," she whispered.

"He doesn't," Vaelen said. "You've taken every piece back. Even the ones that hurt."

She looked up at him, eyes soft, voice daring.

"What if he's watching?"

Vaelen's jaw tensed.

"Then I hope he sees this."

He kissed her slowly — deeply.

"Because this is what power really looks like."

Chapter 98:

It began with a sound.

Not a cry.

Not a scream.

Just a crack.

One that split through the sky like a bone breaking — subtle at first, but unmistakable.

Elira bolted upright in her bed, breath already sharp in her lungs.

She didn't need to ask if Vaelen heard it — he was already standing, sword half-drawn, his rune tattoos glowing faintly across his shoulder.

The Veil had shuddered.

And something was falling through.

By the time they reached the outer wardline, Ilyana and Solen were already there. The forest beyond was warped — twisted light pulsing through the trees, shadows moving wrong.

Kael stepped forward, shielding raised. "Someone's coming through."

Auren added, "But it doesn't feel like someone. It feels like too much."

Then they saw her.

A woman.

Lirian by appearance. Emotion-born by aura.

And utterly, completely unraveled.

She stumbled into the clearing, eyes wide and glowing, hands trembling with uncontrolled magic.

Elira stepped forward instinctively, but the force of pain rolling off the woman stopped her cold.

It wasn't just grief.

It was all of it.

Abandonment. Rage. Betrayal. Yearning.

The woman screamed.

And the trees around her withered.

Vaelen stepped in front of Elira. "She'll tear herself apart."

"No," Elira whispered, pushing past him. "She'll tear everything apart… unless someone shows her it can stop."

Elira walked slowly into the blast radius, her runes glowing silver now, pure and calm. Every step she took was a challenge — not to the woman's power, but to the story she'd been told:

That pain is all there is.

Elira reached out her hand.

The woman flinched back — but didn't strike.

Not yet.

"Do you know who I am?" Elira asked.

The woman shook her head.

"Then let me tell you," Elira whispered. "I'm what happens when you remember and still choose to feel. I'm what they tried to break. And failed."

The woman's sob caught in her throat.

And she dropped to her knees.

Later, in the sanctuary, Solen turned to Elira.

"She didn't come for help," he said. "She came to destroy herself."

Elira nodded. "And the King knew it. He knew if she exploded here, it could destabilize everything I've built."

"Which means…" Vaelen said quietly, "he's getting ready to send someone who can finish what she started."

Elira looked toward the forest.
Her jaw tightened.
And her voice dropped.
"Then we're almost at the end."

Chapter 99:

The sky was clear when he arrived.

No ripples.

No magic.

Just a slow, confident step through the trees.

Malric.

Unarmed.

Unbothered.

And unafraid.

Elira stepped into the clearing first.

She had felt it — his presence. Not a magical disturbance, not a threat.

A wrongness.

He stood casually, as if they were old lovers reunited instead of enemies circling flame.

"I told him this wouldn't work," he said smoothly. "But he insisted. Said I had a connection to you."

Elira didn't flinch.

"I have no connection to corpses," she replied.

Vaelen appeared from the side, silent and tense.

Not close.

Not far.

Just watching.

Malric's eyes flicked to him. "Still playing guard dog?"

Vaelen didn't blink.

But Elira's voice cut in again — cool, sharp, deadly.

"Why are you here?"

Malric stepped forward slowly.

Too close.

His eyes glittered with a kind of hunger Elira remembered too well.

"Because I miss what was mine."

And then—

He reached for her.

Not violently.

Not fast.

But casually.

Fingers brushing the edge of her waist, drifting down her hip.

And that—

That was it.

Vaelen was on him before anyone could breathe.

The crack of impact rang through the trees.

Malric went flying.

He hit the ground hard — but rolled quickly to his feet.

Only to find Vaelen already there.

Already swinging.

The blade wasn't drawn.

Vaelen didn't need it.

He fought with hands, fists, fury — the kind born of possession, protection, love.

Malric tried to speak, to bargain, to reach—

But Vaelen caught him by the throat and slammed him into the trunk of a tree so hard the bark splintered.

"Touch her again," Vaelen snarled, "and I will end you."

Malric coughed, blood on his teeth.

"She's not yours."

Vaelen leaned in.

Eyes wild.

Voice low.

"She chose me. That makes her mine. And I will never let your hands near her again."

Malric laughed — weakly.

A taunt.

"You're just jealous. Because I had her first—"

He didn't finish.

Because Vaelen drove a dagger — his backup blade — straight through Malric's heart.

Silence.

Then:

A gasp.

From Malric.

But not of pain.

Of realization.

He hadn't expected it.

He thought he'd win with words.

With touch.

He thought she'd hesitate.

But it wasn't Elira who struck him down.

It was the one who loved her.

Truly.

Fully.

Fiercely.

Vaelen stepped back as Malric collapsed to the ground — lifeless, blood soaking into the roots.

Elira walked to his side.

Placed a hand on his shoulder.

And whispered:

"You'll never touch what's mine again."

Far away, in the King's Hall, a crystal shattered.

And he screamed.

Chapter 100:

They buried Malric beneath the shattered tree he died against.

No ceremony.

No runes.

No blessings.

Only silence.

And the knowledge that what was taken from Elira would never again rise in his hands.

The sanctuary was still, but not tense.

It was charged.

Solen spoke the words that had been hanging in the air since the moment Malric's body fell still:

"He was the last thread the King had in this realm."

Ilyana's jaw was tight. "And the King felt it snap."

Elira stood at the edge of the roots, overlooking the land they'd built into something close to peace. Vaelen stood behind her — close enough to touch, but not yet.

She was breathing steadily.

But her hands?

Her hands were glowing.

The runes etched into her skin were bright. Brighter than they'd ever been.

"I felt something," she said softly. "When he died."

"Magic?" Solen asked.

"No," she murmured. "Release."

The illusion didn't just lose a soldier.

It lost an anchor.

Across the lands, the Veil flickered.

Not a crack this time.

A shudder.

Whole cities paused.

The King's influence dimmed — just a breath.

But enough.

Enough for people to feel the silence where obedience used to be.

Enough to wonder.

That night, Elira sat beside the fire, Vaelen's arm around her shoulders. Her head against his chest. Her body warm, safe, hers.

"You killed him for me," she said quietly.

"I killed him for you," Vaelen corrected. "And for everything he represented."

She looked up at him, eyes steady. "And if the King had been here instead?"

"I'd have done worse."

She kissed him.

Not for fire.

Not for lust.

But for promise.

And when she pulled back, her runes shimmered silver.

"He's coming," she said. "We've taken too much from him. He'll come in person next."

Vaelen nodded. "Then we finish this."

"No," Elira whispered.

"We begin it."

Chapter 101:

It began with a whisper in the wind.

Not from the sanctuary.

Not even from the Graywood.

But from beyond.

The kind of whisper that spread like wildfire.

Not of terror.

Not of command.

But of hope.

Her name.

Elira.

They spoke it in hushed reverence across distant villages.

In underground caves once used by the resistance that never survived.

In temple ruins where the old gods once fell silent.

"She's real."

"She broke the Seal."

"She made the storm stop."

The Veil began to pulse.

Not break — not yet — but pulse.

Like it was feeling every emotion rising beneath it.

And it did not know how to respond.

In the sanctuary, the emotion-born began arriving faster.

Wandering in, dazed and cracked open.

Their powers weren't calm.

They were dangerous.

But they weren't lost.

Because they were following her.

Vaelen stood by the western gate, arms crossed as he watched another pair arrive — a boy with trembling hands and golden runes, a girl whose sobs seemed to warp the air itself.

"I felt her," the boy whispered. "In my sleep. Like she called me."

Elira stepped forward from the path, her voice clear:

"I did."

⁂

That night, they gathered in the grove.

Hundreds of them now.

Lirians.

Emotion-born.

Exiles.

Healers.

All drawn by a truth they couldn't name.

Elira stood before them, Vaelen by her side, Solen and Ilyana at her flanks.

Her runes glowed bright against the darkness.

And when she spoke, her voice carried through the trees like a promise written into the wind:

"You are not broken."

"You were never too much."

"Your emotions are not curses — they're the King's undoing."

⁂

And far, far away… in a throne room of mirrors and blood…

The King heard her.

Not through spies.

Not through runes.
But through the cracks in the Veil itself.
And he screamed.

Chapter 102:

The training fields had once been quiet.

Now, they pulsed with raw magic.

Lirians and emotion-born sparred side by side, runes crackling, heat rolling off every movement, every breath.

Elira stood at the center, her silver-touched runes glowing steadily as she demonstrated how to tether energy through breath — not force.

"You don't command your emotions," she told them. "You move with them. You honor them."

Some struggled.

Some soared.

And one?

One didn't listen at all.

Her name was Mirae.

Young.

Beautiful.

Broken.

She had no control over her gift — but she didn't want it.

She wanted destruction.

Elira watched her from a distance, heart heavy.

When Mirae moved, her magic came like a storm — unfiltered, chaotic. Shadows and light warping the air around her, rage bleeding into everything she touched.

"I don't want peace," she said once, eyes glowing gold. "I want revenge."

Solen had warned Elira: "She's not like the others. She's the product of what happens when you don't come back."

And Elira?

She saw herself.

The version that could've been.

That evening, after the training ended, Vaelen found Elira sitting alone at the edge of the sanctuary, her knees drawn to her chest, eyes on the darkening sky.

"She's like me," Elira said.

"No," Vaelen answered. "She's who you'd be if you didn't care who you became."

Elira exhaled, voice small. "I don't know if I can reach her."

Vaelen crouched beside her.

"Then don't reach for her."

She looked at him, confused.

"Show her," he said. "Show her what it looks like when you survive and choose love anyway."

Elira watched the last stars blink into view above them.

And for a moment, her voice trembled.

"I'm scared, Vaelen."

He leaned in, pressed his forehead to hers.

"So was I," he whispered. "Until I found you."

She closed her eyes.

And let herself believe — just for tonight — that even the most shattered pieces could be mended.

Because she had once been all edges.

And someone had held her anyway.

Chapter 103:

The sky split open with red light.

It wasn't the Veil this time.

It was Mirae.

Elira had just begun her morning rounds when the pulse hit her chest — not magical, not physical, but emotional. A surge of grief so thick it almost dropped her to her knees.

Solen was already sprinting through the grove when she turned.

"Mirae," he shouted. "She's lost it."

The training field was chaos.

Three emotion-born lay scattered across the grass, gasping for breath, glowing runes twitching under their skin.

And at the center stood Mirae — surrounded by fire that didn't burn.

It screamed.

Elira stepped into the ring of smoke, her runes already humming.

She didn't shout.

She didn't threaten.

She just walked.

"Mirae," she called gently, "what happened?"

Mirae turned slowly — her eyes lit with gold fire, her skin cracked with glowing veins of rage.

"He said I was weak," she snarled.

Elira blinked. "Who?"

"One of them. He laughed at me. Said I couldn't even hold my power."

A tear slipped down Mirae's face.

"So, I showed him."

Elira's breath caught.

Not in fear.

But in grief.

This wasn't an attack.

This was a collapse.

"I know what it's like," Elira said softly, stepping closer. "To be full of fire and think the only way anyone will respect you is if they feel it burn."

Mirae's jaw trembled. "Then why do they listen to you?"

Elira smiled, sad and true. "Because I let them see me before the fire, too."

Mirae faltered.

The magic around her cracked — splintered like a mirror fracturing under too much weight.

And then she collapsed.

Not from a blow.

But from release.

Elira caught her before she hit the ground.

Held her shaking frame against her chest, letting Mirae sob into her shoulder.

"You don't have to destroy everything to be heard," Elira whispered.

"You just have to believe you're worth hearing."

Later, Solen approached as Elira sat by Mirae's side near the healer's quarters.

"She'll recover," he said. "Barely."

Elira nodded, watching Mirae sleep.

"I saw myself in her," she murmured. "The me that almost never found the light."

Solen's eyes softened. "And she saw herself in you. That's why she stopped."

He placed a hand on her shoulder.

"She's not the last one you'll have to pull back from the edge."

"I know."

"Will you have the strength?"

Elira looked up toward the horizon.

Where the Veil shimmered faintly in the rising light.

"I have to."

Chapter 104:

It started with restlessness.

Not fear.

Not panic.

Just a subtle shift in the way people moved.

Eyes glancing over shoulders.

Hands twitching near weapons.

Conversations that stopped when Elira entered the room.

She first noticed it with the newer arrivals — the emotion-born who had come to her after Malric's death.

They should have felt freedom.

But instead… they looked unsettled.

Uncertain.

Solen approached her in the early hours of the morning, his expression unreadable.

"I felt it last night," he said quietly. "Something… pressing in. A whisper."

"From where?" Elira asked.

He shook his head. "Not from outside."

He placed a hand on his chest.

"In here."

Vaelen was already on edge — his presence shadowing Elira more closely than ever. His runes flared anytime someone looked at her too long, said her name with the wrong tone.

He felt it too.

Not words.

But an idea.

A doubt that crept in like rot beneath the skin:

She's dangerous.

She'll lead you to ruin.

She's no savior — she's a spark that will burn you all.

By midday, two emotion-born had argued in the training grounds. One stormed away, shouting:

"You don't see it? We followed her here and now we're targets. She's no protector. She's a beacon for death."

Elira had stood nearby, silent.

And it broke her in a place deeper than bones.

That night, she sat at the edge of the sanctuary, knees drawn to her chest, hands buried in the earth like she could root herself there.

Vaelen knelt beside her.

"You're not the cause of this," he said.

"I'm the reason they're in danger," she whispered.

"No," he said firmly. "You're the reason they've survived this long."

She turned to him, tears burning but not falling.

"They're doubting me."

"They're being poisoned."

"And what if I can't stop it?" she asked. "What if I become exactly what the King says I am?"

Vaelen reached out, cupped her face, and whispered like it was a prayer:

"You're not what he says. You're what you choose."

"And I would follow your choice to the ends of every realm."

She pressed her forehead to his, drawing strength from the place they always returned to: each other.

"I'll show them," she whispered. "Even if it breaks me. I'll remind them what it means to feel. To believe."

And somewhere, through the threads of the Veil… the King smiled.

Because sometimes?

Doubt worked better than blades.

Chapter 105:

The word spread fast.

By nightfall, the clearing was full.

Not just Lirians.

Not just emotion-born.

But everyone.

Those who had followed her from the beginning.

Those who arrived later, unsure of her purpose.

And those who still didn't know what to believe.

Elira stood at the edge of the stone platform near the roots of the sanctuary tree — the place where truth always seemed to echo louder.

She could feel it before she even opened her mouth.

Doubt.

A thick fog. Wrapping around the edges of hearts. Infecting the ones she loved.

She knew the King was watching through them.

Waiting to see if she broke.

Vaelen stood beside her — silent, steady, hers.

Solen gave her a single nod from the crowd.

Ilyana, Kael, Auren… all present.

But tonight, Elira would stand alone.

Because they had to hear it from her.

She didn't raise her voice when she began.

She didn't have to.

It was the quiet that commanded them.

"I know you've heard things," she said. "Whispers. Doubts. Questions you're afraid to ask out loud."

"You wonder if I'm leading you toward something worse. If my fire will get you killed. If I'm the reason the King watches us more closely now."

She stepped forward, her runes glowing silver, slow and soft.

"You're right about one thing."

"I am dangerous."

The crowd tensed.

"But not to you."

"I'm dangerous to the one who told you your feelings were weaknesses. That love made you soft. That intimacy was dirty. That your body, your grief, your joy, your fury—meant nothing."

"I'm dangerous to the one who kept you silent."

Her voice cracked — not with weakness, but with feeling.

"He made you afraid to feel. And now he's afraid because you are."

Murmurs spread through the crowd.

Soft at first.

Then louder.

Solen's eyes gleamed. Vaelen's jaw tightened in pride.

Elira pressed forward.

"I didn't ask to lead. But I will not be quiet. And I will not stop."

"If you believe I'm too much, too powerful, too loud—then you haven't seen what we can do together."

"And if any of you doubt me, you're allowed to walk away. But know this…"

"I will still fight for you."

Silence again.

Then—

Applause.

Scattered.

Growing.

A roar by the time she stepped down.

And she felt it—

A crack in the fog of doubt.

One the King couldn't undo.

That night, Elira lay in Vaelen's arms, silent, breath steady.

She had never felt more vulnerable.

Or surer.

And she knew—

This is where the war truly begins.

Chapter 106:

Mirae didn't clap.

She didn't cry.

She didn't move.

She just stood at the edge of the clearing after Elira's speech, arms crossed, power still pulsing beneath her skin like a second heartbeat.

But her eyes?

Her eyes were softer.

For the first time, they weren't filled with fire.

They were filled with listening.

Solen stepped beside her, arms loose at his sides.

"She reached you," he said quietly.

Mirae scoffed. "I'm not here for her. I'm here for the fall."

Solen tilted his head, unconvinced. "You're here because you want to see if something better rises from it."

She didn't answer.

But she didn't walk away.

In the following days, the shift was palpable.

Emotion-born trained harder. Fewer outbursts. More control. Laughter returned to corners of the sanctuary where silence once lingered.

Kael organized patrols.

Auren reinforced wards.

And Vaelen?

He watched the woods more closely than ever.

"He's too quiet," he told Elira one night. "The King. He hasn't made a move since Malric. That's not peace. That's planning."

And Vaelen was right.

Because what they didn't see was this:

A lone figure slipping past the perimeter.

Wearing the face of a Lirian. Moving like one of their own.

But carrying the King's orders.

Find her.

Get close.

And if you must — break her from within.

That night, Elira stood beneath the trees, tracing the patterns of the stars. Vaelen stepped behind her, arms wrapping gently around her waist.

"Something's coming," she whispered.

"I know," he said.

They stood there a long time.

Two hearts beating in defiance of a crumbling king.

Chapter 107:

The new arrival called herself Thalia.

She came in the night — bloodied, trembling, claiming she had escaped a King's outpost in the South. She said her gift was empathy. That she felt her way here.

Elira wanted to believe her.

But something about her smile didn't reach her eyes.

Thalia settled into the sanctuary easily. Too easily.

She made friends quickly.

Too quickly.

Within two days, she was helping in the kitchens. Laughing with the other emotion-born. Joining sparring sessions. Offering advice.

And yet…

Vaelen watched her like a hawk.

"I don't like it," he said one evening, arms folded across his chest. "Something's wrong."

"She hasn't done anything," Elira said softly.

"Exactly," he replied. "No one comes through that much trauma without scars."

Solen approached Elira later that night, his expression unreadable.

"I can't feel her," he said.

Elira blinked. "What do you mean?"

"She's not empty. She's not overflowing. She's… closed. Like someone turned the feeling off."

The next morning, Auren discovered one of the wards near the eastern perimeter had been tampered with — subtly, expertly. Not enough to fail… but enough to signal someone outside.

And that's when Elira's breath caught.

"She's not just a spy," she whispered. "She's a thread the King is using to reach in."

⁂

That night, Elira entered the grove alone.

And Thalia followed.

Her steps were too soft. Her presence too calm.

Elira turned slowly.

"Why are you really here?"

Thalia smiled. A slow, almost sad tilt of her lips.

"To remind you that the King always finds a way in."

Magic surged.

But Elira was ready.

Her runes flared silver and gold, light blinding as it burst between them.

Thalia's disguise flickered — her eyes turned black for a blink, her form warping — not shifting entirely, but cracking.

Elira's voice came steady and strong:

"You thought I'd let you close."

"But I've learned, finally, what real intuition feels like."

And with a final blast of light, she forced Thalia out — not killed, but cast out, her body thrown back through the Veil as if the very sanctuary rejected her.

Vaelen found Elira moments later, breathless but calm.

"She was inside," she whispered.

He nodded; jaw tight.

"And now?" he asked.

Elira turned, face like flame.

"Now we make sure it never happens again."

Chapter 108:

The grove was quiet again.

Not with fear.

But with reverence.

The Lirians had seen Elira burn with power — and now, they saw her steady with purpose.

Even the emotion-born, once hesitant to meet her eyes, now nodded in passing.

Trust was being rebuilt.

Not from speeches.

But from *truth.*

Elira walked the sanctuary in silence, her fingers brushing the leaves, the stones, the worn wooden railings she and Vaelen had reinforced together. Everything around her felt *lighter.*

And when she returned to their room, he was already waiting.

He didn't say a word when she entered.

Just looked at her — that low, smoldering gaze that said he saw *everything.*

Not just the leader.

But the *woman.*

The girl who had been used, silenced, doubted.

The woman who now stood in the wreckage of a broken world and *chose to rebuild anyway.*

"You're quiet," Elira said softly.

Vaelen reached out, pulled her into his lap, and wrapped his arms around her waist.

"I was just thinking," he murmured into her neck, "how proud I am of you."

Her breath caught — because the words weren't said with fanfare, or expectation. Just truth.

Warm and whole.

She leaned into him. Let her fingers trace the edge of the rune on his collarbone.

"I was afraid," she whispered. "That I wouldn't be enough."

"You were never meant to be *enough*," he said. "You were meant to be **everything.**"

Her throat tightened.

And before she could stop herself, she asked, "Can we just… stay like this for a while?"

They didn't need heat tonight.

Just warmth.

So they sat like that — tangled in each other — for what felt like hours.

No battles.

No speeches.

Just skin and silence and soft touches that meant *more* than words ever could.

But when she looked at him again…

There was something in her eyes.

A question.

A need.

And he saw it.

All of it.

He brushed her hair back and said gently:

"If you want more… just ask."

And her whisper came so softly, so sweetly—

"I want *you*."

Chapter 109:

Vaelen didn't move fast.

He watched her.

Let her set the pace.

His fingers traced her cheek, her collarbone, the place just above her heart where her rune shimmered faintly like moonlight under skin.

"I want to show you," he murmured, voice low and rough, "what it means to be loved."

Elira nodded; her throat tight.

"I trust you."

And that was all it took.

He laid her down slowly, reverently, as if she might shatter — not from weakness, but from being *too precious.*

His hands moved with unspoken vows.

Not rushed.
Not demanding.
But *curious.*

Learning her all over again, like a map he'd never stop exploring.

Every breath she took, he answered with a kiss.
Every shiver, he soothed.
Every ache, he honored.

When he slid his hand between her thighs, she gasped softly.

Not in fear.

In *permission.*

And when he entered her with fingers first, slow and precise, she didn't shrink away.

She *arched into it.*

That's it," he whispered. "Let me feel you."

"Let *you* feel you."

And she did.

He coaxed pleasure from her like it was art.

Made her shake apart in his arms before he even gave her more of himself.

When she was breathless, trembling, already undone…

She reached for him.

"I want *all* of you."

Vaelen kissed her so deeply she moaned into his mouth.

And when he finally slid inside her, he did it slowly — like a promise.

There was no sharpness this time.

No edges.

Only waves.

He moved in long, deep strokes, his forehead pressed to hers, his hands never leaving her skin.

"I love the way you take me in," he said into her neck.

"I love the way you *look* at me when I'm inside you."

"I love… you."

And that?

That's when her tears came.

Soft.

Silent.

And utterly *safe.*

When she came again, she sobbed his name — and he held her through it.

Didn't chase his own release right away.

Just watched her unravel. Felt her tremble around him. Let her *feel it all.*

Only when she was whispering his name like a lifeline did he finally give in.

Afterward, they stayed tangled in each other.

Bare.

Breathless.

Whole.

"You always take care of me," she whispered.

Vaelen brushed his thumb under her eye.

"Because no one ever did for you."

"So, I will. Always."

Chapter 110:

The sun rose quietly, soft gold slipping through the canopy above their bed of woven blankets and furs. It painted Elira's skin in light — like she was being *blessed* by something older than time.

Vaelen was already awake.

But he didn't move.

He just watched her breathe.

Her chest rose and fell with the rhythm of deep, peaceful sleep. One arm curled beneath her head. The other stretched toward him, fingers unconsciously reaching for his skin even in rest.

He smiled.

Gods, he loved her even more like this.

Unburdened.

Unshattered.

Free.

But there was something else too.

He could feel it — the same way his runes always told him when something shifted in the world around him.

A hum.

Faint.

Buried.

But there.

Coming from *her.*

When Elira stirred, her eyes blinked open slowly. She stretched, sighing softly, lips curved in a sleepy smile.

"Mm. You're watching me again."

He leaned in and kissed her forehead.

"Always."

As she sat up and pulled the blanket around her chest, she paused.

Brows knit.

Hands over her stomach.

"...That's strange," she whispered.

Vaelen sat up, alert but calm. "What is?"

"I don't know. Just... a feeling."

She shook her head. "I'm probably just sore again."

His lips quirked. "I *did* warn you."

She rolled her eyes, smirking.

But her hands stayed on her abdomen.

Later that morning, while the others trained in the clearing, Elira wandered to the wellspring — the place where emotions always seemed louder, clearer.

And she felt it again.

A pulse.

Not from her own power.

Something new.

Flickering like a heartbeat.

Solen approached her quietly.

"You feel it too," he said gently.

She turned to him, startled. "You know?"

He didn't answer directly. Just placed a hand lightly over her chest, above the rune that had begun to glow faintly again.

"There is something new blooming in you," he said. "Something alive."

Elira stared at him.

Silent.

And suddenly breathless.

Chapter 111:

Elira didn't tell Vaelen.

Not yet.

There were no symptoms.

No signs.

Just a feeling.

A hum in her magic that wasn't there before — a thread spun of something warmer. Softer.

And *alive*.

Elira didn't tell Vaelen.

Not yet.

There were no symptoms.

No signs.

Just a feeling.

A hum in her magic that wasn't there before — a thread spun of something warmer. Softer.

And *alive*.

Solen had said something was blooming inside her.

But Elira didn't need his confirmation.

She *knew*.

She felt it in the places where her trauma had once lived.

Not like pain.

But like *hope*.

She sat near the Wellspring again, knees tucked to her chest.

She pressed her palm to her lower belly, just beneath the line where her runes began.

"Are you real?" she whispered.

The wind shifted gently through the trees.

And she swore she felt a pulse.

One that wasn't hers.

Meanwhile, across the sanctuary, Vaelen stood at the perimeter wall, staring out into the woods.

He didn't know why he felt so on edge.

Only that something had changed.

Not in the trees.

Not in the wards.

In *Elira.*

The next time she found him — later that evening — she just walked up and slid her arms around his waist from behind.

He stilled.

And then relaxed into her touch.

"I needed this," she whispered.

He turned to face her, brushing her hair back.

"Whatever it is," he said softly, "you can tell me when you're ready."

She nodded against his chest.

"I will. Soon."

Above them, the Veil shimmered again — faint, like a ripple on still water.

But far away, in the shattered throne room of the King, mirrors cracked along their edges.

He felt it.

Life born from love.

A power not even *he* had foreseen.

And it terrified him.

Chapter 112:

Elira found Ilyana tending to the flowering vines near the west wall — coaxing growth from the soil with soft whispers and glowing hands.

She didn't mean to ask.

But the words slipped out before she could stop them.

"Would you have known?"

Ilyana glanced over; brow lifted.

"Known what, my heart?"

Elira hesitated.

Swallowed.

"If you were pregnant. Before the signs. Before the healers."

There was no fear in her voice.

Just a tremble of wonder.

Ilyana stood slowly, brushing her hands clean on her skirts.

She didn't ask why Elira was asking.

She just stepped close, took her daughter's hands, and smiled — soft and knowing.

"Yes," she said. "A mother always knows."

Elira's throat tightened.

She hadn't said it aloud.

But somehow, Ilyana's words made it real.

I'm not alone in this body anymore.

Not in fear.

Not in grief.

But in *creation.*

Tears welled in Elira's eyes, and Ilyana pulled her into her arms.

Held her like she did as a child.

"You don't need proof from a healer, Elira. Your magic told you. Your body told you. *Your heart knew first.*"

Elira clutched the back of Ilyana's robes, holding tight.

"I don't even know what kind of world I'm bringing them into," she whispered.

Ilyana pulled back just enough to look her in the eyes.

"One you're rebuilding. One they'll *never* have to survive the way you did."

That night, Elira sat beside the fire with Vaelen, his arm around her, his body warm and steady.

She didn't speak the words yet.

But her hand drifted to her stomach again.

And this time, when she touched it—

She smiled.

Chapter 113:

It began in sleep.

Not with a nightmare.

But with a whisper.

A lullaby she didn't recognize — sung in a language she shouldn't know, wrapped in a voice that was **not hers.**

Elira turned within the dream, the mist around her thick and silver.

And there it was:

A cradle.

A child inside, cooing softly, skin glowing faintly with runes not unlike her own. Small, perfect fingers reaching toward her.

Her heart swelled.

But then—

The runes began to **crack.**

The cradle turned to ash.

And a cold, hollow voice echoed through the mist.

"You can't protect them."

She dropped to her knees, reaching through smoke, screaming the name she hadn't even spoken aloud yet — one that had only existed in her *dreams.*

"No—don't take them!"

But her arms caught nothing.

Only silence.

Only shadow.

And then he appeared.

Not in form, but in presence.

The **King.**

His voice wrapped around her like a chain:

"Create what you will. Love whom you dare. I will **burn it all.**"

Elira jolted awake, sweat slick on her skin, chest heaving.

Vaelen was there in an instant, gripping her shoulders.

"Elira—what happened?"

She turned to him, shaking.

Eyes wide.

Hands trembling as they wrapped around her middle.

"He knows."

The next day, Solen confirmed it.

"The Veil shivered last night," he said. "But not from weakness. From *fear.*"

Elira stood at the center of the sanctuary, her hands glowing silver and gold, heart pounding.

"He sent me a vision. Of the child. Of what he'd do."

Vaelen's jaw clenched. "He'll never touch you. Or them."

And then, Elira did something she hadn't done since the beginning.

She called for *every* Lirian.

Every emotion-born.

Every soul still fighting beside her.

And she told them the truth.

"I'm carrying life," she said.

"Proof that the Veil is breaking. That love has already *won* something."

There was silence.

And then a single voice whispered in awe:

"She's the beginning of the end."

Chapter 114:

And then, Elira did something she hadn't done since the beginning.

She called for *every* Lirian.

Every emotion-born.

Every soul still fighting beside her.

And she told them the truth.

"I'm carrying life," she said.

"Proof that the Veil is breaking. That love has already *won* something."

There was silence.

And then a single voice whispered in awe:

"She's the beginning of the end."

Elira stood at the edge of the southern ridge, wind lifting her hair as she stared into the far horizon.

The Veil shimmered there — thinner, stranger.

She could *feel* it.

A doorway to something *older*.

Vaelen stepped beside her, eyes dark, arms crossed.

"You're leaving," he said quietly.

"Not for long," she replied. "But I have to go."

"To the ancient places?"

She nodded.

"To the Wells of Flame. To the Ember stone buried in the Forgotten Hollow. There's something there… something that was hidden before the Veil was cast."

"I have to know what it is. For me. For *them*."

Vaelen didn't argue.

Didn't try to stop her.

He just reached out and laced his fingers through hers.

"Then I'm going with you."

They left the next morning.

Elira, Vaelen, and a small circle of chosen emotion-born.

Mirae among them.

Solen stayed behind, holding the sanctuary with Ilyana and the twins.

"Go find what's been hidden," Ilyana told her daughter. "And bring it back into the light."

As they crossed into the broken path that led toward the Forgotten Hollow, Elira felt the hum in her chest grow stronger.

A double pulse.

Her magic.

And the life inside her.

Together.

Beating in rhythm.

Becoming something *more.*

Chapter 115:

As they crossed into the broken path that led toward the Forgotten Hollow, Elira felt the hum in her chest grow stronger.

A double pulse.

Her magic.

And the life inside her.

Together.

Beating in rhythm.

Becoming something *more.*

The Hollow wasn't marked on any map. Not anymore. The King had erased it from records long before Elira was born. But the land remembered. And so did the runes beneath her skin.

Every step forward made them glow brighter.

Silver. Gold.

A pulse she couldn't ignore.

Like the child inside her was calling to something ancient — and it was *calling back.*

As they crested a ridge, the terrain dropped sharply into a vast basin below — the Hollow.

Once, it might've been lush. Sacred. Now it was veiled in mist, lit from beneath by soft, flickering light. Ancient runes were scorched into the stone, barely visible, yet unmistakable.

The emotion-born gasped.

Vaelen stood silent beside her.

"This is it," Elira whispered. "I can feel it."

They made camp on the outer edge. The mist made it too dangerous to enter blindly, even with magic. Elira wanted to wait until morning.

That night, Elira sat beside the fire, one hand on her stomach, the other clutching her journal — the one Vaelen had read, the one that still held her hardest truths.

He came to her quietly, sitting close. So close their shoulders brushed.

"You've felt them move, haven't you?" he asked, eyes on the fire.

Elira blinked.

"...Them?"

Vaelen looked over.

"There's more than one heartbeat now. Yours. Theirs. I don't need a healer to know. I feel it."

Her breath hitched.

She hadn't told him.

And he wasn't angry.

Just *in awe.*

Above them, on the cliffs that overlooked the Hollow, a shadow crouched in silence.

Tall. Hooded. Wrapped in worn leather and ash-stained cloth.

A former enforcer of the King.

But no longer loyal.

His orders were to find Elira. Spy. Report.

But he had come with questions of his own.

Because his dreams had started to whisper her name, too.

Back at the fire, Elira and Vaelen sat in silence.

"I thought it would scare me," she whispered. "Knowing what's coming. The King. This child. The world we might still have to destroy just to rebuild."

Vaelen reached for her hand and squeezed.

"Maybe fear isn't weakness," he said. "Maybe it's proof you still believe it's worth fighting for."

And for the first time in days… she smiled.

Elira turned to Vaelen, her fingers brushing over the inside of his wrist, where his runes always pulsed hardest when he was feeling too much.

"I think you'll be a wonderful father," she said softly.

Vaelen's gaze dropped to the fire. It took him a long moment to speak.

"I don't know how," he said finally. "I don't even remember what a good one looks like."

Her chest ached.

He wasn't pulling away from her — he was pulling *into* himself.

"I had nothing," he continued. "No father. No guide. I don't even know what parts of me were born from love and what parts were born from survival."

He looked up at her then — and gods, there were tears in his eyes.

"What if I'm too broken to raise something whole?"

Elira leaned forward, cupping his face with both hands.

"You're not broken," she whispered. "You're *becoming*."

And then, softer:

"You've already taught me how to love again. You've already protected me. Chosen me. You show up when it's hard. That's what this child will need."

She pressed her forehead to his.
"You're already doing it."
Vaelen exhaled — ragged, aching.
But in that breath, something inside him began to *mend.*

Chapter 116:

Elira turned to Vaelen, her fingers brushing over the inside of his wrist, where his runes always pulsed hardest when he was feeling too much.

"I think you'll be a wonderful father," she said softly.

Vaelen's gaze dropped to the fire. It took him a long moment to speak.

"I don't know how," he said finally. "I don't even remember what a good one looks like."

Her chest ached.

He wasn't pulling away from her — he was pulling *into* himself.

"I had nothing," he continued. "No father. No guide. I don't even know what parts of me were born from love and what parts were born from survival."

He looked up at her then — and gods, there were tears in his eyes.

"What if I'm too broken to raise something whole?"

Elira leaned forward, cupping his face with both hands.

"You're not broken," she whispered. "You're *becoming*."

And then, softer:

"You've already taught me how to love again. You've already protected me. Chosen me. You show up when it's hard. That's what this child will need."

She pressed her forehead to his.

"You're already doing it."

Vaelen exhaled — ragged, aching.

But in that breath, something inside him began to *mend.*

Elira turned to Vaelen, her fingers brushing over the inside of his wrist, where his runes always pulsed hardest when he was feeling too much.

"I think you'll be a wonderful father," she said softly.

Vaelen's gaze dropped to the fire. It took him a long moment to speak.

"I don't know how," he said finally. "I don't even remember what a good one looks like."

Her chest ached.

He wasn't pulling away from her — he was pulling *into* himself.

"I had nothing," he continued. "No father. No guide. I don't even know what parts of me were born from love and what parts were born from survival."

He looked up at her then — and gods, there were tears in his eyes.

"What if I'm too broken to raise something whole?"

Elira leaned forward, cupping his face with both hands.

"You're not broken," she whispered. "You're *becoming*."

And then, softer:

"You've already taught me how to love again. You've already protected me. Chosen me. You show up when it's hard. That's what this child will need."

She pressed her forehead to his.

"You're already doing it."

Vaelen exhaled — ragged, aching.

But in that breath, something inside him began to *mend.*

There, in the center of the Hollow, stood a monolith — ancient and fractured, carved from black stone veined with fire.

At its base, a spiral of symbols surrounded a small pool that shimmered with liquid light.

The moment Elira stepped near it, the runes on her skin ignited.

Not pain.

Not warning.

Recognition.

She knelt beside the pool, reaching toward the glowing surface, and the moment her fingers brushed it—

She saw **her mother.**

Not Ilyana as she was now.

But as she had once been — *fierce*, *powerful*, *unyielding.* She stood before the King, runes blazing, eyes glowing, and said:

"You will never control her."

The vision shattered.

Elira fell backward, gasping.

Vaelen caught her instantly.

"They're showing you the truth," Mirae said, eyes wide. "Not a future. Not a dream. *A legacy.*"

Elira clutched her chest, the runes over her heart humming.

"My mother came here," she whispered. "She planted something. A defense. A truth. A seed that waited for me."

Above, the shadowed figure stepped down from the cliffs, finally crossing into the Hollow.

He didn't hide.

He let himself be seen.

The emotion-born stepped forward to shield Elira — but she raised a hand.

"Let him speak."

The man pulled down his hood.

His face was scarred. Weathered. But not cruel.

"I was once his weapon," he said. "But I left the King because I heard a voice in my dreams. A voice that led me here."

He looked at her.

"It was you."

The wind picked up.

The mist shimmered.

And somewhere deep in the stone beneath their feet, the Hollow whispered:

"She's returned."

Chapter 117:

The scarred man introduced himself simply:

"Ciren."

His voice was gravel and smoke.

But his eyes? They were clear. Steady.

Like someone who had seen ruin… and walked back from it.

The scarred man introduced himself simply:

"Ciren."

His voice was gravel and smoke.

But his eyes? They were clear. Steady.

Like someone who had seen ruin… and walked back from it.

The scarred man introduced himself simply:

"Ciren."

His voice was gravel and smoke.

But his eyes? They were clear. Steady.

Like someone who had seen ruin… and walked back from it.

Elira stared, pulse hammering in her ears.

"Me?"

"You are the culmination of everything she tried to protect. The only vessel strong enough to carry the full truth of what was lost."

"She knew he would come for you. And she hoped… that one day, you'd return here to remember what you were always meant to be."

The Hollow shifted — the runes flaring around them in a slow spiral of light.

And in the silence that followed, a breeze stirred the flames.

Elira's skin prickled.

She looked up—

And standing on the ridge above the fire…

Was **Ashira**.

Not broken. Not spectral.

Whole.

And smiling.

Elira stood; breath caught in her chest.

Ashira stepped forward, eyes wet, voice shaking with the weight of eternity.

"I couldn't reach you before. Not like this."

"But now… you're almost ready."

Elira stepped forward, tears slipping freely.

"You're really here."

Ashira nodded, eyes flicking to Elira's stomach with a warmth that made her tremble.

"You've already broken more than he ever thought you could."

"And there's more waiting."

"The Veil is cracking… but what comes next will cost you. Everything."

Vaelen stepped forward instinctively, standing beside Elira — ready to protect her from even ghosts, if he had to.

But Ashira just smiled at him.

"Thank you for loving her the way she deserves."

Vaelen blinked, chest visibly tightening.

Elira reached for his hand.

And together, they turned to face the fire — the Hollow burning with power beneath their feet, the truth ringing in their bones.

Chapter 118:

Vaelen stepped forward instinctively, standing beside Elira — ready to protect her from even ghosts, if he had to.

But Ashira just smiled at him.

"Thank you for loving her the way she deserves."

Vaelen blinked, chest visibly tightening.

Elira reached for his hand.

And together, they turned to face the fire — the Hollow burning with power beneath their feet, the truth ringing in their bones.

The group leaned in — Mirae tense, Ciren utterly still, Vaelen coiled like steel beside Elira.

Ashira's gaze never left Elira's.

"You were never just meant to destroy the Veil. You were meant to *replace* it."

Elira blinked. "With what?"

Ashira reached for her — not to touch, but to hover her hand above Elira's stomach.

"With truth. With feeling. With *life*."

"What you carry is not just the first child born of love. They are a tether. A light in the darkness. And because of that…"

Her voice faltered.

"…the King will do everything in his power to rip that light from you."

The fire cracked.

Wind swept through the Hollow — sharp and unnatural.

Ashira's form began to flicker.

Elira reached forward, desperate to keep her there. "Don't go. Please."

Ashira smiled, soft and aching.

"You don't need me anymore, Elira. You've already surpassed me."

"But remember this—when the time comes, the Veil won't break with force. It will break with **choice.**"

"And only you can make it."

Then, like smoke drawn into wind, Ashira vanished.

The fire dimmed.

But it didn't go out.

Later, long after the others had gone to rest, Elira and Vaelen stood at the edge of the Hollow's core — a tunnel etched in obsidian stone spiraling deep beneath the earth.

The air pulsed.

Alive.

Calling.

"Are you ready?" he asked her.

Elira looked at him — saw the way his jaw was tight, his shoulders tense. But his eyes were steady.

She took his hand.

"Only if you go with me."

They descended together.

Rune-light lit the path.

The deeper they went, the warmer the air grew. Not heat, exactly — but *power.* A living force.

And at the very bottom, in a chamber carved of fire-veined stone, they found it:

A crystal.

The color of emotion itself.
Swirling.
Beating.
And in its reflection, Elira didn't just see herself—
She saw the *future.*

Chapter 119:

They descended together.

Rune-light lit the path.

The deeper they went, the warmer the air grew. Not heat, exactly — but *power.* A living force.

And at the very bottom, in a chamber carved of fire-veined stone, they found it:

A crystal.

The color of emotion itself.

Swirling.

Beating.

And in its reflection, Elira didn't just see herself—

She saw the *future.*

She wasn't in the Hollow anymore.

She stood in a field, sun-drenched and golden. A soft wind kissed her face. Laughter echoed nearby — high, light, *familiar.*

She turned.

And there — running through wildflowers, rune-glow pulsing gently in her small palms — was a child.

Her child.

She wasn't in the Hollow anymore.

She stood in a field, sun-drenched and golden. A soft wind kissed her face. Laughter echoed nearby — high, light, *familiar.*

She turned.

And there — running through wildflowers, rune-glow pulsing gently in her small palms — was a child.

Her child.

The vision shifted.

Ash.

Flame.

A battlefield.

Bodies strewn.

And at the center — *her* — standing tall, runes blazing, eyes fierce with grief and purpose.

Vaelen beside her.

Wounded. Bleeding.

Still holding her hand.

Behind them, the child.

Alive.

Protected.

This is also possible.

There is always a cost.

Elira fell to her knees as the vision faded, tears streaking silently down her cheeks.

Vaelen caught her before she could hit the stone floor.

"Hey—hey, I've got you," he whispered, arms tight around her, pressing his lips to her temple.

She clung to him, breath shaking.

"She's real, Vaelen."

"She's *real*."

He didn't ask who.

He just nodded.

And for a long time, they stayed like that — in the heart of the Hollow, with the future burning in their chests like fire that refused to be extinguished.

Far away, in the crumbling ruins of his fortress, the King stood before his mirror wall.

One by one, the reflections began to blacken.

Crack.

And the surface of the largest mirror shattered.

"They think they've won something," he growled.

"But all they've done is remind me what I must take next."

Chapter 120:

Far away, in the crumbling ruins of his fortress, the King stood before his mirror wall.

One by one, the reflections began to blacken.

Crack.

And the surface of the largest mirror shattered.

"They think they've won something," he growled.

"But all they've done is remind me what I must take next."

Far away, in the crumbling ruins of his fortress, the King stood before his mirror wall.

One by one, the reflections began to blacken.

Crack.

And the surface of the largest mirror shattered.

"They think they've won something," he growled.

"But all they've done is remind me what I must take next."

Solen met her at the gates, hands clasped over his chest. His smile was quiet, reverent.

"You found it," he said softly.

Elira nodded. "I found… everything."

That evening, the sanctuary gathered.

Vaelen stood beside her. Ilyana and the twins nearby. Mirae, Kael, Auren. Even Ciren, silent and watchful.

And Elira spoke.

"The Veil is weakening. You can feel it — I know you can. The King will strike again. Soon. Harder."

"But we are not what we were."

"We are not fractured. We are not hiding."

"We are *becoming.*"

Her words rang in the air like truth sung from the bones of the world.

And as the crowd dispersed, hearts full and wary and *ready…*

Elira and Vaelen found the quiet again.

Their quiet.

They sat beneath the sanctuary tree, the stars just beginning to stretch across the sky. Elira leaned against his chest, his arms around her. His hands — calloused, careful — resting low on her abdomen.

There was no need for words.

Until—

"There's something I haven't told you," she whispered.

Vaelen tilted his head slightly. "Yeah?"

She guided his hand to the exact place where her rune pulsed beneath her skin.

"I felt it again today. But this time… it was stronger. Like it wanted you to know too."

And then it happened.

A single, steady pulse.

Not hers.

Not magic.

A *heartbeat.*

Vaelen froze.

Then looked at her, awe written across every sharp, war-worn edge of his face.

"Is that—?"

Elira nodded.

Eyes filled with tears.

Voice barely a breath:

"She's real."

"She's *ours.*"

Above them, the Veil rippled.

Not with rage.

Not with fear.

But with **warning.**

Because something had changed.

And for the first time in centuries—

The illusion was *cracking from within.*

Acknowledgements

This book was born from pain — but more importantly, from healing.

To the girl I once was: you were never broken. Only silenced. And now, through these pages, your voice rings clear.

To my husband — my real-life Vaelen — thank you for seeing me, for holding me, and for loving every piece I once thought was unworthy. Your steady presence is everything.

To my readers: you are not alone. If Elira's journey echoes something inside you… that is no accident. May you feel seen, held, and empowered to reclaim your voice too.

To those who believed in me, encouraged me, or simply held space for me while I created this world — thank you. You are part of this magic.

And finally, to the stories still waiting to be told: I'm coming for you.

Character Index:

Elarion

Elira (*EL-ih-rah)*
Ash-gold hair, storm-gray eyes, lean and lithe with a quiet, haunted strength.
Daughter of the King of Elarion and Ilyana. The emotional core of the story — once silenced, now awakening. Elira's journey is one of rediscovery, trauma, rebellion, and learning what it means to truly feel.

King Aurik *(OR-ik)*
Dark, imposing, and shrouded in illusion. Silver eyes that see too much.
Elira's father — ruthless, manipulative, and emotionally void. The architect of the Veil. His control is rooted in the suppression of emotion, and Elira's defiance threatens to unravel everything he's built. A ruler obsessed with order, and terrified of what true emotion can do.

Malric *(MAHL-rick)*
Polished on the outside, predatory underneath. Cold blue eyes, silver-threaded black hair.
Once assigned to marry Elira — a calculated move by the King. His true nature is twisted, cruel, and power-hungry. A monster hiding behind smiles.

Liria

Vaelen ***(VAY-len)***
Dark tousled hair, sharp jaw, deep emerald eyes. Tall, broad-shouldered, always alert.
Elira's protector — and something far deeper. A warrior with a steady hand and a haunted past. His loyalty is unshakable, and his love... transformative. He is her anchor, her storm, and her shield.

Solen ***(SOH-len)***
Sunlight in a body. Sandy-blond curls, golden skin, laughing eyes.
One of the emotion-born, and a guiding light among the Lirians. He's gentle, mischievous, and more powerful than he lets on. He's often the heart when others are falling apart.

Ashira ***(Ah-SHEER-ah)***
Ethereal, glowing presence. Auburn hair in memories, glowing silver in spirit.
Elira's best friend and emotional tether. Though she's no longer of the living, her presence lingers — guiding, warning, and loving from beyond the Veil.

Ilyana ***(Ill-YAH-nah)***
Long silver-blonde hair, deep violet eyes, regal bearing even in exile.
Elira's mother, once the most powerful Lirian ever born. She seduced the King as part of a covert rebellion. Exiled when the

plan failed, she lives with the hope that her daughter will succeed where she could not.

Auren ***(OR-en)***
One of Elira's twin siblings. Wild, unpredictable, and emotionally intense.
Bright copper hair, eyes like wildfire. His power is potent and sometimes volatile — but fiercely protective.

Kael ***(KAY-uhl)***
Auren's twin. Quiet, intuitive, and steady.
Pale hair, soft features, storm-silver eyes. While Auren burns hot, Kael soothes. Her magic balances perfectly — especially when joined with Elira.

Others/The In-Between

Alari ***(Ah-LAH-ree)***
Dark-skinned, silver-eyed woman with gentle grace.
The first known expectant mother of a child conceived from true love in generations. Her pregnancy is a sign the Veil is breaking. A living symbol of hope.

The Emotion-Born
Various appearances. Each one represents a pure emotion. Born of feeling, not flesh. Allies to Elira and reminders of the power the King has tried to suppress.

About the Author

Geneveive McPartlin-Bryant is a trauma-informed writer who blends deep emotional truth with the sweeping power of fantasy. She is the author of two nonfiction self-help books that walk alongside survivors of narcissistic abuse and now brings that same voice to fiction — fierce, vulnerable, and free.

Her stories explore healing, love, and identity in a world that tries to erase both.

She lives in a small town in Illinois, with her husband and children, where she spends her time reading, dreaming, and breaking every illusion meant to silence her.

www.ingramcontent.com/pod-product-compliance
Lightning Source LLC
Chambersburg PA
CBHW060758310726
48980CB00002B/148

* 9 7 9 8 9 9 8 5 8 4 0 2 2 *